THE DEMONS WITHIN

GRIMLUK, DEMON HUNTER VOL 3

ASHE ARMSTRONG

I0629220

First Edition, October 2018

ISBN: 0-9963409-4-7
ISBN-13: 978-0-9963409-4-6

DEDICATION

To my fellow orcs. We're not what we seem. Yes, even the Tolkien line.

We live, we love, we burn with life.

CONTENTS

ACKNOWLEDGMENTS

A very special thanks to the following folks:
Laura Hughes for her editing. You didn't have to say all those nice things after the job was done. It meant a lot. Krista Ball for CONTINUING to be a supportive peer who offers advice and new opportunities. Bob Kehl, once again, for his work on my cover and absolutely knocking this one out of the damn park. Gem for her cheerproofing. Garrett for being such a good DM that it inspires me. You're all wickedly rad people.

Chapter 1

A burst of freezing air slammed into Grimluk as he made his way down the hill into the town below. The tails of his long black coat snapped out as the wind howled, threatening to blow his hat away if he failed to keep it secured. The coat was buttoned tight on his chest, keeping the plain, wool scarf wrapped around his neck in place, enough to help keep him warm while still allowing him to get to the heavy revolver on his hip if he needed it.

He passed a sign with "Welcome to Arbortown, the Greenest Town in the Valley" carved into it and was relieved to have finally arrived. The sun had set an hour before, and the cold began to move in like a predator, nipping at his heels. Even Grimluk's orcish constitution couldn't protect him outdoors on a winter night, much to his annoyance. Every winter, he contemplated holing up somewhere warm, maybe heading back to Hunter's Hollow and spending time with family. But every winter, new jobs continued to crop up on the bounty boards. Demons didn't care about the cold. Or the heat, for that matter. Demons cared only for chaos and carnage, for souls and blood. Grimluk was all too happy to oblige their desire for carnage.

For blood, too. And here he was, ready to oblige once more.

The little farming town was fairly out of the way. The closest other town was a few days walk back the other direction, farther west and back into New Gilead. To his knowledge, no one had claimed the bounty posted for Arbortown. That was fine. Not every demon hunter was quite as stubborn as Grimluk was about the job. Though after making the trek, he was more than ready to be done with the outdoors for a night or two. A thick tent had served him as he traveled between towns. He never minded sleeping on the ground, but the cold had a way of seeping through blankets and coats. Grimluk wanted away from the cold, if only for a bit. The tips of his ears were nearly numb, a fact that pricked at his desire to stay put and not be such a mule-headed ass.

The town itself was more of a hub than a real town. It had the usual staples: a small hotel, a saloon, peacekeepers' office, general store, nothing out of the ordinary. Except that the peacekeepers' office had a huge hole in the front wall. Grimluk's throat rumbled at the sight of it. Something big clearly made that hole. He just didn't know what it was yet. A sign hung on the untouched door that read "In saloon until further notice."

The saloon was directly across from the office, sitting next door to the meager hotel. The batwing doors had two very heavy blankets hanging up behind them to block the cold. Grimluk pushed the blankets aside as he walked in. A gruff voice met him on the other side.

"Pray thee hold, stranger."

Grimluk stopped, looking to the owner of the voice. There stood a thin, black–skinned elf dressed in what could be called the typical dress of peace-keepers; pants, tall boots, a work shirt and a vest with a shield badge pinned to it. Eyes like twin bon-fires studied Grimluk. The elf was tall, though Grimluk still stood over him, and his coarse hair was styled square and high, adding a few inches to his height. A roomful of people watched Grimluk from various tables and spots at the bar.

He touched the brim of his hat. "Howdy," he called before knocking a bit of snow off himself.

"What is thine business here, orc?" the elf con-tinued, hand clearly on the butt of his gun.

Old speech, definitely not a younger elf. Grim-luk took in the area as he answered, noting mostly humans and a few halflings. "Reckon I'm here to kill your demon, if that's still a problem. Name's Grimluk." He held out a hand.

The elf regarded him silently for a moment, looking down at Grimluk's outstretched hand with clear disdain. "Sheriff Shalvine," the elf said. "Dost thou speak true?"

Grimluk sighed and lowered his hand. "That's my aim, at least. Always possible the damned thing kills me and carries on, but if I can kill it, I'll kill it."

Shalvine nodded, relaxing his hand from his gun. "Wise to avoid unnecessary pride. The crea-ture hath proved perilous in the short time it hath plagued us. Come, we will commune on the mat-ter."

"Lead the way, Sheriff," Grimluk said with a

nod, adjusting the elk-skin bag hanging off his shoulder.

The sheriff led him to a desk in a back corner of the main room with two chairs in front of it and one behind. The desktop was sparse and stained lightly, just enough to protect the wood. Nothing fancy, but peacekeeping–like demon hunting–wasn't fancy work. A simple desk got the job done. Grimluk did note that his host preferred a quill and ink to the more modern fountain pens that were all too common. Not entirely unsurprising given his way of speaking. The older an elf got, the less likely they were to change their habits.

He motioned for Grimluk to have a seat before taking his own. "Forgive any perceived discourtesy to thine entrance. Strangers art not always as they seem, is it not so? And, well, thou knowest thine history, I am sure."

Grimluk sighed quietly. Definitely an old elf. "Reckon so. About the demon?"

"Yes, yes," Shalvine said, leaning back. "I am eager to declare this beast slain. What dost thee need to make it so?"

"Information, first and foremost. Sightings, attacks, any particular uses of magic or particularly powerful feats. Does it travel with smaller, winged demons? Huge black dogs? Have you seen anyone acting strangely? Anyone acting paranoid and secretive?"

Shalvine nodded. "A challenge easily bested. In truth, the beast hath proven more...vexing than dangerous. Even so, it slew one of our folk and harmed still more. Verily, we wouldst see thee end this fiend with haste."

"Certainly do my best. What about the hole in your office?"

"Ah," Shalvine said with a dismissive wave of his hand. "Over-eager deputy, hunter. Inconsequential to thy matters. Pray thee patience while I consider how best to recount this tale," Shalvine said, steepling his fingers bowing his head. "The demon manifested some months back, before the snows arrived. Always alone, to my knowledge. I have witnessed no strangeness among my neighbors, encounters with the beast aside. Truly, a mighty creature. but..."

"Yes?" Grimluk asked, brow furrowed. Shalvine looked as if he were fighting back embarrassment.

"I pray thee believe me when I say the foul beast is—" He paused. "Well, it is witless."

"Witless?" Grimluk asked, cocking an eyebrow.

"Truly a clay-brained creature if ever there was one. Never have I seen a living thing so inept in its goals."

Grimluk blinked for a moment before frowning. "An inept demon, eh? Reckon that's a first on my list, Sheriff. Worst I ever deal with are ghouls. Relatively speaking." He sighed. "They're just...so damn tedious."

"Ghouls art demons?"

"Very weak, but yes. If you could continue, though. As many details as you can give. Or anyone you think could help. You say it's inept, but it still killed and hurt you folks?"

The sheriff nodded. "As thou ask."

Shalvine mostly provided information about the general nature of the incidents; how the demon would be found scratching at windows or generally lurking and being an unsettling nuisance. The one death credited to the demon happened, by all accounts, by accident. A woman named Bonnie had spotted the thing on top of the hotel.

"Dear Bonnie did endeavor to, uh, shoo the demon. Her efforts shocked the beast, rending it from the roof where it plummeted to her death."

Grimluk didn't really buy that the demon had fallen by accident but he nodded all the same. Shalvine then gathered a few of the other patrons up and offered to let them fill in the holes.

A pair of young, shaggy-haired human boys, not quite adults yet, told him the thing had attacked them while they'd been out walking together. Several times, it seemed. Didn't hurt either of them, necessarily, just shoved one of them repeatedly and growled at them. Even drooled on the other boy. When the taller boy, Ike, decided he'd had enough, he'd taken a swing at the demon. Despite breaking his hand on its jaw, Ike seemed to knock the wind out of the demon. It'd roared and struck back, slicing the boy's arm before it fled, leaping into the air and gliding away.

Grimluk just scratched his jaw at that and ordered a shot of whiskey. In all his years hunting, even as an apprentice hunter, he'd never heard such a ridiculous story. He could easily believe a demon toying with two defenseless people but, the fact that the boy had struck it and gotten away with only a sliced-up arm was peculiar to say the least.

"Did it come at you again?" he asked.

"No, sai," Ike said. "Leastways, not so direct. Next time we really seened it, it was just trailin' us."

"Huh."

"But…" the other boy spoke up.

"Yeah?"

"Ike here found his cat strung up by her guts in his doorway not long after."

"I see. Anything else?"

"No, sai," they said in unison.

"Thank you both."

After them was an old widow named Margaret, also human and owner of the general store. She had a head of gray hair, with a hawkish face and fading blue eyes that, taken all together, gave the appearance of someone with a sharp temper. All she had to say on the matter was that the demon was a "gods-damned thief," and that it had eaten a whole bolt of gingham.

"A whole bolt of gingham?" Grimluk repeated. "I'm hearing you right, ma'am?"

"A whole damned bolt, son. Just appeared in the store, picked it up, looked dead at me, and then stuffed the whole thing down its gods-damned throat. Damned thing was likely as thick as your leg and the gods-damned demon opened up its maw and just shoved it down. May the Old Ones curse that bolt to rot."

Grimluk took his hat off and ran a hand through shaggy hair, his winter style in place of his usual, mostly shorn head. He let out a long sigh before ordering another shot of whiskey for good measure. Shalvine introduced one of his deputies, a halfling in similar dress as Shalvine. Like Margaret, he had pale skin but a head—and feet and knuckles—of golden-blond hair. Grimluk stopped him before he could begin his story.

"If you tell me the thing shit in your dinner or kicked your dog, I'm afraid I might bust a gut from laughter. Be gentle."

The halfling gave a crooked smile and looked up at Grimluk. "No, sai, didn't shit on my dinner none."

"Well, that's good, 'cause I was real afraid I'd die right here."

"It serenaded my dog."

Grimluk just looked at the deputy in shock for a moment before laughter began to rise out of him like a fire springing to life. "It did what?"

"Well, sir, I gots me a good dog, see. Bigger'n me, but minds real good and she came into heat recently. And, well, I come out one night two weeks past, 'cause this gods-awful racket was comin' from behind my hole. And there it was, prolly big as you and singin' to my dog."

"Suppose it brought a gift, too," Grimluk replied with a chuckle.

"A big ol' bone, matter a fact."

Grimluk had to swallow hard to keep from roaring with laughter. He'd seen and heard some strange things, but damn if this didn't beat them all. "Okay, okay. I get the point." He slipped his hat back on and paid for his whiskey. "I know you folks are kind of out of the way, and you've said it killed someone and hurt others, so I reckon you ain't just wastin' my time with some fool joke. Still hard to believe."

The widow huffed while the deputy looked on a bit sheepishly. Shalvine sighed. "I swear to thee, hunter, we speak true. I did warn thee of the fool-ishness the beast hath wrought."

"I know, but can you blame me? I've been all over New Gilead, wandered in and out of the Terri-tories and the Wastes. Been at it for a decade now and I've never heard of a demon like this before." He sighed and ran his tongue along his tusks. "Any-thing else I should know?"

"We did endeavor to slay the beast in our way," Shalvine said with a shrug. "Success was not with us."

"That's what the Hunters are for. All right, I'll take the job. Minimum fee is usually ten gluts, but let's just call it two gluts and a room while I'm here. If this thing is as pathetic as you say, I don't reckon I'll be long."

"Thou art more than accommodating, hunter," Shalvine said with a slight bow. "We have an accord."

"Reckon so," Grimluk replied.

It took several days for the demon of Arbortown to appear. Grimluk spent his time playing cards in the saloon or just wandering around looking for signs of his prey. He spent more time doing that after being jolted out of bed the second night by a dis-tant, but loud, explosion. No one reported anything demon-related to him or the sheriff, so he continued hunting and waiting. He found some old foot-prints in random places or near where they'd been reported to him: big, taloned prints in the snow, perfectly preserved. Grimluk figured it'd be easy to spot the thing given the townsfolks' descriptions, especially against snow.

Outside of its size, they'd told him it was red-skinned, bright red like fresh paint, with blackened hands and feet and a long tail and wings. Of course, its hands and feet had sharp claws and its teeth were likewise predatory. Yellow eyes and horns completed the description. Nothing particularly sur-prising to Grimluk. It basically amounted to a giant-sized imp, one of the most common types of demons you could find. He seriously wondered if the damn thing was a giant imp, but that didn't seem accurate. He'd seen plenty of reasonably clever imps. Devious little bastards. He hadn't yet seen this thing, though. Not in town, out of town, or flying around above it.

When he left the hotel on the fourth morning, ready to make his rounds again, Grimluk was astounded to find his prey out and clearly visible. The damned thing was looking into one of the saloon windows. For the first time he could remem-ber, he didn't shoot first or react to an attack. The thing didn't even seem to notice him. Curiosity welled up in Grimluk, urging him on. He walked quietly toward the big red creature.

The demon made no movement at the sound of Grimluk's boots on the hotel's porch, or maybe it just didn't care. It stood there, tail flicking idly like a cat's, breath flaring out in plumes that fogged up the window. Grimluk pulled his coat away from his hip, readying his revolver for a draw and cleared his throat, expecting the demon to whirl on him and attack. It still didn't move, save to tap on the glass lightly with one clawed finger. Grimluk's head tilted as he looked at the thing he was here to kill. The widow's story flashed in his mind. He was beginning to see why Shalvine had made such an effort to explain things before actually explaining things.

"Little far from the Abyss, aren't ya?" Grimluk called, his curiosity still piqued.

This time, the demon did turn to him. "Ah-beess?" it said, its voice incredibly low and gravelly. "Bashuurga escape Abyss. Bashuurga did not like it. Too noisy."

"Reckon I should apologize in advance for sending you back then," Grimluk said, unholstering his gun. The thing was just gonna stand there and let him kill it.

It sniffed at him for a moment and then began growling, its yellow eyes letting off a smoking glow. "Smell Bashuurga on you. You want to send Bashu-urga back! Will not go back!" It roared and leaped through the awning into the air.

"Well, shit." He dropped the heavy revolver back in its holster and shook his head. "Ain't that just a kick in the head." The one time Grimluk allows for curiosity and the thing escapes. He sighed, knowing he should have just shot it.

The saloon denizens spilled out of the batwing doors. The bar-man, cook, and Shalvine with a couple of his deputies looked up at the red body flying away and then over at Grimluk.

"What didst thou do?" Shalvine asked.

"Spooked it, apparently." Grimluk walked into the street, running his tongue over his gums as he thought. "Sheriff?"

"Hunter?"

"Got an idea to fix this. A few, actually. Mind if we go in and talk? I could use some breakfast."

Shalvine studied Grimluk for a moment before replying, "As thou wilt."

The group went back into the saloon, parting the blankets. The bar-man, who owned the place, started to voice his anger at the awning being destroyed. Grimluk was hungry and annoyed and didn't want to hear it, so he flicked the man a silver bilt. That seemed to settle him down in a hurry.

Grimluk joined Shalvine at the desk again. The sheriff just kind of stared at him, looking rather shocked that the demon had been so close and that Grimluk had failed to take it down right then and there. Grimluk was frustrated with himself for such an apprentice-level mistake, but the whole thing had been so strange he found it difficult to be harder on himself. Shalvine waited patiently while Grimluk ordered breakfast. Once that was taken care of, he asked the question that was filling the air.

"How didst thou fail—ah, 'spook' the beast?"

Grimluk shook his head and gave a little laugh. "Be real honest with you, Sheriff. Gettin' the slip on a demon and it not tryin' to rip my head off was a new experience. Damn thing even spoke to me. Won't happen a second time, though." He pointed to the teeth on his hat band. "Reckon it got a whiff of these. Demon teeth. Trophies of sorts."

"Hunter, thine attitude vexes me."

"Chalk it up to curiosity. As I said, though, I have a few ideas on how to handle this now that I've seen the beast."

"Yes? I beg thee enlighten me."

"First things first," Grimluk started, "we'll need blood. A chicken or a pig, something expendable."

Shalvine cocked his head. "Thou meanst to summon the beast?"

"More or less. Think of it like a dinner bell."

"I see. And then?"

A young girl brought Grimluk a plate and a mug. He slipped her a penny and took his breakfast. "Recently acquired a rather helpful tool for my profession and I reckon this is as good a time to prove it as any. But the basics of it are we put the carcass and the blood in the center of a demon trap. Demon'll come for the blood and stay for the trap."

Shalvine nodded. "Thou could not make use of this trap at the onset?"

"Not rightly. I wasn't exactly expectin' to walk out for breakfast and stumble on the thing. If the free meal doesn't work, I'll try something else."

"As thou wilt. I shalt acquire thy blood."

Grimluk nodded and ate some of his food. "Reckon if we can set this trap up for dusk we'll have the best chance of luring it in. Might be a little more dangerous come dark, but if everything works like it should, the trap will hold tight."

"Dusk, then," Shalvine said flatly.

Grimluk tilted his mug toward the sheriff in a small salute. Now he just had to make sure everything was ready.

A flame lit up the night sky above the currently occupied outhouse. The fire burned bright enough to catch the occupant's attention while he did his business. He could see the light plainly through the little crescent hole in the door, like it was aiming straight for him. He hoisted up his breeches with a quick jerk, catching the tip of his black beard in the waist because of his hurry. The dwarf winced and cursed but shoved the door open all the same, hoping to get a proper look at the oddity streaking through the sky. It seemed to be descending rapidly and with all the force of a cannonball. And it was getting bigger.

By the time that realization dawned on him, it was too late. The flame shot right over the man's head, making him duck in instinctual fear despite it being several feet above his head. A thunderous explosion sounded behind him, followed by a rush of wind and bits of debris that knocked him onto his face, ass pointing at the winter sky. Before he could process that, a second explosion followed the first, practically deafening him. He rolled over off his face and rubbed his nose while he lay there panting in a thinning layer of snow, breath coming out in rapid puffs.

The dwarf got to his feet a moment later and nearly jumped out of his skin when a hand grabbed his shoulder. Another dwarf, slightly shorter, but with similarly dark hair, looked at him with wide eyes, mouthing something at him. The words were hard to understand. Another dwarf joined them, beard intricately braided into a head of dirty blond hair.

Faintly, he heard his name. "Nahum!"

"Can't hear ya, Dar!" he shouted at the other dwarf. "Shittin' explosion fucked my ears! They're ringin' like someone put a dinner bell in 'em!"

Dar nodded and pointed toward where the explosion came from.

"Don't fuckin' know what it was. Big ball of fire." Nahum shook his head in a vain effort to clear his ears. That ringing was really pushing on his nerves. He grunted in frustration. "One o' ya come with me, the other go make sure the kids is all right."

The blond dwarf stepped forward as Dar turned around and headed back into the house. She looked at him and then toward the fireball's impact and gulped. Nahum followed her gaze apprehensively. A cloud of hazy smoke, or maybe steam, billowed into the sky some ways away where their well had once stood. He looked at her in surprise. She mouthed something at him, a little clearer now than before but still mostly inaudible from the ringing.

"Still can't hear ya, Maisy." He was fairly sick of shouting. He didn't even like shouting during harvests, but at least then it served a purpose. "Guess we should look to it, eh?"

Maisy gave a shrug but led the way. Nahum followed close behind, trying once again to solve his hearing issue, this time with a finger in one of his ears. The stones and mortar that had once been the well were scattered all around, singed, some of them still smoking. As the two dwarves followed the rubble, they came to the ruined well. The majority of it was demolished but parts of it still stood. Looked like the fireball – or whatever it was – had crashed through the canopy and ripped through the rest on impact.

Nahum let out an annoyed sigh. Bad enough his ears were ringing, but now the well needed repairing or replacing and he felt like he was freezing his stones off. No one wanted to be out in the dark of winter in nothing but their underwear and breeches. At least he had his boots on.

"You reckon we can rebuild what's left?" he shouted.

Maisy looked it over and shrugged halfheartedly.

"My thoughts as well."

Near the well was a smallish crater. The two of them circled around it. The warmth wrapping over the edges felt nice. Nahum contemplated sitting down in the center of it but that seemed like a possibly dangerous idea.

Maisy leaned out over the crater as she looked around through the smoke, waving her hand in an effort to push it away. Nahum walked around to join her, letting out an unconscious whistle he couldn't quite hear.

"...rock..." he heard Maisy say. He told her so. Instead of trying to repeat herself, she slid down into the shallow crater, the tails of her coat scraping the dirt. She scooted towards the center, where most of the smoke was concentrated. She pointed down and waved the smoke away, revealing a strange-looking rock. She tapped it with the toe of her boot.

"Don't!" Nahum shouted, afraid of what might happen.

A few moments passed, confirming that nothing had happened, so he slid down to join her. She looked at him, but he could only shrug at her.

"Damned if I know, Maze." Thankfully, it seemed his hearing was starting to clear up some.

Maisy bent down to the rock to try and inspect it, holding a hand over it in an effort to gauge the heat rolling off it. The smoke and steam were getting wispier by the minute, probably from the cold night air. She walked over to the crater edge and gathered up a few big handfuls of snow, dumping it all onto the rock. New plumes of steam rose up in rapid flashes.

Nahum heard a dim pop, and flinched when Maisy yelped and jerked away as well. She climbed out of the crater and gathered up more snow to repeat the scenario. Nahum decided to help, and soon, the steam rose slower before stopping entirely.

Satisfied, he bent down along with Maisy as she reached out to touch the rock. He held one hand out. There was still some heat, but it was pleasant and warmed his hand. Maisy picked up the rock, bouncing it from hand to hand for a moment before settling. They carried it out of the still-smoking crater to get a better look at it.

It was mostly round, almost like a ball, with what looked like little craters of its own dotting the outside and something like a seam running through it. Nahum reached out cautiously and touched it. As much as it looked like a rock, it didn't quite feel like one. He didn't know how to put it into words properly, though. Maisy didn't seem to either.

"Reckon it's—" Nahum's ears popped violently before he could finish his thought, making him yelp and grab Maisy's shoulder. "Fuck me! Gods-damn it, that hurt! Fuck!"

"Are you all right?" Maisy asked, concern washing over her face. She clutched the rock to her side with one arm and reached out to stroke Nahum's cheek.

"I guess so. Least I can hear again. Fuck me." He worked his jaw for a moment to readjust. "As I was sayin', you reckon maybe it's valuable? Maybe like one of them rocks your grandpap turned into swords? What were it he called 'em? Starblades?"

Maisy shook her head. "I don't think so. I felt one of them rocks once and it didn't feel like this. Felt more like a regular bit o' rock, just with iron in it." She held the rock back up where they could see it in the moonlight. "I don't rightly know what this is."

"Definitely don't look like no iron rock, that's for damn sure." He touched it again, and frowned in confusion. He just could not figure this little thing out. "It feels...springy."

Maisy turned it over in her hands, looking carefully and closely at its surface. She stopped. "Lookit."

She pointed at part of the seam, cracked open just a touch. Just enough to be noticeable. Something dripped out and fell on one of the well stones. A moment later, the seam cracked and a strange gas spewed out into Maisy's face. The dwarf woman shrieked and dropped the rock, which bounced off the stones and rolled away.

"Maze!" Nahum shouted. "Come on, come on, get out of this." He did his best to pull her away from the cloud, which seemed almost to cling to her. As he tried to direct his partner away and back inside the house, he heard a loud splash and looked down. The rock, whatever it was, had rolled into the well.

"Ah, fuck."

When they got back inside the house, Maisy started having a coughing fit. Dar had gotten the kids back to sleep by the time they got back in and hovered over her as Nahum got her into their shared bed.

"Get her somethin' to drink," Nahum told his other partner rather insistently. Dar found a pitcher of tea and poured a glass, rushing it back over. Some of it sloshed over the rim, but that was a concern for later.

Gently, Dar tipped the glass back to put a little liquid down Maisy's throat. It seemed to help. She took one big breath and sank back against the headboard. She tried to drink on her own the second time and spilled some of it down her braids.

"Feels like my chest is burnin'," she managed to say after another coughing fit. It sounded mercifully weaker, but none too pleasant all the same.

"What happened?" Dar asked. Nahum told him about the rock and the gas. "Gods-damn. I'll get more tea, Maisy, dear."

For the next hour, Nahum and Dar doted on the mother of their children until she felt fine enough to get to sleep. Once Maisy curled up, the two joined her. Nahum sighed and hoped they could all get some rest. It'd been one strange night.

CHAPTER 2

Far from the reluctance to help that Grimluk had expected, the townsfolk came together to do what he asked. He was offered two old pigs and whatever other help he needed. Given the demon's behavior, he wondered if he couldn't make use of a crowd. He found a spot in the center of the street, outside of the hotel, and began clearing away the snow. The ground had had plenty of time to harden in the cold so the mud was minimal. He asked that a few folks gather up a wheelbarrow of snow. Two of the deputies set themselves to the task.

"I pray thee, what use dost thou have for snow?" Shalvine asked, his deputies shoveling snow into the wheelbarrow.

"It'll serve as cover," Grimluk responded simply.

"For?"

The wheelbarrow rolled up just as he began to answer. "For this." Grimluk dug a thick wool blanket, tightly rolled, from his elk-skin bag, tipping it toward the sheriff. "This is the new tool I mentioned."

"A blanket?"

"A blanket." Grimluk unfurled it with a snap

21

and spread it across the little clearing he'd made. The majority of the blanket was covered in a pentacle and five sigils, embroidered in white.

"Thy trap?" the sheriff asked.

"The trap. Demon steps in a trap and it's bound until it's released or the trap's destroyed. Now we just cover it with snow. Come dusk, we spread the blood around it. Reckon we can tie the other pig down, too, if you folks are that keen to make use of it."

The pig's owners nodded. "It'll be worth it to be rid of that big fucker."

"Then we just kill some time now. Anyone got a deck of cards?"

After an afternoon of no-stakes poker, dusk rolled around. Grimluk had the pig farmer slit the old pig's throat. Together, the two of them spread the flowing blood around the hidden blanket, steam from breath and blood puffing in the cold. The farmer staked the other pig down with a short tether and disappeared back into the saloon on Grimluk's instruction. Grimluk slipped into the hotel and waited.

Thankfully, he didn't have to wait long. The sound of huge, flapping wings came from overhead, heralding the demon's arrival. It landed near the trap with a heavy thump.

"Bashuurga knew, knew the smell. Fresh blood," the demon called, practically cooing in its gravelly voice.

Grimluk peeked out of the lobby window. The demon was down on its hands and knees, lapping up the blood from the snow. And somehow managing to not touch anywhere near the trap.

Grimluk growled. "That thing has a devil's own luck." He would usually laugh at the saying when he encountered it, but it seemed rather fitting here.

The demon flopped back on its butt, tail curling around out of the way as it reached for the other pig. The hog squealed with all its might and tried to break the tether. The rope held though. Until the demon snagged it with a taloned finger. Grimluk's jaw fell.

"Gods-damn," he muttered. The demon just laughed as the pig ran. Grimluk's patience finally started to wear thin. This beast had strange luck and an odd demeanor; maybe Grimluk could use that demeanor to his advantage. He made his way back outside and walked right up behind the big red bastard.

As before, it paid him no heed. Grimluk looked down at the pig's corpse, untouched in the center of the trap. He sighed. Then he stomped hard on the demon's tail. It shrieked, pulling its tail away and nearly toppling Grimluk in the process, and attempted to jump away.

It bounced right onto the dead pig.

The demon let out a second shriek as it realized it'd been trapped. It thrashed and roared, snarling in anger and surprise before it turned to face Grimluk. It roared at him then, trying to swing a clawed hand at Grimluk's face, only to slam into an invisible wall. The mystical barrier contained the demon with abject efficiency. Only Grimluk could release it now.

"Finally," Grimluk said. "I was really beginnin' to worry you were gonna be more trouble than I was led to believe." He stepped back and unholstered his revolver. The gun barked and the demon's head exploded from the back. It slumped to its knees, a ragged growl escaping its maw, and Grimluk fired twice more, another shot to the head and one to the heart.

The beast let out a death rattle that shook the windows around it, roaring with pain and ebbing fury as its body burned up in a burst of light. Flames poured out of its insides as its skin melted away. Grimluk slid the revolver back in its holster and watched as a rotten-looking skeleton collapsed into a neat pile on the center of the blanket. He bent down and scooped up what was left of the demon's horned skull. Shalvine approached cautiously as Grimluk held it up for the sheriff to see. His first bullet had blown a hole through the back, while the second had ruined the jaw completely. It was still quite a large chunk of bone all the same.

"Always nice when the job is simple."

"As thou say, hunter. The beast is slain, then?"

"Dead as dead," Grimluk replied. "Reckon I give this to you as proof of the kill."

"Not as such. Arbortown is without its own magi-tell and bounty board. Thou wilt return whence thee came, else continue on to Downingville. I wilt send a writ with thee, whatever thy choice, and the peacekeepers shalt pay thee."

Grimluk nodded and set the skull back down. "Reckon I'll head on, once morning comes."

He didn't mind having to travel on. It happened. In New Gilead, the smaller towns rarely had magi-tell stations in place, and courier riders were usually slowed down in the snow. The magi-tell system allowed for limited but near instantaneous communication through magic. Messages had to be brief and straight to the point, as it took a fair amount of energy and effort to transmit the messages to every other station on the continent. Amazingly, the Borderlands were covered with the stations, allowing border towns to keep current for hunters of all types and anyone desperate enough for work they'd consider being near to or right in the Wastelands. The latter were extreme cases. There were towns that still existed in the Wastes, but they were scattered, with few remaining well enough for use. When the Sundering happened and the Wastelands were born, most of the frontier settlements were overrun with demons and the monsters they created.

"What wouldst thou have us do with…this?" Shalvine motioned to the pile of smoking bones.

"Fertilizer," Grimluk replied with a nod.

Shalvine's eyes went wide. "Thou wouldst mock me?"

"It sounds ridiculous, I know, but some of the loremasters have done tests on the stuff. Without the demon to maintain the form's power, it loses the taint of the Abyss. Make you some of the biggest flowers you've ever seen. Surprisingly helpful for pumpkins, too, of all things."

Shalvine scratched at a pointed ear absently before shrugging. "As thou say, hunter."

Grimluk bent down again and set about

retrieving his blanket. He gathered up each corner and lifted, rolling the snow, bones, and blood into a neat pile. He found the wheelbarrow and dumped the contents in, sending the bones clattering against each other and the wood. After folding the blanket back up, Grimluk plucked the skull back out of the pile.

"Dost thou foresee an early journey?" the sheriff inquired.

"Reckon so. No rest for a demon hunter, after all."

Shalvine nodded. "The writ shall be held at the innkeeper's desk, then. I will endeavor to complete the paperwork this eve."

"Appreciate the effort, Sheriff."

"Should I not be the one to offer thanks?"

Grimluk gave a low, amused huff. "Reckon we could thank each other and be off."

"Truly, thou art a strange one. Are all hunters as such, or is this purely an orcish quirk?"

Grimluk slipped the skull into his bag. "Comes with the territory, I reckon. It's dire work."

"As thou say, hunter. I beg thy pardon and bid thee enjoy thy night." Shalvine followed the sentiment with a polite, if slightly formal, bow and returned to the saloon. Grimluk headed back to his room in the hotel. He appreciated simple jobs, but in truth, he hoped the next one had a little more substance. It'd been a lean winter. Then again, he supposed, maybe that wasn't such a bad thing.

It took Grimluk three days to find his way to

Downingville. Thankfully, there'd been a few waystations along the way to give him respite from the winter chill. The sight of Downingville surprised him. The town was big. Far bigger than he was expecting, though still not as big as New Gilead's capital, Varnerton. Grimluk had never been to this part of the province, so he hadn't known what to expect. Downingville, by all appearances, was a thriving town built near the Cold River, which served as a natural border between the southern edges of New Gilead and Westlynth and the northern edge of what was generally known as the Southern Territories, which was home to a large tribal confederacy. He vaguely recalled that the border into Westlynth was not far beyond the town.

There was more to the town than just a street or two and a few shops or a saloon and a hotel. Downingville had houses scattered all around it. Grimluk passed through the outer section, filled with people of all races. The flat, painted fronts of halfling mounds dotted the area along with the more traditional brick and stone and wood homes of the larger folk. Some were clearly dwarven in design, with a myriad of geometric patterns chiseled in to add some personality, and rocks of varying colors in place of paint. The windows were small and square and touched with frost that sparkled in the setting sun.

The wooden structures were varied in appearance, some painted in the simple colors Grimluk was most familiar with in New Gilead while others were untouched. Most likely these were of human design, though he'd heard human architects often took certain design cues from the dwarves and the elves. One of the larger houses was a striking blue and white, and seemed to be an example of that mix. Every home, mound or not, had smoke piping from the chimney. A few of the locals glared at Grimluk, either unsure of the outsider or maybe guessing at his profession. The average person was wary of what they thought might be a hunter, whether demon or some other supernatural threat. Hunters could mean trouble, even if their goal was to help. Grimluk had met his fair share of folks who denied their problems even as imps circled overhead.

Of course, there were always those that just flat out disliked orcs. A thousand years since the Great War and the old prejudices refused to die.

A few of the younger halflings spotted him, getting as close as they dared, ogling this oddity, this black-clad orc. He smiled to himself and looked their way. They scattered, all except the youngest and smallest, fur not yet covering their little feet or knuckles. The little halfling looked up at him, eyes huge with wonder.

Grimluk touched the brim of his hat and gave an exaggerated wink, sending the little one fleeing with a giggle, shouting at the other kids.

Up ahead, a sign read "Welcome to Downingville" and under that, "Population 3000." A little hut sat behind the sign with the outline of a shield on the door. Peacekeepers. The door opened and a halfling wandered out, gray-haired and feet furry enough Grimluk could've sworn he had some sort of animal tied to them. The old halfling waved at Grimluk.

He touched the brim of his hat and continued

on with the diminutive peacekeeper making no sign to stop him. Grimluk was grateful he hadn't had to deal with anymore aggressive halflings since the summer. Gods willing, spring would come, bringing a new year, and that bit of good fortune would continue.

A thought occurred to Grimluk and he stopped and turned back to the Peacekeeper. "Pardon, friend."

"Ayuh?" the halfling replied in a soft, slow voice.

"Comin' through to collect on a bounty from Arbortown. Have my proof and a letter from the sheriff there. Reckon I might need to be directed to the board. Never been this way before. Might also need a local recommendation for the best saloon in town."

The peacekeeper nodded. "Ayuh, stranger. Bounty board's straight down next tuh McCree's Dry Goods, just down that way." He scratched his chin absently, digging through a thinning beard. "Heard Arbortown had a bit o' demon troubles. You kilt it?"

"I did. Strangest one I've seen to boot."

"Say true ya?" the deputy said with a phlegm-filled snort. "Ah, as fer drink, best in town's the Comin' Conqueror. Follow the street past the board and take north at the split. Can't miss it. Look fer Emerald an' tell 'er Amos sent ya."

"Thank you kindly," Grimluk replied with a nod.

"Ayuh. And mind yerself, stranger. This here's a good town with good folk."

Grimluk held up his hand as he walked away. "Do my best, sir."

Downingville was apparently laid out for ease of use. The main street stretched out the entire length of the town in a mostly straight line. Here and there, streets split off to his left. Grimluk found McCree's easily enough, in its own little square along with the Wales Family General Store and the bounty board office, which was bigger than any other he'd seen. When he stepped inside, he saw why. This office shared its space with a courier service named Courier Six. A young human sat behind a desk near the bounty board, a ledger open in front of him. Behind him was a row of desks each with a small, crystalline sphere. Various people sat behind the desks, touching the spheres when they began to glow and scribbling down information and the messages they received.

"So that's how the magi-tell works," he mumbled to himself. He'd never seen an office this size before.

"May I help you, uh, sai?" the boy asked.

"Pardon, yes, I'm here to claim the demon bounty from Arbortown. Job's been completed."

The young man gaped for a moment but nodded. "You have verification?"

Grimluk pulled the demon skull and Shalvine's letter from his bag and handed them over. The boy squinted at the letter after he opened it.

"Uh, can't make two licks of the writing but the seal is official. Good enough." The boy stamped the letter and laid it aside before reaching into a desk drawer and retrieving another ledger, much smaller than the one already open on his desk. "Name?"

"Grimluk."

"Guild affiliation?"

"New Gilead, Hunter's Hollow."

The boy scribbled in the ledger and then yelled over his shoulder. "Maro! Arbortown demon job is clear!"

"Yar!" came the reply.

The boy stamped the letter again and returned it to Grimluk. "Take this to the peacekeeper station across the way and they'll pay you."

Grimluk took the letter back and nodded. "Appreciate it."

Once in the peacekeepers' station, Grimluk offered the skull for disposal, hacking a piece of its horn off first. It was common practice to take pieces of fallen demons. In the event someone tried to resurrect them, the ritual, if successful, would render the demon far weaker than it had been. Once that was done, Grimluk received his pay and tried to find his way to the Coming Conqueror. A few days back out on the road and that creeping desire to hole up somewhere warm was upon him again. He still had the money for it, too. Hopefully there'd be a decent hotel near the Conqueror with some big, orc-sized beds. Grimluk occasionally preferred hard ground to a small bed he couldn't stretch out in.

Course, unless the place was owned by an orc, they usually charged extra for the bigger beds. That got under his skin, but one nomadic hunter wasn't about to change such a common practice. Grimluk sighed and continued on, hoping for the best.

In the week following the meteorite, Nahum and Dar set to repairing their busted well. Most of the rubble had either been scattered or buried by the impact. He and Dar tried to fish the meteorite out of the water but after a lack of success, Dar declared it had either sunk to the bottom or they just had the worst luck. Thankfully, it really only took a day's worth of work to rebuild the well, a small bit of fortune given the stature of the thing. Nahum was pleased to find the winch was still in working order, so he wouldn't have to build a new one. That likely would've meant a trip to Arbortown, which he was fairly against given they still had their demon problem. He was also relieved to find that the impact hadn't affected the pump connected to the trough in the barn. Trying to water a herd of animals with a bucket could, understandably, be a giant pain in the ass.

Maisy was not so easily mended, though. The poor woman seemed fine a couple of mornings after her coughing fit. She'd always been stout and her partners had been sure she'd pull through quickly. Instead, she'd nearly passed out on her way to the chicken coop. Nahum and Dar got her back in bed as quick as they could, their two daughters, did their best to help, holding the door open as the men carried Maisy back inside. They were still young though and the sight of their mother cough-ing in bed upset them terribly.

While the two dwarves had a quiet dinner together, Nahum sighed. "Dar, I reckon we might need to get the girls to help with things for the time bein'."

Dar grunted. "Ayuh. Least there's not as much what needs doin' at present."

Nahum rolled his spoon through a pile of baked beans as he thought. "Maybe we just take shifts. The girls is big enough they can handle Maze while we tend the barn."

"Seems straight," Dar said, shoveling a heap of beans into his mouth.

The next day, after Nahum finished placing the winch and bucket back into the well, Maisy wan-dered out of the house in nothing but her sleeping gown. Nahum rushed over to her.

"Maze, dear, this cold ain't gonna help ya none right now. Let's get you back inside." He could see the girls standing in the doorway, frowns on their bare little faces.

Maisy looked past him and all but walked right through him as she headed for the well. She seized the rope and hauled the bucket up with furious tugs. Maisy tipped the bucket back and dumped water down her throat, soaking her gown. Nahum just watched, dumbfounded as she did it. He called for Dar a moment later, for once not feeling uncomfortable for yelling. Maisy dropped the bucket back down the well for a refill while Nahum tugged on her arm to try and get her back inside.

"Maze, c'mon now, you're scarin' the girls. I

can bring ya some water if you're so thir–" Maisy's hand interrupted him with a forceful shove.

Nahum stumbled back and looked on. Maisy being a bit rough was not entirely a strange occurrence. She liked a good wrestle on occasion. What was strange was how she did it. Even when they wrestled, she took care not to really hurt anyone. The shove nearly pushed Nahum's shoulder out of its socket, though.

Dar rushed over to check on him, utter confusion painted on his bearded face. "What'd you do?"

"Nothin'! I just pulled on her arm and she near knocked my shoulder off. Help me get her back in. Figure we'll have to carry her. I just…" Nahum was afraid of one of the possibilities of Maisy's sickness. With demon activity so nearby, a part of him couldn't help but wonder if she was possessed. He didn't have a clue how that would've happened. Meteorite aside, they'd had no contact with the demon plaguing Arbortown. They were far enough away it wasn't really a concern. He hoped that wasn't the case and held the thought back for now. Maybe, he thought, if he kept it to himself, it'd just be a nonsense bit of anxiety.

Dar looked over at Maisy, guzzling another bucket of water. "Reckon so. How you wanna do it?"

"Just get her up and we go." He looked back at his daughters. They looked utterly beside themselves. "Girls, we're gonna get yer ma back inside. Hold the door for us. We need ya to be strong for a bit, okay? I know you're scared and I can see the tears, but keep 'em back 'til we get her back inside, okay?"

They nodded in unison and pulled the screen door back together.

Nahum and Dar readied themselves and then set on their partner quick, before she could react. Nahum hauled her back by her arms while Dar scooped up her feet. A moment later, she started thrashing and nearly kicked Dar in the mouth. They got her back inside with some effort while she yelled and struggled. The two of them spent over an hour fighting to keep Maisy in bed where she could rest. When it became clear there would be no more resting for Maisy, Nahum had Dar help flip her onto her stomach.

"Get the girls outta their room and shutter the window," he said, climbing onto Maisy and pinning her down. "Make it quick, if ya can!"

Dar hurried out to do so. Nahum could hear him talking to the girls.

"Ma's real sick, girls. We gotta put her in your room for now, okay? I know, my gem, I know. We don't know what else to do. Come now, quick quick."

The three of them were mercifully quick. Dar returned shortly after and the two of them hauled Maisy up again and took her into their daughters' room. Nahum felt like a monster just tossing her in there and slamming the door, turning the lock with a loud click. Maisy was at the door a moment later, banging on it and screaming like a banshee.

Nahum, Dar, and their crying daughters all climbed up into the trio's bed and curled up together with the girls between Nahum and Dar. Each man held onto a child and the four of them sat in quiet sorrow while Maisy continued to scream and bang on the door.

Chapter 3

Amos had been spot on when he'd said Grimluk couldn't miss the place. The Coming Conquerer sat at the end of its own little street near what was probably the center of Downingville. It stood three stories tall and bright even in the early evening darkness, painted up with reds and whites and golds. The front side was split into two prongs, one side marked with a "Hotel" sign and the other "Saloon." That suited him just fine. Two imps with one bullet, as it were. And the place was inviting to boot. Piano music and song poured out of the saloon side to greet him.

Unlike Arbortown, the bat-wing doors were uncovered. When Grimluk passed through, he knew why. It wasn't a strong sensation, but it was there: a magical barrier to keep the heat in. Maybe he'd get a comfortable bed after all.

Cigar smoke met him immediately but faded enough to mingle with the smell of whiskey. No one seemed to pay him any mind as he looked about. Everyone was busy drinking or gambling or singing around the little piano. Grimluk cut toward the bar in the back, passing by several poker tables, each covered in soft green or red or blue felt.

Wooden chips clicked and clacked against each other while the players took their chances with bluffs aplenty. The smell of the place shifted near the bar, filling his nostrils with the scents of beer and, strangely, just a hint of flowery perfume.

The bar was long and well polished, covered in bronze accents and a fine stone top. Maybe marble? Grimluk didn't really know much about rocks. If it'd been steel, he'd have had a better chance, but he liked the stone, whatever it was. It was dark and speckled with gold and silver.

Grimluk stepped up and waited his turn as several others gave their orders to the barmen on duty. He looked up at the mirror hanging behind the bar and noticed an orc talking with a human to his left.

When it was his turn, Grimluk ordered two tankards of the house brew and a shot of their best whiskey. The man talking to the orc bumped into Grimluk but didn't seem to notice or care. The orc wore a dress of reds and golds, a similar color scheme as the barmen and a few others Grimluk had noticed, showing what some might describe as a generous amount of cleavage. She was frowning heavily, with hands on hips. The look and her stance made Grimluk pay attention.

"I said no, Roscoe," she said.

"Think yer shit dun stink?" the man asked angrily. "Think yer better 'n me?"

For a moment, it sounded like his words were slurred with drink but Grimluk realized the man's accent was helping out as well.

The woman didn't answer, which seemed to make the man madder. The human hauled back like he would slap the orc but Grimluk caught his wrist as the barman set his drinks down.

"Pardon, friend, but I reckon this might be a foolish course of action," Grimluk said. The barman watched with a cautious glare.

The man ripped his hand free and spun on Grimluk. "The fuck you say, gerblin?"

Grimluk's throat rumbled and he ran his tongue along one of his tusks. "Reckon I said your behavior might not be the best. Reckon that's double now."

"Ain't your woman, goblin." He made a clear effort to enunciate the word this time. "Ain't no point in protectin' her none, neither!"

Grimluk downed the shot of whiskey and turned to face the man proper. "Not protectin' her, friend. Tryin' to protect you. I reckon you could say I know a thing or two about orcs. Here's what I know, friend. You hit her and she's gonna break your hand. And you say that ugly word around either of us again, and I reckon she'll break something else, too. Now, if I were you, I'd take a walk outside and let the wind cool me down a bit before somethin' bad happened."

The man opened his mouth to protest more but Grimluk cut him off with a growl. "Before something bad happened. Friend."

A conflict of emotions warred on the man's ruddy face as he weighed the situation. "Fah! Troll fuckers!" he shouted before wandering away to some dark corner, no doubt to tend to his wounded ego.

Grimluk nodded to the woman and turned back to his brew.

The barman set another shot of whiskey down. "On the house."

Grimluk held the glass up in a small salute and downed it.

"Didn't have to do that, stranger," the woman said, moving closer to him. "Barrier spell in here prohibits violence. He'd have been turned away 'fore he hit me."

Grimluk shrugged and set his hat down. "He might be an ass, but there wasn't a need even for that. He'll either rethink his strategy next time or else the spell will do whatever it does and he'll learn the hard way."

She gave him a momentary laugh and a smile. He thought both were beautiful. Her tusks were clean and strong, if a little on the thin side, and framed by lips that were painted bright red. He couldn't help but think of the now-dead demon, but he'd learned long ago to let thoughts like that slip away. He smiled back.

"Ain't you a real sweetie," she said, giving a wink. Her eyes were a dark red, made all the more striking with the help of her makeup. A pale green hand brushed Grimluk's sleeve.

This close, he could see her eyes better. Among orcs, there were certain physical characteristics con- sidered particularly beautiful. Grimluk saw such a feature in her eyes. Orc pupils were usually dia- mond-shaped, but sometimes, the points of those diamonds stretched out a little, resembling a shining star.

"Well," he started, "I see enough violence." He shrugged. "I figure a saloon should be a haven. Doesn't always happen that way, but that's my view all the same. Especially given my proclivity for travel."

"Aaah, I bet you're a cardsharp, ain't ya? Clean house and then move on, am I right?"

He grinned again. "Sometimes. Speaking of travel, though, does this place have any free rooms? Given your presence, maybe even something comfortable for an orc? Deputy Amos told me to find someone named Emerald, too."

She nodded and gave another smile. "Matter of fact, I'm Emerald, hun. And we do have a nice room for a fine gentleman like yourself. If you'd like, I could show it to ya. What's your name?"

"Thank you kindly," he said, gathering his hat and remaining drink. "Name's Grimluk. Lead the way, Miss."

Emerald led him through the throng to a stairwell he'd missed when he entered. She made her way down a long hall that connected both sides of the building, her hips moving rather exaggeratedly. Grimluk wondered if maybe she'd hurt herself at some point, but the thought drifted away. Wasn't any of his business either way and he appreciated her kindness.

She stopped and opened a door before disappearing inside. "Illumo," she said as he followed. The lamps around the room flared up, along with a small wood stove in one of the corners. It was easily the biggest hotel room Grimluk had ever seen in his travels, aside from one trip to Varnerton. He knew it was a modestly sized room, though. The type easily found in towns of this size. Still, it had a couple of high-backed chairs, a table, a dresser and chest, and, as he'd hoped, a bed that would fit him well. Soft wallpaper lined the walls and thick red curtains hung across the windows. Everything looked quite comfortable. Plush even.

"What do ya think? Nice enough?" Emerald asked after he finished taking in the room.

"It's very nice. Only one nicer was in Varnerton."

"You've been to the capital? Goodness, hun, you really do like to travel."

He nodded once. "That's the life."

"Maybe you can tell me about it later. Now, it's a bilt for two hours, three for the evening, and ten for the night."

His throat rumbled as he frowned. "A mite on the expensive side, ain't it? Ah, well. It's warm and your drinks are damn good."

"Expensive?" Emerald said, the sweetness draining from her voice. "Excuse me?"

"Reckon so," Grimluk replied, unbuttoning his coat. "Usually get a night for a bilt, maybe two." He slipped out of the coat and hung it up on a nearby rack along with his hat.

"Expensive? What a pile of troll shit. I'll have you know I've gotten extra pay for a night!"

Grimluk's brow furrowed. "Extra for the night?"

"Damn right."

"Why?"

Emerald's eyes narrowed and she marched over

to Grimluk, every inch of her suddenly fierce and aggressive. "Cause I'm gods-damned worth it! And I don't care how big your gun is, if you don't agree, then get the fuck outta here, mister! Gun or no gun, I'll whoop ya good!"

Realization struck Grimluk. "You're a Companion?"

"The fuck else would I be? You asked for a room!"

Grimluk had to steady himself as the laughter rolled through him, heavy and sincere. Emerald looked at him like she would knock his head clean off. He held up his free hand in a sign of surrender. She looked at him warily but stepped back. Her own face lit up for a moment.

"Oh. Maybe you don't like girls, then?"

"No, no, it's not that. I like girls just fine. Don't really have a preference one way or another. I really was just lookin' for a room, though. I didn't realize you were a Companion." Another chuckle rolled out of him. "I've no doubt you're well worth your prices, though."

"Didn't realize…" Now it was Emerald's turn to laugh. "I'm so sorry! I just thought…"

"I know, I know. Reckon a little miscommunication goes a long way." He sipped some of his brew. "Been a while since I seen another orc. How 'bout I pay you for your time and we can just sit and talk? Still need a room, too, if these are actually for rent."

Emerald blinked a few times and then ran a hand through her dark hair. "You sure? I mean, I threatened to whoop ya."

"Not the first time someone's told me that. Won't be the last." He motioned for her to take a seat in one of the chairs. Emerald glided over and slid down gracefully. Grimluk took the opposite chair, plopping down with a grunt. "Wouldn't be much of a hunter if I couldn't handle myself."

"A hunter? What kind of hunter?" The interest in her voice seemed genuine.

"Demons, usually. Just came from a job, in fact."

"Was that why you were in Varnerton?"

Grimluk gulped down the rest of his brew and set the tankard aside. "It was at the time. Governor Feely wanted me to come up and give a full report on an incident over the summer."

"What was he like?"

"Generous. And worried, given what happened. It was…bad." Memories bubbled in his mind. He sighed and pushed them away. "Anyways, Varnerton's a pretty city but I've spent more time wandering New Gilead's smaller towns, and the Borderlands. Even the Wastes more than a few times. Those folk tend to have more problems than the bigger towns, like here. Easier to summon somethin' out in the sticks where no one will see."

Emerald looked at him with open astonishment. "I've never met a hunter before. Rangers pass through sometimes, since the border to Westlynth is so close. One of them's a friend of mine, shares stories but nothin' ever like that." She looked him over for a moment. "I think I might have another service you could make use of."

"What might that be?"

"When's the last time you had some relief rubbed into your muscles?"

Grimluk thought about his answer. The truth of it was more of a technicality given that he'd been in a demonically induced sleep. To fight atrophy, the healer had plied his muscles while he was out. Mint had a way with hands-on healing like that. Elvish techniques were borderline miraculous. "Reckon it's been a while."

"All right," Emerald said with a determined nod as she stood back up. "Hop up on the bed and take off your shirt. Gun's up to you." She gave a playful wink.

The tiniest hint of heat filled Grimluk's cheeks. Emerald climbed onto the bed and patted the blanket in front of her. Grimluk stood and unbuckled his gun belt, laying it in the chair. The bed didn't have a footboard of any kind, so he sat on the edge before pulling the warm, winter shirt off in a smooth motion.

Emerald let out a short gasp. Her fingers made a gentle line down his shoulder blade as he set his shirt aside.

"What happened?" she asked quietly. "Demons?"

Grimluk sighed through his nose. He'd forgotten about his back. He had numerous scars, some worse than others. You didn't hunt demons and not survive without a sign of the struggle, but most of them had faded down to a barely noticeable softness thanks to the salve he used. It was one of the few bits of alchemy he knew, though the scar fading was more of a side-effect of the healing. The scars on his back had been too numerous, though, and hadn't been treated with the same care. They would likely never fade.

"Long story," he said softly, not looking back at her. "Not worth tellin', either."

Emerald held her hand against his back for a long moment as they sat in silence.

"Well," she began, clearing her throat. "Said I knew what to do for you and I ain't never gone sour on a job before unless they earned it."

The hand slipped away from his back. Emerald muttered something and then pressed both hands into his shoulders, digging her fingers in. The muscles underneath flexed of their own accord rhythmically, steadily growing in tightness before relaxing again. A light crackle rose to his ears and Grimluk turned his head. Emerald's hands were glowing as she dug her fingers a little deeper into his shoulder. The muscles twitched faster and then tightened up with a sudden force. When they released, a new warmth spread out from her palms.

Grimluk let out a long, low rumble of pleasure, shoulders slumping slightly. Those warm hands moved down his back, fingers that could never be called dainty digging in, pushing in currents of heat as they went, occasionally a little shock to tighten and release the muscle as she went along. Grimluk's pleasurable rumble grew as Emerald pushed more heat into his lower back. For a moment, he thought he would collapse back into her. That hardly seemed like a bad thing.

And he suspected she was grinning at him for it.

Sometime in the late hours of the night, or maybe the early hours of the morning, Nahum gingerly rolled his youngest off his lap, hoping not to wake her. His girls had finally fallen asleep from exhaustion and, with the uneasy quiet filling the house, he decided to check on Maisy. As he approached the door, a frail voice called his name from behind it. Nahum stood his ground, conflict ripping through his mind. He wanted to fling the door open and embrace his partner. The thought made his heart ache, but Maisy had been so violent. He squatted down in front of the door and called her name.

"Nahum…why am I in here?"

"You don't 'member?"

"I don't remember anything."

He sighed. "You wandered outside in your gown. You…you got a bit rough. Uh, violent."

Maisy was silent for a long time. "Did I hurt the girls?"

"No, no, the girls are fine. Dar's asleep with them. How are ya feelin', Maze?" The key was heavy in his hand. "Wasn't sure if you fell asleep. You were thumpin' and yellin' somethin' fierce until, I don't know, a few hours or so ago."

"I'm okay. I think. Cold. Can you let me out now?"

"You're not…not thirsty, are ya?"

"No, just hungry. Eat a whole cow, I think."

Nahum nodded to himself, a smile trying to

creep across his face, and stood. "Yeah, Maze, let's get you changed and fed."

He was fairly afraid Maisy would be blue from the cold. It was the middle of the night and he had no idea whether or not she'd had enough sense to grab a blanket or just get into one of the beds since they hadn't had time to stoke the oven in the girls' room. When the lock clicked and the door slid open, Maisy all but fell into his arms. He pulled her back and looked at her face. Her lips were their usual rosy hue. He felt her cheeks, which were a little cool but not terrifyingly so. Nahum lifted her hands up, looking for blue fingers. Satisfied, he kissed each hand and shuffled her off toward the kitchen, one arm around her protectively.

They passed by their own bedroom. Nahum smiled at the sight of Dar and their daughters sleeping, or mostly sleeping. Dar looked up at him groggily and nodded inquisitively. Nahum shook his head and motioned silently with one hand for Dar to go back to sleep.

Nahum pulled a chair out for Maisy and helped her into it before disappearing back into the bedroom to grab a spare blanket and some fresh socks for her. She seemed to have relaxed a touch when he returned. He looked up to see her smiling down at him after he'd changed her socks for her. Once he'd spread the blanket around her like a cloak, he set about the pantry, gathering a bag of beans and some corn muffins. The muffins were starting to go stale, but they were still good. He figured Maisy might as well finish them off after being locked in the bedroom for so many hours. Maisy was as ravenous as she'd claimed and devoured every morsel he put in front of her. She ate nearly the whole pot of beans and every muffin he put down.

He started to go get a few sausages to fry up, but a hideous noise drew his attention. It sounded like a horse. A similar noise followed it, a touch fainter. Another followed after that until Nahum had no doubt something was going on in the barn. He gave Maisy the last of the beans and hopped into his boots. This time, he thought ahead and slipped into a coat before rushing out into the freezing winter night.

When he got into the barn, all he could see were thrashing shadows, but the sound of the animals, clearly in immense pain, slammed into his ears almost as hard as the boom from the meteorite. Nahum lit a lamp as quick as he could. He had no talent for magic so tried to keep matches on him whenever he could. The kerosene-soaked wick caught immediately, filling the barn with its soft, orange glow. The horses, actually a breed of pony favored by dwarves and halflings, shook and stamped but the movements were jagged and stiff. The goats lay on their sides, bleating and twitching. One of the cows had collapsed and taken a divider wall with it. The sight and stench of it all threatened to overwhelm him.

Nahum's head spun. The sight would've been horrid in the daylight but the shadows made it worse. The stink made it all the more sinister. It was like they made the painful movements bigger. He rushed to the nearest creature.

The goat couldn't even look at him. It just bleated incessantly, desperately, like maybe it was giving birth to something big and spiny. Nahum tried to pet it, to calm it, but it just screamed harder.

He backed away from the goat. Maybe Dar could help. He was better with the animals, knew more about their care than Nahum ever had. It was part of why he loved the man. He turned and smacked into Maisy. He thought for sure he'd hurt her, but she didn't budge, didn't even flinch. She wheezed, visibly shaking with each breath. He couldn't hear it over the animals, but he could see it. See her shadow shaking behind her.

She was on him before he could speak.

Maisy had him pinned as soon as he hit the straw-covered ground. She leaned down over his face, shuddering wheezes racking her body but not diminishing her strength. Nahum looked up in confusion. Terror was there as well, creeping in the back of his mind. The confusion mixed with it and he suddenly remembered his private fear. Maisy was possessed. She had to be.

Then why does she look so sad and hurt? he wondered.

She convulsed and retched above him. Nahum watched helplessly as Maisy's eyes rolled back, suddenly sunken and strange. She retched again, and her face split open, the skin sloughing off in an explosion of gore that covered Nahum. Nahum bucked and tried to move out from under his partner, tried to free himself, but she just pushed harder, seemingly spurned on by her convulsions and retching. He screamed at the sight of her skull under a sheen of something iridescent.

The bubble that rolled out of the gaping hole

of her mouth was shining and thick. Too thick to be saliva and too light to be bile. Nahum watched, terror and awe transfixing his gaze, as the stuff poured out. He was sure it reached out for him.

The bubble shifted, and he realized he was right; it was reaching for him. It was now a long and crawling tendril that slipped into his mouth and nostrils. He wanted to scream, tried to scream with everything in him, but whatever the oozing thing was, it stuffed itself down his throat, shutting off his access to air. He bucked again in panic and this time, Maisy fell away, long strands of the slime stretching out from the ruins of her face to his. As Nahum struggled to his feet, the world started to go black. The animals had grown silent again, the goat he'd tried to calm now split open, the iridescent slime spilling out of its guts. Nahum hit the dirt again, landing next to Maisy. As the world faded, he saw yellow eyes watching him below a mouth full of gleaming white teeth.

Nahum had been right about a demon, then. Before he could think much more on it, darkness folded over him, burying him in pain and silence.

Chapter 4

After the massage, Grimluk and Emerald spent the evening just talking. Grimluk gave her a single gold glut for her time – more than enough for several nights of her time, in fact. She woke him the next morning with a big, meaty breakfast and an offer to show him around town. He had no reason to object and needed to check the bounty board again in any case.

Grimluk found Emerald immensely easy to talk to. He knew some of that was her training as a Companion. From what he knew of them, Companions were taught the art of conversation as well as the arts of physical pleasure. Even still, her wit and charm were self-evident.

In the cold morning air, she wore her skirts down, covering her legs, and kept her chest covered by a warm coat. Grimluk didn't bother to button his own coat up, instead opting to wrap his scarf high on his neck. When Emerald slipped her arm through his, the tips of his ears warmed slightly.

She took him to the Downingville Market, a unique sight in his travels through New Gilead. The market was a huge square that took up a fair chunk of the town, with small fires to help shoppers stay warm in the cold. The square was filled with all manner of people, including several stalls run by groups Grimluk knew were from the Southern Territories. Humans, elves and halflings with dark hair and deeply tanned skin, dressed in buckskins and furs, beads and feathers, selling artwork and jewelry and clothing. Grimluk had always loved the jewelry that came out of the Territories and the tribes that dotted the provinces. No one else on Ornesea could replicate the style properly, rendering fakes easy to spot. Now he saw a stunning array of crafts that, while similar in composition, all had a unique feel.

As the pair walked, passing masons and cobblers and musicians, Grimluk couldn't shake the feeling he was being watched. Eventually, he noticed a human staring at him from the square's center. The man was hatless and dressed all in black, his coat long and tight with a collar of white that hugged his neck. He held a large tome bound in dull red leather. Pale blue eyes bore into Grimluk's with an intense gaze, as the man spoke loudly and clearly to the crowd.

"Repent for your ignorance," the man in black cried, still staring at Grimluk. "Repent, though you do not understand the knowledge you lack! You blasphemers! You do not see the truth!" He thumped the book for emphasis.

Grimluk watched him silently, the mystical tattoo on the crown of his skull tingling uncomfortably. He could feel a presence pushing against his mind. The man smiled at him, lips peeling back from crooked teeth. Grimluk turned his gaze away with a grunt.

"Who's the human with the book?" he asked Emerald, softly.

She huffed. "Him. Won't give anyone his name. Showed up a week or so back. Just spouts off about blasphemy and repentance and truth and sometimes sin."

Grimluk's throat rumbled.

"Peacekeepers tried to shoo him off after he started up. Hear tell he just said, 'I preach the words of truth for the true gods,' so now folks just call him the Preacher. Don't seem to eat or sleep, just stands out here with that big damn book and his big damn mouth."

"I see," Grimluk replied, letting out a steamy puff of breath as he looked around at the other sellers. A familiar word caught his ear among the crowd. Someone said something about demons and he followed the sound of the voice, Emerald trailing along with him until he found the speaker.

A human man with a graying beard and blue eyes was holding up a blue-bladed knife. Grimluk snorted to himself. He knew right away that underneath the man's furry hat was a balding head.

"That's right, friends, these are gen-u-ine demon killers! Grab one now before a beast catches you unaware!" The merchant made a dramatic move, miming a pouncing cat toward two children watching him.

Though the children laughed, Grimluk approached the man with a sour frown.

"Ah, a customer! Step right up, my friend, don't be shy."

"It's Sal, isn't it?"

"I see my reputation precedes...me..." The man's face dropped as realization filled his eyes. "You! Get away from my stall! The last time I saw you, you broke one of my blades! That was ten bilts of damage!"

"I sincerely doubt that, Sal. Why don't you do these folks a favor and sell something more useful?"

"Friend of yours?" Emerald asked, eyebrows raised and a playful grin across her face.

Grimluk let out an amused growl. "Mm. Ran into him over the summer out at the edge of the Wastelands, hawking these useless pieces of shit he claims are demon killers."

"Really now?" She feigned a look of surprise. "I assume, then, that they are of unrivaled quality."

"One can only assume. Where was it you said you got them, Sal?"

Sal looked back and forth between the orcs. "Uh, I didn't. My, uh, supplier likes to remain private. But just between us, I get them from the two best smiths in the land, Flytena and Thor."

Grimluk stared at the man for a long time before sighing through his nose. "Ythena and Flor?"

"That's what I said."

Grimluk tsked. "If you thought me breaking one of your blades was bad, you'd really hate to see what those two would do to your shop if they knew you were trying to pass these off as their work." He leaned toward Sal and continued speaking, softer now. "And truth be told, I'd really prefer you didn't get anyone killed from ineffective weapons. It makes demon hunters like me look bad."

"...Oh," Sal said, a sudden burst of uncomfortable laughter pouring out his round face.

"Yeah."

Sal continued his nervous giggling before swallowing hard and stepping back. "Gen-u-ine chef's knives! Cut up a thousand potatoes with these beauties. Yes, sai. They can even cut up an onion without making you cry! Gen-u-ine chef's knives!"

When the merchant looked at Grimluk for approval, he gave a toothy, semi-sarcastic smile before walking away with a snickering Emerald.

"Everyone knows his knives don't do shit," Emerald informed Grimluk. "Though I do like the color."

"Maybe so, but it's the principle of it. Met plenty of folk that weren't keen on hunters even after their children had been saved. Don't need any more reasons for fear and distrust. Especially for us."

Sadness filled Emerald's eyes for a moment, and she nodded. She was silent as she led him through another row of shops and stalls.

"Can I ask you somethin' a little personal?" Emerald asked.

"Reckon so," he replied as he took in the shops, passing by a furniture store for halflings.

"Well, um, how to put this..."

"I usually prefer the direct approach."

"I don't want to seem rude, 'cause I don't mean this to be rude, but aren't you a bit too, uh, friendly? For a demon hunter, I mean?"

Grimluk stopped and looked at her with knitted brows. "Too friendly?"

"Yeah, I guess. I once heard demon hunters are purged of emotions. Only way to fight a demon or some such. But you're most certainly not emotionless."

A little laugh slipped between Grimluk's tusks, his eyes closing in amusement. "That old rumor? Gods, is it still floating around? Been a long time since I heard it. Every hunter I know, our people especially, is vibrant and full of life." He held his right arm up and pulled his coat sleeve back with a sigh, giving Emerald a clear view of the studded, black leather bracer. "This belonged to a friend like that. He was...intense."

"I'm sorry he's gone."

"Died a hero. Guess you could even say a warrior's death." He lowered his arm again. "Hazard of the job."

"Why do it, then?"

Grimluk's throat rumbled, as he mulled over a potential answer. Before he could answer, something caught his eye at the back of the square. It was massive and covered in dense fur. A bulbous red nose swayed with its movements as it picked up a crate in front of a halfling.

"Troll!" Grimluk blurted out before launching into a dead sprint.

"Troll?" Emerald started to ask before he took off. "Grimluk, wait! That's just—Stop!"

The hunter rushed up to the disgusting creature, which was holding the crate over the halfling's head. The halfling's chestnut ponytail bobbed as they pointed. Grimluk ripped the halfling away, causing them to yelp and squirm in his grip. The troll turned at the yelp. Its bulbous nose wobbled gently, while dark, beady eyes regarded Grimluk. As he pulled his gun, it bared its teeth.

"Help!" the halfling called.

Emerald ran up and got in between Grimluk and the troll. "Stop that, you big ass!"

Grimluk set the halfling down in one smooth motion and pulled Emerald out of the way. "Careful!"

The troll roared, "Help Margy!"

Emerald gave Grimluk a sharp slap to his cheek. "I said stop, Grimluk."

Grimluk blinked at the sudden heat radiating in his cheek and looked at Emerald, lowering his gun. "It talks."

"That's just Bart," she said, pointing at the troll, her other hand on her hip. "He helps Margy here."

"Barty help good!" the troll rumbled, seeming to calm down when Grimluk lowered his gun. Bart set the crate down where he'd been told to and patted his belly with satisfaction. "Barty helped."

"It talks," Grimluk repeated, slightly dazed. He looked around in stunned silence at the staring crowd and spotted several peacekeepers headed their way.

"Em? What's going on?" Margy asked.

"Hi, Margy, fellas. We're terribly sorry. Grimluk here's new to town, he didn't know about Bart. We're going now. Say hi to your sister for me. Hope she recovers quick. Orin's really missin' her behind the bar." Emerald pulled Grimluk by the arm as she walked off.

He followed dumbly for a moment before holstering his gun and turning back around to touch the brim of his hat at the halfling. "Apologies, miss." He stepped backward with Emerald, watching the troll a few moments longer before turning away. The brief interruption to their routines ended, the denizens of the market continued on, the dull roar of conversation and action blanketing the square once more.

"Ain't that a kick in the head," Grimluk finally said.

"You always so thick-headed when you get a mind to do somethin'?"

"Trolls aren't usually so well-behaved in my experience, and hesitation with a demon will get you killed."

"Well, that's fair enough, I s'pose."

"Didn't mean to cause a scene," Grimluk said, turning to look at the troll again. "Bart? Really?"

"Really. He's a sweetheart, too."

"Bart the troll. Cenka's not gonna believe that."

"Who's that?" Emerald asked as she looked through a jeweler's stall.

"I guess you'd say my mother."

"You guess?" she asked with a dubious look.

"Gave birth to me but ze's not a man, not a woman. Reckon some folks would say it's 'complicated' but ze's just hirself."

"Aaaah, not that complicated, then," she said with a wink. "Tulip's like that, too. You know, like a lot of elves get. What do you think of this?" She held up a silver necklace with a jeweled pendant.

"Reckon it's nice, though I don't know too much about jewelry and such. Can't imagine much not looking good on you, though."

"Why, Grimluk, you'll make a woman blush," Emerald replied with a coy smile before inquiring about the price.

"Two bilts," the jeweler replied.

"Well, we are a good-lookin' people and you do your people a real credit."

Emerald nodded, unable to hide her smile. She pulled two silver coins from her coin pouch and dropped the necklace into the pouch before tucking it away again. Then she reached over and took Grimluk's arm. "I think I'm done with my shopping for now. I was thinking maybe I'd show you through the town a bit more, if you're interested."

"Lead on," he replied with a nod.

The tour of Downingville was an utter treat for Grimluk. It was rare he spent enough time anywhere to actually see the sights, and the smaller towns could be explored by turning in a circle. The only places he could claim to know with any sincerity were Hunter's Hollow and Eagle Point. Though the vast majority of this town was residential, Grimluk reveled in getting to see it from a local point of view. They spent a few hours strolling around Downingville's edge, and Emerald showed him the budding train station. Grimluk had heard about the project several years prior. The governors' council had decided to push forward on building tracks across the provinces. It made sense to him; trains could allow for greater travel and speedier deliveries. So now, here was Downingville, land being cleared for tracks while the platform was standing there waiting to fulfill its purpose.

"Don't suppose you heard whether or not they figured out how to make the elemental steam engine work?" Grimluk asked as he looked down the pathway of cleared earth.

"Elemental engine? No, I'm sorry. I just assumed they were working with boilers. We have a pretty big one at the Conqueror. For baths and such."

He grunted. "Really wondered about that. Heard the folks buildin' these things were lookin' to use elementals. Water and fire spirits tend to be difficult to deal with when they're mad. The problem is they tend to make each other mad. Reckon a regular old boiler engine would do the trick, though. How are the baths?"

"I'm not just sayin' this 'cause I work there, but they're pretty amazing. Local magician worked out an alchemical treatment for the wood to let it burn for a long time without stoking. You could practically live in a hot bath."

Grimluk couldn't help but grin at that. "Cold as it's been, that sounds like a downright holy experience. You know, the good kind."

A peal of laughter spilled out of Emerald. "The good kind of holy? There's a bad kind?"

Grimluk shrugged. "I've not had a good experience with anyone claiming to be holy."

"Well, most folk keep their worship in their homes out here so I'd wager you won't have to worry about that."

"What about the Preacher?"

Emerald sighed. "I'd forgotten about him. Don't recall if he ever called himself holy, though."

Grimluk offered his arm to her again and gave her forearm a soft pat when she took it. "You go on forgettin' him for now, then. Reckon maybe we should head back. Reckon my glut's probably been spent by now."

"I suppose it has. Though my free time is my own, I do have some callers who've been waiting for my time. We can go this way. There's a back door through the kitchen."

After they'd returned to the Conqueror, and while Emerald saw to her callers, Grimluk occupied his time with a game of poker. He joined a table with some halflings and a drunken dwarf who seemed rather determined to lose as much money as she was able. The penny pot turned into bilts rather quickly because of it, and though he tried to encourage the woman to fold and wait off the booze, she wouldn't have it, offering some rather heated comments for his efforts. He couldn't help but sigh and roll his eyes, but he was grateful she never resorted to racial slurs. She really did seem nice enough, if terrible at poker.

In the end, he and one of the halflings split the pot and raked in their winnings. Grimluk slipped a handful of pennies into the dwarf's cup when she wasn't looking and wandered off before anyone could say anything.

One of the barmen rang a bell and called out an announcement. "Time's about six, folks. This evening's song is set to start soon in the showroom. Emerald will be your host tonight."

"A show, eh?" Grimluk muttered. Emerald had told him about the Conqueror's theater, where shows from a variety of performers took place. There were jokesters and illusionists on occasion, but mostly there were musicians and dancers, and once a week, the Companions would put on a crowd-pleasing show full of bawdy songs and innuendo and dancing.

He followed the crowd back into the showroom and found a comfortable spot to wait for the show to start. Patrons trickled in steadily until the floor was packed. A piano started up, eliciting hoots and hollers aplenty. The curtains peeled back and revealed Emerald standing in front of a line of Companions, each one with their skirts pulled up or their chests bared or some combination thereof. The crowd cheered and whistled at the motley crew. They were mostly humans but there were others as well; a couple of halflings, a pair of dwarf twins, and an elf so beautiful Grimluk wasn't sure whether they were using a glamor or not.

"How y'all doin' tonight? You ready for the show?" Emerald called from center stage, wiggling her hips suggestively.

Whistles and yips filled the room again and Grimluk couldn't help but smile a full, tusky smile. As the crowd quieted, the piano player transitioned into a new song.

"If you're a regular around here, you know what to do. If you're new, you'll catch on fast! Pro-

vided you can pick your jaws off the floor first."
She turned and pushed her hip out, punctuating her
statement with the move and eliciting several more
yelps and yips.

When Emerald turned around once more, it
was to lead the first verse of the song:

> "When you come a ridin' right into
> town
> For sweet recreation you surely are
> bound.
> Find us all waitin', your journey is
> through
> The Coming Conqueror is the right
> place for you."

The crowd let out a chorus of approving yips
and hollers at the start of the song. Emerald's
singing voice had a similarly husky quality to her
work voice, no doubt for the same reasons.

> "Come right on in, come on up to
> the bar,
> We promise that you won't have to
> look very far;
> One of our sais will bring you a
> boon,
> Here at the Coming Conqueror hotel
> and saloon.
>
> "Lumberjack or cowpoke, we really
> don't care,

No matter the person, we'll treat you
right fair.
We got the best booze and we got
the best shows,
Especially when they involve a lack
of our clothes.

"We're always warm and always open
for you;
Down at the Conqueror, you'll never
be blue.
Men or women, those outside and in
between,
We'll make you quite happy, on that
we're quite keen."

The crowd clapped and cheered and sang along
with such force Grimluk could hardly hear Emerald. In response to the uproar, she offered her hand
to the elf and the two twirled around each other
before coming to a stop with Emerald standing
behind them, looking oh so very shocked. One of
the humans tiptoed out exaggeratedly and gave
Emerald's rear a pinch, causing her to thrust her
pelvis forward and shove the elf away. Emerald
looked upon the crowd with a satisfied smirk and
motioned for them to quiet down. Several Companions joined her across the stage, shushing the
patrons theatrically.

"So give us a kiss and we'll give you
a rub;

Maybe we'll do both down in a brass tub.
At the Coming Conqueror, there's one thing to know:
We'll make you feel great from your head to your toe.

"And on the next morning, when you bid us goodbye,
Feeling so good you might kiss the sky;
We kept up our promise, you knew we'd be true.
The Coming Conqueror was the right place for you."

At the end of the final verse, the patrons erupted into another round of yips and hollers and high whistles. The Companions stood in a line across the stage and bowed as one to the chorus. Those with breasts gave an extra little jiggle and a wink to the crowd up front, receiving more whistles and the unmistakable sounds of fists thumping tables. Grimluk clapped as well and admired the show and Emerald's command of the crowd. He figured there'd be more to come but decided to slip out before everyone else. He stood in the doorway to the saloon for a moment and looked at the stage again with a smile before heading to his room.

Slime bubbled up out of the animal carcasses, burning and ripping through meat and skin with ease, setting off wet snaps and pops. The slime rolled around in its meals, something like satisfaction filling the dim thoughts of its mind. The animals in the barn had been nourishing, and had given the slime strength after its journey through the darkness. It had no concept of how much time had passed before it landed. Though it never would have known otherwise, its birth had gone smoothly.

As it fed on the dwarves, its perceptions started to change slowly.

As the slime rolled out of the one called Maisy's skull and in the one called Nahum's mouth, it took with it some rudimentary knowledge, absorbed a portion of the woman's mind. It knew some basic facets of the world it now inhabited. Maisy had been a loving partner and mother. The slime's understanding of the concepts was loose, but it knew them after feeding on her, gaining its strength. It knew she loved Nahum and fought the slime's influence even as it compelled her to pin the man down. As it dug into Nahum's flesh, that strength continued to grow.

Each carcass contained some part of the slime, all separate but at once still very much a singular entity. The slime slurped as it gorged, sucking every last fiber of meat and skin and hair off the creatures it devoured. New knowledge bubbled up as it fed on Nahum. It now knew that it was on something called a farm and that it was devouring farm animals. It knew, between Nahum and Maisy, that the pair of them were something called dwarves and that there were other dwarves outside the barn, in something called a house. The slime wondered what they would taste like. It wondered what love was. Did love make things taste better? Maisy and Nahum had tasted wonderful and it knew from eating them that they loved each other very much. And they loved the others in the house.

One of the dwarves approached. The slime could feel it with its every sense, soaking up the approaching life. It was the one called Dar. Dar was making strange sounds, a lot like the ones the animals made when it had started feeding on them. It didn't like those sounds, but there was still plenty to eat off the animals and the two dwarves right now. It could wait. It could finish this meal first.

It felt Dar take a step toward the bodies of Nahum and Maisy. The slime had no intention of approaching Dar at the moment, but if he wanted to come now and feed himself to it, the slime would enjoy him now, too. A strange, jumbled thought rose in its mind. "Don't lick a gift horse in the kettle." It didn't know what that meant but it felt the sentiment clearly enough. Dar did not feed himself to the slime, though. Instead, he ran back into the house. That was fine, too.

When the slime finished its meal in the barn, it congealed into one solid mass. Bones lay strewn about, perfectly clean and neat, a touch scorched in various places and piled up where the bodies had been previously. The great mass rolled out of the barn and into the whiteness beyond, then let out a gurgling hiss of pain. The ground outside felt like it would rip the slime apart. It retreated back into the safety of the barn.

It sat for a while, looking at the expanse of

whiteness that stretched out between the barn and the house. Tentatively, the slime reached out two long tendrils and tested the ground. The pain was less intense this time, but it was still sharp enough that it squelched and pulled the tendrils away. What was this, that it could hurt so much? The slime bubbled in thought.

The dwarves had walked across this white stuff. It had moved Maisy's body across it without any problems, following after Nahum. Maybe it had to do with their shapes. All the things it had eaten had appendages supporting them when they moved. Weren't they called logs? There had been long, hard things inside the logs, though. It couldn't recall what they were called but the slime wondered if maybe it could use the hard things to get across the hurtful whiteness.

It swallowed up Nahum and Maisy back into itself and took the biggest, longest of their hard things – buns? Borns? Then it spat out the rest before spreading them out under itself. Surely this would let it get to the house where its next meal was waiting. The slime tried out its new plan to leave the barn again but the borns just fell away when it moved, clattering against the barn floor. It had assumed that moving with them was all it had to do. Maisy had simply moved forward, after all.

The slime tried again, focusing on the log borns this time. It pulled them into itself and pushed them back out. With great effort, the slime held on to them and tried to emulate Maisy, undulating the protrusions in different ways, turning this way and that.

Eventually, the slime discerned a method of

locomotion. Tentatively, it left the barn once more and started across the white stuff to the house. It moved slowly, and it seemed its efforts were a success, but the slime was disappointed to learn that while the outside wasn't as cold as the ground, the air was still frigid and hurt, too. It was more bearable, though. The slime worked its way to the back door of the house, turning itself inside-out several times along the way in an effort to fight the cold air.

Its progress was halted by the door itself. It did not yet know about doors. It did know about holes and cracks, though, and pushed against the door, seeking out the small spaces. Bit by bit, the slime pushed itself through the cracks and crevices of the frame. It dropped its logs when it no longer needed them and, before long, the bulk of the thing had poured itself into the house.

It could sense Dar and the two other dwarves somewhere else in the house. A fresh hunger boiled in the slime, demanding attention, demanding to be sated. The roiling blob had worked so hard to get in, and now it could see if love made things taste better. It slithered across the floorboards, following the sound of Dar's voice. Another door was in the way. That was fine. It knew about doors now. It pushed itself under the bottom of the bedroom door much quicker than it had the back door. Dar was pointing something at it as it came through. The thing roared and something hit the slime. Hot metal pellets filled the slime's body. It didn't like the taste of those, so it spat them back out.

The slime reared up, taller than Dar, and flared itself out like a giant, viscous hood. The hunger roared, demanding food. The slime gladly obeyed. What else was there but food? And here was its next meal. Dar pointed the strange thing at the slime again. It made the loud noise once more and out the little metal pellets came. The slime still did not like their taste.

The little dwarves were making the bad animal sounds. The slime descended upon them all at once. Garbled shrieks filled its body as it covered the last of the little farming family.

Chapter 5

The creature held on to the things it now knew were called bones. If those first few had helped it cross the cold ground, the slime felt certain that more would provide some further use, and it had a lot more now. It knew more about doors now, as well. One hard bash knocked them open, broken and hanging strangely but no longer an obstacle. The great, viscous blob slithered back out into the cold evening air, pushing and pulling its new tools in and out of its body like a massive centipede. When the smallest bones – from hands and toes – proved useless to the endeavor, it pushed them to another part of itself and continued on. They might provide some other use later.

It was hungry again. Always hungry. The slime knew no other way to be and while it absorbed some of the knowledge of the dwarves, most of it lacked context or faded away. It had been disappointed to learn that love did not make things taste better. But that was okay.

As the blob skittered along on its bone-limbs, something caught its attention. A voice.

"You have been a most interesting sight, creature. I have never seen such gluttony in anything but my kin. I wonder what you are?"

It continued its trek but reached out with its senses, looking for the source of the voice. Maybe the voice would be food.

"I am not food," the voice rumbled. "I felt your presence, watched as you devoured those frail mortals. I can sense your hunger. Perhaps I can help you with that."

The slime let out a gurgling groan in reply. All it knew were its own desires, but the creatures it had eaten had made noises to communicate. Maybe this would satisfy the strange voice.

A slim red form covered in scales and black claws and horns descended in front of the slime. Membranous wings beat at its back as it regarded the slime with cold, black eyes. "You do not have to try and speak to me, creature. You have enough of a mind that I am able to communicate with you. As for your hunger...come. I would see more of you."

The blob bristled with excitement and followed the red thing happily. It led the blob to another farmhouse. For a moment, the slime thought it had been led back to where it started, but it sensed the presence of living things once again. This was a different place, then, with different things to eat. It hurried to the barn with all the speed the rolling bones could provide it, the white protrusions undulating furiously from under its slick, pinkish form.

The animals all screamed in their ways. The barn was warm, so the hungry blob let the bones drift inside itself as it reared up and wrapped around a cow. The red creature laughed aloud as the slime devoured the animal. A memory drifted up from Nahum and his family. Laughs meant pleasure. The red thing liked helping it eat.

Maybe the red thing would show it more food after this.

It sensed more beings approaching. Things like the dwarves, but taller. It heard them scream and yell and one of them pointed a weapon at it like Dar had. The blob gurgled in annoyance and hurled a part of itself at its attacker's face. The piece wrapped around its attacker's head and began to feast, dissolving the skin and hair and glorious meat. Its meal dropped to their knees, clawing at the slime, screams muffled by its gelatinous form.

The blob spread more of itself out, globules slithering about the barn floor and attaching to living things that hadn't gotten away. The red creature flapped its wings, staying in the air as it watched and laughed its rumbling laugh again. The blob gurgled and smacked, burning its way through its meals. And it learned something new.

The red creature was a demon. It learned that from the head of the tall dwarf, which was not, in fact, a tall dwarf. These were called humans. The other humans gave the slime more knowledge. Demons were, according to their memories, things to be feared. They were evil.

That didn't make sense to the blob, though. It didn't know what evil was, and besides, the demon had helped it find this new meal and learn these new things. The thought slipped away, useless and unwanted and replaced with rapture as the slime spread over the last animal and last human. This it wanted. Its hunger boiled and burned within.

The demon laughed as the slime ate. "Yes, feast well. I, Sheogorath, have found the key to my vengeance."

Once the blob finished its meal, Sheogorath led it to another farm. In the dark of night, the slime crashed through the door, splitting apart again. It found beings similar to dwarves but smaller. Halflings, it learned. They didn't have a barn full of animals, but there were enough of the halflings in their dirt dwelling that the slime cared little. Though it wouldn't have cared either way. Food was food. As long as it got to eat, that was all that mattered. As it devoured all it found, it pushed one of the halflings up against a window where Sheogorath was watching. The demon just laughed its harsh laugh and tapped its clawed fingers against the glass.

"Come along," Sheogorath growled once the slime had eaten the halflings. "Dear creature, you have a new meal waiting near. Then I will take you to a true feast. Yes...and then I will be the one fed."

The slime grew sluggish after the third farm. The family was big. Four generations of dwarves along with a huge barn full of livestock. The slime felt something close to satiation after that. The hunger still bubbled deep within while rolling waves of new thoughts churned in its mind. The demon hovered above the slime, watching it intently.

"I trust you are satisfied for the moment." It picked up a massive table and hurled it through a wall, shattering glass and masonry alike. As the dust settled, the demon pointed a taloned finger toward the quiet, snow-covered fields. "That is where we will go next. My dear kin's ruined corpse lies beyond. As does your feast." It descended and got close to the slime's body. "You, marvelous creature, will be the instrument of my vengeance. I can feel the hunger burn in you, unquenchable, immutable as the Abyss. Your," Sheogorath gave a sharp-toothed grin, "appetite for destruction is comparable only to my Elders'."

The blob listened and rolled the demon's words around in its mind. Vengeance. It didn't really understand that concept. It wasn't something the minds of the people it'd eaten had showed it. It knew, for instance, that almost every piece of masonry in the area had been built by the family it had devoured. It even knew, now, what masonry actually was. But vengeance? Could you eat it? If love didn't make things taste better, would vengeance? It bubbled in thought.

It sucked the bones of the animals back into itself and pushed them out. A ripple ran through them as they adjusted to an even distribution. It knew now that snow was temporary and, in another month, it would all be gone as warmth began to fill the land. The slime moved forward in the direction the demon had pointed with the sun beginning to rise ahead of them.

The demon hissed. "Yes. Together we will make the mortals pay. I lay claim to the one who killed my dear Bashuurga. I will suck out their soul and show it an eternity of pain!"

The slime wondered about wild game and birds, something else it had learned about. It had devoured a whole coop of chickens, but the halflings they'd belonged to had enjoyed other birds more. The human family before that had been fond of something called venison. The slime wanted to try these things.

It stopped. The bones serving as its feet rippled again, clacking against each other and crunching the snow lightly. It appreciated the demon's help in feeding it, but now it would find its own meals. It shifted the mass of its gray-and-pink body and turned in a new direction.

The demon let out a low growl. "That is the wrong direction."

The slime ignored the demon. Where could it find a venison? And pheasant? Or elk? Were elk like birds? Something told it that elk were bigger but that didn't always mean much. Maybe that meant they had more taste. Maybe not. The dwarves had more taste than the humans, even though they were smaller.

The demon landed in front of the slime, growling much louder. "That. Is the wrong. Direction."

The slime skittered around the demon, uncaring and focused on its goal of new foods and flavors. It still wasn't sure when it started tasting its food, but it did, and it liked it. It was a new sensation that only added to the joy of feeding.

A wall of black fire erupted in front of the slime. It bubbled at the sight before skittering through the flames. Though the fire blackened its outside layer slightly, it didn't hurt like the cold snow did.

The demon roared. "No! You will do as I say,

creature! I found you, I fed you! You find yourself in my debt now! Sheogorath does not forget a debt."

The slime's movements slowed, each protruding bone forcing its way forward as though something was holding it back. Its focus shifted to Sheogorath. The demon's eyes were alight in a sickly yellow glow, its teeth bared in an angry grimace. The slime pushed harder and regained control of its movements, skittering away once more.

The demon let out another furious roar before landing on the slime. "Fool! You will serve me!"

Sheogorath's taloned fingers dug into the middle of the slime's mass, dark energy pulsing around them and into the viscous fluids of the creature's form. The slime squelched in pain and tried to pull away with every ounce of strength in it. The demon's grip held. Red wings beat rapidly and suddenly the slime was rising above the ground. It squelched again, struggling and pulling as Sheogorath aimed in the direction it had commanded they go. New buildings started coming into view, bigger than houses and more numerous than the farms the slime had visited over the past few days.

It pulled again, trying to remove itself from Sheogorath's grip, but the demon's power would not wane. Deep in the blob, its hunger stirred and combined with its desire for freedom. Instead of pulling away, the slime started pushing against the demon. Gray-pink flesh oozed up Sheogorath's arms, slowly at first, and then all in a rush.

The single-minded demon didn't notice until the slime had wrapped itself around its head, and then it was screaming and biting while it flew higher. The bites only served to let the slime get inside the demon. It pushed part of itself down the demon's throat while the rest wrapped around Sheogorath's body, crushing its wings with a constricting spasm.

A crackle of energy ripped through the blob's body, agonizing and euphoric all at once. The energy crackled again, filling the thing's body with eldritch light as it plummeted out of the sky.

For the second time, the slime crashed into the earth below, in the middle of the place it had seen from the air. Bits of its body sprayed out on impact while the intact mass expanded and then imploded with an unearthly shriek. A taloned hand shot out of the oozing mass for a moment, sending a single bolt of purple energy into the sky. Clouds raced in from nowhere, black and thunderous, and returned the bolt back into the slime, crashing down in a deafening strike that shattered every window around and forced Sheogorath's hand back into the roiling mass. Within the slime's body, something split and cracked, a dark force spilling out like blood from a deep wound.

Its body started to boil and hiss, darkening similarly to the way it had from Sheogorath's black flames. Bubbles began to rise all over the mass of its body, bursting at the surface, a moment of sharp pain that shifted in an instant to form mouths and eyes at random. The mouths took every possible shape a mouth could take. Some had teeth like those it had feasted on, some like cows, others like Sheogorath's mouth, and still others took the form of sharp needles and suckers, while the eyes were every size and color and shape an eye could be, having and lacking pupils or forming them and then losing them.

As one of its new eyes burst through the surface of its body, it saw people around it. A black-skinned elf pointed a gun at it.

"What art thou?" the elf asked.

One of the mouths bubbled forth, yellow teeth gnashing in reply. Another mouth bubbled out from within the first, garbled, bubbly words tumbling forth unbidden and malicious, both its own yet foreign.

"Ssshhhhoggoth...Vvvveeeenn–" The mouth burst before the words could finish.

The oozing mass of its body reached out toward the elf with a long, probing tendril the color of a dark bruise. The elf jumped back and its weapon flashed, releasing its own thunderclap, and something slammed into the slime's body. It was getting tired of people shooting it.

"Vvvvennnjuuusshh!" several of its mouths tried to roar in unison. Vengeance. It wanted vengeance. Hungered for vengeance. These mortals killed its sibling. They would pay. They would sate its hunger. They would experience untold agony at its hands.

The creature reared up like a great hood, mouths rising and falling in eager anticipation before popping like boils with angry hisses. Others joined the elf, weapons in hand, yelling and rushing all around the slime. It called the missing pieces of itself, willed them to return through a path of resistance, a path of pain. The missing pieces of the slime's body rolled toward it, each globule striking the swarming mortals as it sought to rejoin the whole. The pieces sliced and pierced. One of the chunks turned into a mouth and bit through the calf of a halfling. Another, larger piece drilled into the back of a human and out through the stomach, dragging its victim into its gleaming black body and waiting mouths.

The elf fired again and again. Others hurled stones and bottles. The slime roared with all its mouths, the sound like a massive, drowning beast. It hated all. It hungered for all. Hungered so deeply, beyond anything it had ever known before. It collapsed toward the elf, who again leapt away as the slime slapped the ground with the force of a dropped boulder. Tendrils lashed out, attacking and dragging those foolish enough to get near it, swallowing them up until only it and the elf were left in the street.

The slime rolled in on itself, bubbling and growling, immense in its new girth. It moved forward with alarming speed, barreling down on the elf, who ran and fired his ridiculous gun, leaping away with the slimmest margins of escape until at last a furious tendril lashed out and pierced the elf through the chest. Quickly, the tendril spread around the frail body in a gluttonous embrace. The elf struggled and screamed but there was no escape. Oily black ooze filled the elf's mouth and then all was silent as the body disappeared into the writhing mass, one free hand clawing at the now dark flesh until it, too, disappeared.

As it fed on the people of Arbortown, the slime pushed its body through each building, searching for whatever remaining mortals still lingered in hiding. It found and devoured them. As the whole of the town sat burning in the blob's innards, a single detail began to shine through in its mind.

Grimluk.

The name echoed in the mind of its victims. Grimluk, the orc. Grimluk, Bashuurga's murderer. Downingville. The killer had fled to another town with Bashuurga's head.

The slime burst out of the hotel, shattering the entirety of the building's front with its massive bulk, and began rolling in the direction of Downingville. It would find this Grimluk. It would find him, make him pay for his transgressions, his mortal arrogance. It would devour him completely.

There were screams all around, but Grimluk couldn't see who was making them. He chased a shifting demon through a wall of fire, his gun barking, following the beast with stinging lead.

The demon disappeared, but Grimluk wasn't alone. Corpses surrounded him, reached out for him, begged him to save them. He reached down for the nearest one, taking its hand, and pulled. The effort was futile. He flexed every muscle, straining with every ounce of his considerable strength, but the harder he pulled, the weaker he felt. He might as well have been trying to lift a mountain. Tears rolled down Grimluk's face as he screamed in frustration. Frantically, he moved on, trying desperately to pull another corpse out of the flames and mud, but each new tug made the victim sink deeper.

The demon returned, mocking laughter spilling out of its twisting maw as it seized Grimluk's neck and squeezed. Grimluk hurled his fist at the thing's face but as it neared impact, it slowed to a crawl while he moaned in agonized frustration. The demon squeezed his throat.

His body spasmed hard enough that it ripped Grimluk away from sleep in one violent motion. It took a moment to reorient himself. There were no flames, no corpses, no demon. He was safe in his room at the Coming Conqueror.

He let out a sigh. "Fucking nightmares."

The dream held tightly to his mind, but the waking world demanded his attention now. Gunfire crackled in the distance, staccato thunderbolts rousing him in a hurry. He sat up, turning the wick on his bedside lantern up. A massive, bone-white moth fluttered away from lamp's lip, suddenly casting a monstrous shadow on the wall.

"Shoo," Grimluk said as he listened. It was quite common to hear the report of a revolver at night, but it was usually no more than a shot or two from a drunk or a warning shot from a peacekeeper to get someone's attention. This was no drunk or warning shot. Instinct kicked in and he dressed without thought. More than likely it was a band of rustlers for the halfling goat farm Emerald had shown him, or a pack of thieves trying their luck with the peacekeepers but, as his cenka was fond of saying, it was better to have something and not need it than to need it and not have it. Grimluk always preferred to have his gun when he was able.

The heavy canvas of his coat settled on his shoulders, reassuring and familiar after the dream. It was followed by his bag as he slipped quickly out of his room. Long strides carried him into the frigid night air, where the curious gathered on the porch of the Conquerer to peer into the dark toward the sounds of battle – sounds that were much louder now that Grimluk was outside. Screams pierced the dark, reminding him too much of the nightmare.

The strange roar that followed sent chills down his spine.

"Everyone get back inside!" he shouted at the onlookers. "Now!"

Several looked at him like they were about to start arguing, but when he pulled his gun out they all bolted back into the Conqueror. Grimluk took off in a dead sprint once the hotel's door slammed closed again, rounding the corner and heading for the gunfire and screams. Several people passed him as he ran, yelling incoherently, some of them bleed-ing. Far ahead, near where Grimluk had come into town, something massive shifted, reflecting glints of lantern light off its body. No sooner had the glimmers faded than more screams filled the night. If he hadn't known better, he'd have thought it was mist rolling down a hill, but mist didn't tend to reflect lantern light like that. Of course, screams and frantic gunfire at whatever it was certainly helped solidify that assessment.

Grimluk rushed forward, readying himself for battle. The sound of gunfire had begun to die down, but the screams hadn't. Some of them had shifted into gurgling wails that were snuffed out almost as soon as they started. He stopped next to a halfling just in time for the man's gun to bark out five shots.

"What's going on?" Grimluk shouted.

The halfling looked at him, eyes wide and frantic. It was Amos, the deputy who greeted him. "It took 'em! It took 'em, gods-damn it, it took 'em all!

"What took them?"

"Amos!" someone shouted from near the writhing thing.

"Marty!" Amos cried out as he sprinted forward, furry feet carrying him off before he could reply to Grimluk. He was faster than Grimluk expected.

"Amos! Gods-damn it," Grimluk growled. The old man shrieked, calling for help as he toppled over.

Grimluk dashed forward. Something dark and slimy had Amos by the legs. It pulsed almost like the heartbeat in a raised vein. Grimluk grabbed Amos's outstretched hand and pulled. Whatever had the Peacekeeper held tight, though, and Grimluk pulled harder. Memories of the nightmare threatened to overwhelm him, but he shoved them away with another throaty growl.

"Hold on to me, Amos," he said as calmly as he could while Amos clawed at his arm with his other hand. Grimluk took aim carefully and fired at the slimy appendage. A squelching roar sliced through the air. The grip on Amos started to loosen and Grimluk wrenched. Amos let out another scream as he slid free of the thing's grip.

As Grimluk pulled him away, firing twice more into the dark, Amos kept screaming. Grimluk hoped the demon was hesitating from further attack but that wouldn't last long. And he hoped Amos was only screaming in fear. He hauled Amos into the little booth the halfling had been manning when Grimluk arrived and tried to lean him gently against the wall. After a flick of the lamp's wick for more light, Grimluk saw why Amos was screaming.

Amos's pant legs were shredded along with the flesh beneath. Bits of muscle twitched as the light cast its orange glow on the bloody mess. His left leg ended in an oozing nub above where his ankle should have been. His right leg was missing below the knee, and the muscle above was gone, exposing the femur, light glinting off the blood. Amos slumped over, muttering, eyes rolling in his skull.

"My legs, oh gods, my legs, my legs," he kept repeating over and over.

Grimluk hesitated, not wanting to leave the man defenseless but knowing whatever was coming would be on them any second. He shut the door tight and marched back into the street. The mass of writhing darkness rolled forward, glistening in the light of the streetlamps on either side.

"Reckon you and I got business tonight, demon," Grimluk called out, swapping the three spent shells in the chamber for fresh ones. His fingers worked nimbly, perfectly practiced, a trick that almost looked like an illusion.

The thing seemed to pause. Grimluk could see a strange flashing across its surface. It looked like dozens of reflections, all blinking rapidly like moonlight reflecting in the eyes of hidden animals.

It rolled closer, drawing itself near one of the street lamps. Grimluk's jaw set hard at the sight of so many shifting eyes. And mouths. He'd never seen anything like this. The oily surface of its body seemed to be boiling, constantly roiling and shifting like blood and oil mixing. Eyes formed on eyes, mouths in mouths, nothing permanent or fixed. It almost reminded Grimluk of an Abyssal womb except that it was moving around on its own. It also wasn't spitting out demons, a small mercy for which he was grateful.

He lifted his revolver and pulled the hammer back as something in the center of the thing bulged out. Maybe he'd spoken too soon about it not being a womb. Something that looked all too familiar formed in the bulge, pushing forward, reaching out for him. Horns and claws and toothy maw. It looked almost exactly like the demon he'd killed in Arbortown.

"Grim...luk," the shape said in a long, squelching, and viscous growl.

Grimluk had never been so revolted by his own name before. The sound sent chills through him. Some part of him demanded he flee but he ignored it. There was work to be done.

"You want me, demon? Suits me just fine." The gun barked twice, provoking another roar. Tentacles lashed out. Grimluk met them with bullets as he dodged away. "Let's go, you filthy sack of troll shit!"

With that, he turned and ran in the opposite direction. He had to lead the gods-damned thing out of town. It knew his name, was focused on him.

He just had to get it away. And he just had to hope no one stumbled into their path while he did it.

As he ran, he had to slow to fire and yell at wandering people to run. A few of them were drunk and looked at him in disbelief before running away screaming at the writhing mass of midnight roaring toward them, the form of Bashuurga leading the way. The demon's form lashed out, both connected and disconnected from the rest of the creature as it rolled forward.

It roared his name again, no longer a mere growl or some sort of an accusation. There was fury now, plain and clear to Grimluk's ears. The fury seemed to make it move faster. If not for the occasionally rune-empowered bullet from his gun, the thing would have quickly overtaken him. The gun packed a heavy punch, though, and each impact slowed the thing long enough for Grimluk to regain the distance. But it was a losing prospect: he would fall to attrition.

The next time he looked back to fire, the great, gelatinous mass was gone. For the next eternity, Grimluk stayed where he was, sweeping the revolver's barrel around, ready for his foe to break out and attack. From where, he hadn't a damn clue. He was in the middle of the market square, stalls and stands all around, nowhere to hide for something so big. The nearest building was a dozen yards away. He pulled his knife as an extra precaution. The massive, gleaming blade shone like a dark rainbow even at night.

Grimluk crept forward, weapons and body at the ready. He could be stealthy when he needed to be, but this was altogether something different.

Even for a demon. Demons rarely just vanished. They might sneak around you, but always with a taunt. A cruel laugh. An illusion. A trick of the senses. Even then, their size was still a factor. A small hill didn't just vanish.

A gust of winter wind cut down the street as he walked, kicking the tails of his coat around. He kept far away from heavy shadows and tall porches with plenty of space underneath. A light shiver ran down his spine. He wasn't sure if it was cold or nervous energy. Ultimately, it didn't matter. Years of training made sure of that. He moved on, back the way he'd come, back toward Amos's guard shack.

Several of the streetlamps shuddered but most were still lit as he approached. Another gust hit him, followed by a low bang up ahead as the wind caught the door of the little shack. He trained the barrel of his revolver on the door. A faint trail of blood caught Grimluk's eye on the porch. As quietly as he could, Grimluk pulled the door open using the tip of his knife. The bloody trail led to a puddle, but Amos was nowhere to be seen.

"Ah, shit," Grimluk muttered. He latched the door back and looked out to where the thing had been when he arrived. There were a few bodies strewn about. One of the halfling burrows had collapsed. Some of the windows of the other houses began to light up as he stared, filling with the forms of the dwellers within. He could see a few people creeping out onto their porches.

He fired once into the air and they scrambled back inside, followed quickly by the dimming of lamps. He hated to scare people but now was definitely not the time for gawking.

He hurried back toward the peacekeepers' office. Every lamp was lit but the place was empty when he peeked inside. Grimluk's throat rumbled. "Balls." He hurried back toward the Conqueror, turning sweeping circles every so often as he did. Better overcautious than dead when dealing with something you'd never dealt with before.

All the drunks who had retreated back inside seemed to be sobering up. Several of the other Companions were up and around, bringing coffee and offering sympathetic words. Grimluk scanned the room and noticed a human woman looking at him with wide eyes. Emerald was standing next to her. She motioned quickly for him when she saw him.

He put his weapons away, though left his coat tail behind the holster of his gun. Everything in him screamed to stay ready.

"What's going on?" Emerald asked in a hushed voice.

Grimluk grunted. "Demon. Beyond that, I can't rightly say at the moment."

"I thought you knew all about them?"

Grimluk chewed on his words for a moment. The woman was still looking at him. Maybe she'd seen the thing chasing him when he'd run past. He just nodded. "Ma'am, uh, sai." Emerald was still looking at him expectantly. "Never seen anything like it so I can't say for sure. It's gods-damned dangerous, whatever it is."

He stepped away from the woman, gently leading Emerald by the arm. "I think most of the peacekeepers are dead," he whispered. "Do you think the enchantment in here is strong enough to counteract a demon?"

Emerald blinked rapidly, confusion blanketing her face. Her tusks wobbled as she worked her mouth in thought. "I...don't rightly know. Not somethin' we've ever had to test." She paused. "Are ya sure they're dead?"

"If not dead, then badly wounded at the front of town. I thought I'd managed to save Amos, but he disappeared from the guard shack where I left him."

"Amos?" She let out a sigh. "So that's where he was. He came in a few minutes before you did. Looked like something had hit him...well, everywhere. Like a walking bruise, almost. He seemed a touch stunned but otherwise fine."

Grimluk's eyes narrowed. "Nothing wrong with him at all?"

"Other than the bruises, he looked well to me."

He leaned in close. "Nothing wrong with his legs?"

"No?" Emerald replied as quietly as she could.

Grimluk's lip peeled back in a light sneer. "Where?"

Emerald walked around Grimluk and scanned the room. "He was...I–I just saw him. He went to sit in the corner all by his lonesome. I just thought he needed to compose himself. H–he was right over there."

Grimluk scanned the saloon as well but saw no sign of the peacekeeper. "I need to find him. Now."

"Why? What's wrong with Amos?"

Grimluk looked down at Emerald, he knew his

face was probably too hard, so he forced a touch of compassion out. "Tell the other Companions to make sure everyone stays in here."

"Why? Tell me what the fuck is going on!" She appeared to struggle to keep her voice low.

"I left him in the shack at the front of town, Em. He was missin' both his feet. The man you saw wasn't Amos."

Chapter 6

The pair set out to find Not-Amos as quickly and quietly as they could. Grimluk led, hand on the butt of his gun, while Emerald followed silently. Grimluk's mind stayed focused on whether or not the anti-violence enchantment protecting the Coming Conqueror would extend to demons, and, if violence arrived, how it would react to him. That kind of inhibition could make saving a building full of people a mite difficult. He'd just have to deal with it when it happened.

They headed for the theater first. Grimluk hesitated at the door, wondering what to do with Emerald. He could tell her to stay at the door, but if the thing masquerading as Amos slipped by, it could grab her. On the other hand, she could get in his way if they found it. He grunted.

He looked at Emerald over his shoulder. "Stick close. Try to mind your surroundings, including me."

She acted like she was about to speak, but seemed to swallow whatever she'd been about to say and gave a tense smile and a nod.

Better close by and easier to save, Grimluk thought with a sigh.

The theater was dimly lit, giving Grimluk further pause.

"Oh!" Emerald said in a quiet gasp. "Um, illumo."

With that, the lights came to life, now brighter than they'd been during the show that evening. The shadows of the tables concealed no monstrous, writhing masses. The ceiling seemed likewise clear. The curtains behind the stage rustled as the barrel of Grimluk's gun pointed in their direction. The barrel froze there, waiting like a steel sentinel. A hand rolled out from underneath the curtain. Grimluk darted up to the stage, grabbing the hand and yanking, gun trained and ready. A dwarf with a messily braided beard came sliding out.

The dwarf yawned. "The fuck y'all doin'?"

Grimluk let out a heavy sigh. It was the drunken gambler he'd beaten and given money back to. He guessed she'd wandered back here in a drunken daze and fallen asleep behind the curtain somehow.

"You need to head into the saloon," Grimluk told her. "There's…a situation."

She yawned and wiped drool away from her beard. "I was sleepin'. Go away."

Grimluk pulled the dwarf to her feet. "It's very important that you do as I tell you, miss."

Emerald added, "Please, go to the saloon. Tell whoever's behind the bar that Emerald said you could have a drink on the house."

The woman looked from Grimluk to Emerald. "Free drink? Why the shit didn't y'all say so in the first place?" She stumbled off toward the saloon.

"We need to keep everyone together if we can," he told Emerald. "Reckon we oughta check upstairs, too," he muttered as he scanned the curtains for further movement.

"R–right," was all Emerald said, her voice shaking a little.

"There many people using the hotel services right now besides me?" It was helpful information and he hoped that maybe talking would help calm Emerald's nerves.

"Um, only two others are actually staying right now. Most of the track layers went back to Cold River to get the rails goin' again once it warms back up."

"Can we go and get those two?"

"I just need the skeleton key from the office," she replied, pace quickening.

It seemed Grimluk's hope had paid off. He followed closely behind, gun still out but pointed at the ground. With so many people around, he had to maintain discipline even more. This was no time for a stray shot.

"We should probably get the cooks out of the kitchen as well, if they're still in there this late," he added. They passed the dwarf woman at the bar, who raised her mug in their direction.

"The kitchen. Right, yes." Emerald stopped at the end of the bar for a moment and motioned for another Companion, a red-haired human woman. "Get everyone else together and keep the patrons in here."

"What? Why?"

Emerald looked at Grimluk. "We have a situation."

The red-haired woman looked between the two of them. "You mean…" Her eyes went wide and she nodded.

Emerald continued down the hall under the stairs that joined the saloon and the hotel together. "Midge'll be in the kitchen tonight. Maybe Denny." She stopped at the door in the middle of the hall, knocked twice, and slipped in before an answer came. The office sat empty but Emerald didn't seem to notice. She got into the desk and pulled out an ornate metal key. "Okay, up we go."

The crowd was getting restless and confused as the other Companions corralled them into the saloon. Several people complained at Emerald as they made their way to the stairs. Grimluk noticed the human man from his arrival sneering at them. Roscoe, he thought Emerald had called him. Roscoe glared at them, not moving his eyes when Grimluk looked into them. Experience told Grimluk that Roscoe was about to make himself an unnecessary complication.

"We gots to stay in here, but them goblins is rollin' off for a fuck? If that ain't a pile a troll shit, I don't know what is."

Grimluk growled. He didn't have long to contemplate any reply, though. Emerald tugged at his hand and pleaded with her eyes. He nodded and holstered his gun, following as she led him into the hotel. She took him to a room a few doors from his own and knocked twice.

"Hello? I'm Emerald. I work here. Um, there's

a bit of an emergency." When no one answered, Emerald used the skeleton key and opened the door. The room was mostly dark, except for one lamp burning low by the bed.

"Hello? I'm sorry about botherin' y'all so late." She started to step inside, but Grimluk stopped her and entered instead.

The gun came back out as he looked the room over for any signs of the writhing mass or Amos. Luggage sat in front of the bed, a large traveler's chest and a multicolored carpet bag. The bed looked occupied, so Grimluk stepped over and started to reach down to rouse the sleeper. Then a glimmer caught his eye. He turned the lamp up. The pillow was soaked with blood and a strange substance, dark and shimmering, and far heavier than the blood. Grimluk pulled the blanket back farther to reveal the occupant. The sleeper was missing their head. And a good chunk of their body. Blood soaked the sheets. No doubt the mattress would need to be replaced after soaking up the guts of this poor soul.

"Emerald," he said, not looking away, "do not come over here." He turned the lamp low again and walked away. He looked at Emerald in the hallway, her brows high, eyes questioning. "Go to the next room," he said gently. "There's nothing we can do here."

Her eyes went wide but she nodded silently and started for the next room. Grimluk closed the door behind them with a sigh. Gods knew how many peacekeepers had been killed, and now a traveler. Whatever this thing was, the situation was already well out of control.

And Grimluk still didn't know just what on Arkod he was dealing with. His best guess at the moment was a shapeshifter of some kind.

Emerald walked faster. Grimluk wondered if the dead patron was pushing her or if it was just fear. He wasn't even sure what was happening, and he was trained to deal with this sort of thing; he couldn't fathom just how powerless she must feel. How they all felt, really. He kept that feeling locked into his mind every time he set out for a new bounty.

Emerald knocked more urgently at the second door, rapping four times in rapid succession. "Hello?" She knocked again. "My name is Emerald. I work here. There's an emergency, please open up."

Before she could slip the key into the lock, the door opened and a face peered out. "Em?" It was the beautiful elf from the show.

"Tulip! Is your patron in? There's an emergency and we need everyone in the saloon. There's trouble."

"Em, what's—"

Grimluk spoke up. "There's a demon."

Tulip's eyebrows raised ever so slightly. The door closed. When it reopened a minute or so later, the tall elf exited the room followed by a human man. Both wore red and gold robes. The man wiped sleep from his eyes and looked up at Grimluk with a sour frown.

"To the bar, if you would," Grimluk said, his tone polite but insistent.

"Bah," the man said and clunked away in his

boots and robe. Tulip and Emerald followed, Grim-luk trailing behind.

The crowd was even more restless than before. The other Companions had done their best to keep everyone in the saloon calm and occupied. The now-sober drunks and late-night patrons had begun to wonder what was going on. Grimluk scanned the faces from his vantage on the stairs but Amos was still nowhere to be found. A dull roar filled the room as people talked and gossiped.

Grimluk moved to stand behind the bar. He needed to get their attention before things got out of hand. He let out a whistle through his teeth, something he'd had to practice years to do reliably when he needed it. It was harsh and loud, a sound that immediately grabbed the attention of anyone who heard it.

"Beg a pardon from you folks for keeping you waiting and questioning." He looked from face to face slowly. "There's been an attack. Reckon most of you heard the gunfire. Reckon some of you might've even seen me runnin' down the street."

The woman Emerald had been tending to when he'd arrived looked at him from the left. "What...was that thing?" Her eyes were still wide.

"Short answer? A demon. I don't know much more than that."

The din of the patrons returned, less dull and much more frantic. It didn't take an expert to sense the panic beginning to rise. The feeling of a crowd's tension thickening and preparing to burst was something you had to learn to recognize as a demon hunter. Grimluk hoped he could find the right words to stem it before it broke and they got themselves hurt or killed.

He whistled again. Silence flooded in. He looked around the room, meeting eyes, breathing calmly. If he didn't appear calm, they'd definitely panic. "I am a demon hunter," he said, letting the words linger. "I have reason to suspect the thing is a shapeshifter. That is why I've asked you all to stay together. Each of us will need to be tested to verify our identities. Until I find it, we must remain calm and together. Do you understand?"

Several heads nodded dumbly, along with a few quiet affirmations.

"That's real nice, goblin," Roscoe started, "but what says you ain't the shifter? What says you ain't about to skin and—"

A shriek cut him off.

As Roscoe spoke, Grimluk had produced his knife and proceeded to drag the blade across his forearm where everyone could see it clearly. Blood welled up from the cut and Grimluk smeared it across the flat of the blade and held it up. "This knife is a tool of the hunt, designed to hurt demons and ward off demonic influence."

"That's...that's..." Roscoe had apparently lost his tongue.

"And on a personal note, friend, I would once again politely request that you not utter that word again." Grimluk stared at the man hard, eyes full of steel. "If you refuse, then I would also politely request that you step up and be the second confirmed."

Roscoe glared at Grimluk, but the man's anger withered as Companions and patrons alike stared him down. He went quiet and folded his arms across his chest, sulking.

Emerald and Tulip stepped forward and offered their forearms. "I'll be second," Emerald said calmly, loud enough for everyone to hear.

Grimluk nodded, wiping the blade clean on his coat arm. "Shouldn't hurt. Blade's mighty sharp and I know how to use it." He nicked the pair of them in quick succession, small cuts purely for show. The blood welled up in little beads of crimson and he grunted. "Clean."

Emerald circled around the bar to stand next to him. She pulled down a bottle of whiskey from the shelf and then four small glasses, filling them each with shots. "Everyone who takes the test will get a shot on the house. And you must give your consent to Grimluk. If y'all don't consent to the cut, the protection enchantment will toss him out."

Grimluk couldn't help the grin that tugged at his lips as he gave Emerald a satisfied nod.

An hour later, almost everyone in the room had a tiny cut on their forearm and a shot of whiskey in their belly. The Companions had done their best to help Grimluk, shepherding people toward the back and out of the way as new people came up. Someone would step forward, hold their arm out, and then down their shot before heading to a seat or spot away from the bar. The dwarf twins worked through the crowd, thanking everyone for their cooperation and offering a complimentary kiss to go with their shots of whiskey.

Grimluk appreciated the help immensely. Without the Companions, he doubted he would have been able to keep the crowd nearly as calm. He'd have to pay them for it. Or at least offer them credit. Wasn't often a hunter was the one to owe money.

Roscoe was the last one left.

Grimluk had watched him as the others stepped forward to be tested. The man refused to get near Grimluk. Refused to move or be moved, so everyone moved around him, like a creek over a stone. Then they were done and everyone glared at Roscoe, nervously glancing at each other in pregnant silence.

"The fuck y'all lookin' at me fur, eh?" Roscoe growled. Crossed arms seemed to cross tighter and planted feet seemed to dig deeper, like a stubborn weed. He just stared at his feet and ground his teeth, the very picture of obstinacy.

If Roscoe kept this up, the patrons would finally panic. Everyone around him was slowly edging away, trying to move away from the potential threat. Grimluk could see thoughts of attacking the stubborn man pass across some of the faces. He looked at Emerald, who'd readied the last shot of whiskey for the colossal pain in their asses.

"Word of advice, friend," Grimluk said, breaking some of the tension. "You're in a room full of folks who have bled themselves willingly. Don't give them a reason to fear you."

Roscoe shrank at the admonishment, but just tightened up more, hunching up, knuckles turning white. "Fuck you, ya gobby shit."

"Emerald?" Grimluk said without looking away from the man.

"Hm?"

"Reckon one of your peers would be willing to make the cut?"

"Um, Tulip?"

"No, Em. A human. Reckon this fellow ain't too keen on anyone else touching him. And as much as I'd like his explicit consent in this, I don't see him giving it. So he can either let a human do it, or I can walk over there and make him do it."

Roscoe squeezed his eyes shut and bared his teeth. "Gods-damned right human only," he said through his teeth.

The red-haired Companion from earlier stepped up nervously. Her brown eyes were alert but crowned with worry. She gave an anxious tug at the skirt of her red dress before pulling the bodice down a touch as well.

Grimluk nodded at her. "What's your name?"

"Rebecca."

He held up the knife, close to the tip. "I'll show you a little trick, Rebecca. You can hold the knife like this, no need for much pressure. I know it's a heavy blade, so just hold it this way and let this bit of edge do the work. Understand?"

She nodded and he handed the knife over.

Rebecca approached Roscoe cautiously. "Sai, may I have your arm?"

He stood unmoving for a long moment – too long on such an anxious night – before pulling a hand free just enough so she could get to it and no more. "Better not get no gods-damned goblin disease from this."

If the situation were different, Grimluk would've given serious consideration to dragging the man outside and dropping him like a sack of potatoes. That wouldn't help the situation, though. He knew the asshole was scared more than anything. Bigotry and fear were probably the worst combination a hunter could encounter during a hunt, but with a demon in their midst, the fear would be stronger.

At least, that was Grimluk's hope.

Rebecca held the knife to Roscoe's forearm, her off-hand taking the weight of the handle. A scream ripped through the building and Grimluk's gun was out before his next breath, pointed at toward his right. Toward the kitchen.

"Gods-damn it, woman, ya gods-damned mauk, ya nearly sliced my fuckin' arm off!" Roscoe shouted.

"Knife," Grimluk said, holding out his hand. The horn handle slid into his palm from a shaking Rebecca. "Appreciate the help. Get him cleaned up. Looks worse than it is," he said, glancing at the cut before he stalked off to the kitchen, revolver held at the ready.

A tall, batwing door, worn almost as much as the door into the saloon side, concealed the kitchen. Dull light spilled out from the lamps within, flickering lightly. Grimluk thumbed the hammer on the revolver back and pushed the door forward with his knife. A halfling was sprawled out ahead of him, staring at the ceiling. Grimluk looked up.

An elvenoid shape was pinned to the ceiling, covered in a thin layer of the dark ooze Grimluk had seen on the dead sleeper's pillow. Grimluk reached up, using his height and the size of the knife to slashed at the slime, attempting to free the person trapped beneath. The ooze sizzled and squelched in protest, ripping away wherever Grimluk cut it. The chunks fell away. Some fell toward him, but he slapped them away with the revolver. The slimy substance pulled away from the body and it dropped into Grimluk's arms, bloody and limp. Liquid darkness slid down the wall toward the water pump before disappearing down the pipe.

He watched the pipe for a long moment, waiting to see if an attack was coming. When none came, he reset the hammer and holstered the gun before sliding the limp body to the floor. He then looked at the halfling, a woman from the looks of it.

"Midge?" he asked.

Wide, terror-filled eyes regarded him, her mouth twitching.

He sighed. "Midge, I'm Grimluk. I'm a demon hunter. That thing is a demon and I think it can shapeshift. I need to use my knife to make sure you're mortal. I know this is a lot to take in, but I need your permission to avoid the protection enchantment." He held up the knife as non-threateningly as he could. "This is a hunting tool. Do you understand?"

She stared at him. Her eyes wandered down to the body on the floor. A sob choked out of her. "Oh, gods," she whispered. "Denny, no..."

"Midge, please, I have to make sure. Everyone else is in the saloon. I need your permission."

Midge looked at him, confused, like she was seeing him for the first time. Her eyes rolled back down to Denny, tears welling up in her eyes. She nodded numbly.

Grimluk took her left hand in his. He didn't bother to draw blood this time. That had mostly been for show before. Occasionally, a demon hunter had to embellish their actions. Blood always made for a strong show. Just dragging the blade along her skin would reveal the truth. He sighed when there was no reaction.

"Can you stand?" he asked her.

She looked at her legs, as if only just remembering she had them. She stood slowly, with a wobble, but of her own power.

"Head on in with everyone else. Tell Emerald I tested you."

Midge wiped away tears and wandered slowly out of the kitchen. Grimluk looked down at Denny's bloody body. He'd seen the man's skin pulled off but the doubt of the situation was too big to ignore. Gently, Grimluk touched the flat of his blade to Denny's chest. Nothing. He wiped the blood away on his sleeve before the knife found its sheath once more. Grimluk lifted Denny's body with little effort. The blood was sticky now, drying bit by bit, clinging to his shirt and coat in the spots where skin and muscle had been laid bare.

Grimluk carried Denny into the saloon and laid him down on the bartop. A chorus of gasps filled the room as people saw the man. Grimluk found several towels under the bar and began gently wiping blood away from what looked to be the worst of the injuries. Denny's breaths came out in shallow spurts. Only time would tell whether or not he survived.

"I tested him as well as Midge. Do we have a healer?" Grimluk asked quietly, soaking one of the rags in a bit of whiskey before he used it. Emerald and several other Companions stood nearby.

Rebecca stepped forward again. "I was an apprentice before I became a Companion."

He nodded. "Quite the talented one, Rebecca. Do what you can to help him."

"What will you do?" she asked, taking the towel from Grimluk.

"Hunt."

The Coming Conqueror's bath cellar was everything Emerald said it would be. There were a number of steam rooms lining the walls, as well as bathing tubs in the center of the room. Pipes ran overhead, dipping into and out of the steam rooms and converging around a huge boiler at the back. After seeing the demonic blob retreat into the water pump, Grimluk wondered if it might be hiding down here, or if it was still in the pipes themselves.

The air hung thick and humid. He could hear

the water flowing through the pipes in a steady thrum as he moved toward the boiler. Gun and knife were out and ready as he moved. Grimluk walked with the grace of a hunter, each step silent and deliberate. Mostly, the use of stealth was a habit formed from years of training. He was well aware that whatever this demon was, it had the advantage over him. Grimluk felt quite sure it was watching him, making his efforts irrelevant.

As he crept, he peeked through the bath curtains, double-checking for signs of the oozing monstrosity or missed patrons. A couple of the tubs still had water in them. One of them looked oily. He dipped the tip of his knife into the water and dragged it through.

Nothing. He nodded, and moved on toward the boiler.

As Grimluk looked the boiler over, he had an idea. The demon trap wasn't the only tool of its kind. There was another that worked in the opposite manner. Instead of confining a demon, it would expel them. Mostly, the expulsion circle was used to facilitate exorcisms, so he wondered if it might also work on inanimate objects and containers. If the shapeless demon was hiding in the boiler or the pipes, this might flush it out.

Grimluk slipped his knife into a loop on his coat, letting it dangle where he could get to it easily. He swapped the revolver into his freed hand and reached into a breast pocket in his coat, withdrawing a small, metal cylinder. He twisted the body counter-clockwise, producing two barely audible clicks as he did, revealing a small bit of chalk at the tip.

He found a clear spot on the boiler and held his hand close to it to check how hot it might be. Very little heat seemed to be coming from the immense metal body.

"Hm, proper Schmiedehand boiler," he muttered. The best dwarven boilers had been designed by the Schmiedehand family to make use of volcanic activity. Whether through thermal vents or heating water with magma, they minimized the risk of getting burned nearly completely. They were common in areas that could afford them. Clearly, the Conqueror did good business.

Grimluk set to work, starting with the five-pointed star that served as the base for both the trap and the expeller. His hand moved as if circling the star, as he would do for the trap, but staggered the circle instead, creating breaks. Under those breaks, in the space between the lines of each point, he wrote a sigil. The last sign would, under normal circumstances, activate the expulsion circle. Results were instantly apparent when used in a normal exorcism. The demon would fight to maintain its hold on the host, and, unlike the trap, the expeller was not guaranteed to work, owing its success to factors such as the host and the demon's own strength.

An agreeable host would result in only minor discomfort for possessor and possessed. A demon of sufficient power might even rip the host's soul out, leaving a disconnected husk behind, a living being whose body would grow and age and die but whose essence would be forever dimmed, usually falling into a vegetative state. That result was mercifully rare. Usually, the expeller worked and that was that.

Grimluk watched the boiler for what felt like far too long before he saw any sign of effect. The minutes drew out slowly until, finally, several of the pipes bucked and shuddered as screeching filled them.

"Got you."

Grimluk hurried back upstairs, ready to find the thing wherever the pipes spat it out and hopefully end the impromptu hunt.

Chapter 7

Great shudders rocked the Coming Conqueror, filled with the sounds of groaning wood and dim roars as Grimluk climbed back up to the saloon. Screams from the patrons practically slammed into him as he exited the cellar. The demon-thing would either be expelled back out into the kitchen or it would force its way out in some other, more violent direction. Grimluk hoped for the former.

The Conqueror gave one last, violent shake before stillness took its place back. Bits of dust tumbled down, freed from years of captivity between floorboards and in every other nook and cranny the building had. As Grimluk passed the crowd of patrons and Companions, he attempted to hush them with a finger over his lips. Most of them went quiet immediately, but a few couldn't contain the laughter of the confused and frightened.

"Stay quiet and stay still," he told them. He thumbed the hammer of his revolver back and headed for the kitchen.

A great black blob covered the wall and part of the ceiling near the water pump, eyes bubbling over its surface as quick as boiling water and as slow as molasses all at once. A faint pulsing glow of dark energy rippled under the surface. Mouths and maws of all shapes formed similarly, snapping as they did so. Whether they were aimed at him or not, Grimluk could only speculate.

"Gods-damn," Grimluk muttered to himself. A dozen eyes locked on him at the sound.

A portion of the blob rolled across the ceiling. The demonic form that had called his name poured out from it, drooping down headfirst before suddenly rolling right-side up.

The revolver barked, and a gaping hole formed in the chest of the demon.

The writhing mass of eyes and teeth shuddered and squelched, loosing a cacophonous chorus of growls. The hole closed slowly, even a touch laboriously. The demon shook its head.

"I know what you're supposed to look like, you foul abomination, but you ain't it." Grimluk sneered at the thing before him. "I still got one of its horns."

A word that sounded like "feast" came from one of the mouths while the others hissed or growled or gnashed. The word seemed to come out like someone trying to speak with mud in their mouth. "Shoggoth...wilve...vengshhhhaaa."

The demon's hand shot out at Grimluk. Without thinking, his right arm jerked up in defense, revealing the studded bracer on his forearm. Inky blackness slammed into the bracer, pushing him back a few feet, the sound of sizzling flesh filling the air. The writhing form let out a bubbling squeal of pain and pulled away hastily.

Grimluk fired twice more. The bullets ripped

into the oozing form with thunderous slaps and squicks. The demon's face seemed to roar at him but made no sound. Instead, the oozing darkness sucked up into the ceiling all at once, dripping in reverse. The demon's roaring face was the last thing to slip between the spaces in the ceiling, and then it was gone. Three bullet holes were clearly visible in the wall.

"Shit." Grimluk turned and rushed back into the saloon. "New plan. Everyone out. Now!"

"What happened?" Emerald asked.

"Did you kill it?" someone else asked.

"Ain't a goblin born what's capable o' doin' a gods-damned thing right," Roscoe announced loudly, a sneer plastered across his face.

Grimluk turned to the man. "Out. Now. Or I take you out." A yelp pulled his attention away.

"There's something over the door!" shouted one of the human Companions.

Bubbling darkness filled the doorway, sucking the batwing doors off their hinges.

"Get away!" Grimluk shouted, too late for it to matter. Tendrils grabbed the Companion and drew them into a roiling maw of swirling, jagged teeth, the scream deafening the saloon. "Back! Stay away from the door!"

"Grimluk!"

He turned to the voice. It was Emerald.

"It's coming out of the ceiling!"

He looked up to see more of the oozing demon seeping through the cracks in the ceiling. His eyes darted around the room, panic beginning to fill his mind. There wasn't enough time to move over two dozen people to safety, if there was even safety to get to at this point.

An idea jolted him. Grimluk turned to Emerald. "Hit someone. Surprise them."

"What the fuck—" her eyes went wide before she finished "—Oh!" Emerald turned suddenly and slapped the nearest person she could reach square in the mouth. The crack of palm hitting cheek barely rang out before Emerald disappeared in a red flash.

"Everyone!" Grimluk roared, "Fight! Your lives depend on it!"

A mob of very frightened people fell into each other with panicked vigor, hurling fists and open-handed slaps with every ounce of what was clearly a very primal fear. Flashes of red cascaded one after the other and then Grimluk was alone, black death oozing all around him. He sliced at dripping tendrils and mouths with his knife.

"Come on, you filthy bag of pus. Come and get me!"

The Conqueror shook as the demon bellowed its rage. Wood began groaning as Grimluk ran for the stairs, firing at a grasping, blobby arm that reached for him. The arm ripped away and slammed into the wall. A dozen tiny eyes formed as it slid down the wall, every one of them fixed on Grimluk as he passed.

"Come and get me, you useless puddle of puke!"

Wood started shattering behind him as the thing pushed inward. The stairwell splintered and busted under the weight of the colossal thing rolling up it. Grimluk fired again and the demon let out a liquidy roar, slowing for a moment before hurling itself forward again. It barreled toward him, mouths snapping and dripping with malice. Grim-luk turned down the hallway with rooms pointing to the outside wall of the building and slammed into the nearest door, busting through shoulder first. Two glass doors led out to a small balcony and Grimluk crashed through those as well, sending bits of glass and wood flying everywhere, nicking his cheeks and hands, setting trickles of blood flow-ing. He ignored it all and leapt off the balcony railing with every ounce of strength he had, aiming for the roof across the way.

His fists slammed into the roof, followed by his body slamming into the edge. Grimluk only grunted with effort. The shingles were rough, wet with snow, and sticky with pitch as he hauled him-self up, rolling on his side for a moment before climbing to his feet.

Time was not on his side this night. The demon latched onto the roof seconds later, pulling the rest of itself over the gap in a hurry. Grimluk put boot to roof and ran.

Death seemed utterly assured when the demon hunter told Emerald to hit someone. She started to protest, her mind reeling, wondering for a too-long moment if he'd lied, if he'd gone mad in the cellar.

The words started out of her mouth, and then Emerald realized what his goal was.

She spun on the man closest to her, a human she practically towered over. He looked up at her in surprise, his eyes going wide as she raised her hand. It wasn't a practiced, measured slap, like some customers would ask for on rare occasions. It was a hard, fearful strike. Harder than was probably necessary, but not hard enough to really hurt him. At least, she hoped not. The impact stung her fingertips before it rolled up her forearm, but it worked. The enchantment seized her in a flash of red light that immobilized her, and then she landed on her butt in the middle of the not-quite-muddy courtyard in front of the Coming Conqueror.

Lamplight reflected off snow and cast a dull orange haze on the night, allowing her to see without too much effort. She immediately wished for pitch-black darkness.

The nightmarish thing attached to the front of the building assaulted her eyes. She'd seen a demon once, a long time ago. A dead imp killed by an apprentice hunter. It had been a small thing, with black, rocky skin, little horns, and sharp claws on its hands and feet. It was hard to forget, but it had hardly seemed like it should have been. Not like this.

Not a colossal mass of pulsing ooze that seemed like diseased, liquidy flesh that still had life to it. The eyes and mouths snapping into and out of existence across its surface seared themselves into Emerald's mind. Each eye that formed seemed to roll across the body, toward the interior of the building, ignoring her. Ignoring the sudden crowd that joined her.

The flashes of red light slammed her mind back into her body, giving her the anchor she needed to keep the fear and revulsion from sending her screaming into the river. Companions and patrons fell around her while gunfire thundered from behind the mass of black. It was muted, but what else could it be but Grimluk's huge revolver? Emerald scrambled to her feet and looked around, helping people around her to their feet. Emerald hoped to whatever gods might listen that the demon wouldn't notice them. She hushed everyone who tried to speak, imploring them with her eyes. The urge to fall to her knees – babbling, begging for silence, begging for the thing to ignore them – tried to fight its way out, but she held it down. She tried to focus on keeping her breathing steady with marginal success.

The crackling of wood caught her attention as the thing forced its way back inside with a sudden rush and a roar. The entranceway buckled slightly. She heard another gunshot, louder now that the demon wasn't blocking the open doorway.

"Everyone, to the peacekeepers' office, now! Run!" Emerald surprised herself with the order. No one argued, not even Roscoe. They all just turned and fled as one, a sudden herd in front of her, stampeding away. She started to follow, suddenly dwelling on the thought of slugging Roscoe for managing to make a demon attack even more of an ordeal than it already was.

Glass shattered. Emerald looked to the source in time to see Grimluk soar across the alleyway and slam into the roof of the building across from the Conqueror. The demon was right on his heels.

Emerald ran. The thing was chasing him, and it could still chase her if she didn't get away from it first. The only thing she knew to do was run for the magi-tell office. If she could send out an emergency call to the rangers, maybe they could stop the thing, or bring in more demon hunters. Anything.

She was thankful the mud wasn't bad as she ran, passing around some of the crowd as she did. The ground had set well when winter rolled in months prior, allowing for only a thin layer of muck to form. There was little chance she'd slip in her haste, snap an ankle or some other impediment. Small blessings.

Emerald burst into the magi-tell office. "Call the Rangers!" she cried. "We're under attack!" This late at night, only a few people were in the office, for just the reason she was there.

The other gasped. "We'd heard the guns. What happened?"

"Just call the rangers!" Emerald pleaded.

The operator nodded and went to work immediately, wrapping her little hand around the crystal and speaking. "Emergency! Downingville requires ranger assistance! Repeat, Downingville, New Gilead requires ranger assistance! We are under attack. This is not a drill!"

The crystal glowed in the halfling's hand. It stayed that way for a good minute and then she spoke again. "Acknowledged."

Emerald nearly collapsed when the woman nodded to her. She was suddenly very tired. She wobbled a little but leaned against the doorway to steady herself.

"They're dispatching now but require more details," the woman added. "What can you tell us?"

"I think most of the peacekeepers are dead. It's a demon, I think. Probably. The demon hunter that came through recently was fighting it, but it...he..." She didn't know what else to add. She didn't even know if Grimluk was still alive. "It was chasing him."

The operators looked at each other. "Dead?" the first operator said.

"Everyone from the Conqueror should be in the peacekeepers' office by now," Emerald said quietly after a moment of silence. "It was the only place I could think to send them. You should come, too. It's not safe."

"One of us has to listen for messages, especially now," the second operator said.

Emerald understood, but the part of her still running on adrenaline pushed her to act instead. She marched over and picked each woman up under her arms. She did it so fast and surprised them so thoroughly that she'd made it halfway to the peacekeepers' building before either of them uttered a protest.

"I'm very sorry, but it's not safe and we have to stay together," she heard herself saying sharply. "You can bill me later. Free massages if we survive."

She set the women down on the porch of the peacekeeper building and ushered them in. Something moved in the corner of her vision, dragging her attention away. Emerald gasped at the sight of Amos walking slowly toward her, still looking slightly dark and bruised, both legs whole. The breath caught in her throat as she remembered what Grimluk had told her. Emerald tried to squeak out a word at the group huddled inside, but nothing came out.

Amos drew closer. Close enough Emerald could see a wet sheen to his skin and beads of something on top of the sheen. She took a step back and still no words came out. Amos reached out for her with one hand. His fingers were too long. Halflings had small hands. His face seemed to be melting, too. Something round rolled out of his mouth. It shivered and then opened to look at her with a red slit of a pupil.

The dam in her mind finally broke and Emerald screamed an animalistic scream of terror.

As Amos neared her, his fingers seeming to grow longer with each step, she threw her hands out as if to push him away, squeezing her eyes shut. She wanted Amos far away. He'd been a good customer before, but this wasn't him and she wanted him – it – gone. She wanted her life to be normal again. No demons. No dead people. No writhing black masses that threatened to rip her mind to pieces just looking at them. Pleasuring clients and spending her time how she pleased. She didn't want to be a hero. She didn't want to be responsible for anyone else but herself unless she was being paid for it.

More than anything, Emerald did not want to die. Especially not in the street, and most especially not to a demon pretending to be one of her regulars.

When she opened her eyes, wondering if she'd been killed and just hadn't realized it, Emerald saw Amos reaching out for her, nearly frozen completely still. His face was contorted in agony, his body covered in a thin layer of ice that made his movements sluggish.

Not-Amos's fingers stretched further out, still reaching for her slowly, the ice crackling as they did. Emerald was dimly aware of people watching her from the door as she screamed again and threw her hands out. She'd never tried using her magic this much before, but frost blew into the demonic doppelganger and the fingers stopped.

"No!" she bellowed at him, fear mingling with her will, her powerful need for survival. Another blast of frigid air and snow flurries wrapped around the thing's form as she pushed the magic as hard as she could. Her whole body clenched against the effort while ice crystals spread across Not-Amos's body with sudden ferocity until a clear layer had formed, utterly cocooning the abomination in ice.

Emerald collapsed to her knees, slumping hard, wobbling before the rest of her tipped forward and joined her knees on the porch. Her eyes rolled in her head and then everything slipped away in a dim haze. She felt hands on her arms and tried to pull away, tried to scream, but dazed murmurs were the only thing that came out before darkness rushed in and carried her away to unconsciousness.

As the demon climbed onto the roof behind him, Grimluk fired his last round and ran. He didn't bother to look back. The thing was too big to miss at this range. As he leapt to the next roof, he flipped the cylinder out and dumped the shells into the alley below. His fingers set to work reloading, moving swiftly, deftly, utterly confident and precise in their movements, practiced and honed over the years, even while moving.

The demon hesitated crossing the new gap after him. It let out a series of grumbles and squelches before swiping out against the thin layer of snow on the roof. The hesitation gave Grimluk more time to work, time to think. He had to get the thing out of town. That hadn't changed. It was behind him again, and he meant to keep it that way this time. He stopped, watching the thing's tendrils probe the snow. Maybe he could goad it.

"You that other demon's mate?" he asked, his gun readied with fresh shells. "Sibling? Parent? Reckon it went down like a simple pest. No more difficult than swatting an annoying imp."

That seemed to catch its attention. The familiar shape lurched out again, dragging the rest of the oozing blackness with it.

"That's it, then, eh? Revenge? Not that you'll survive it. You know how many of your kind I've destroyed?" The gun barked once. "More than I care to remember!" Grimluk took off again, sliding toward the edge of the roof and then off, into the street again, the tails of his coat billowing out as he dropped and snapping down on his landing.

"Come on and get me, then," he yelled, not standing still. "You'll never do it. You ain't got it in you to take me out! Reckon you ain't even got brains enough to tell dung from honey."

The demon roared its muddy roar. A few moments later, Grimluk heard it slam into the ground and start after him again.

"Come at me whole hog this time!" Grimluk shouted, running for all he was worth. There was a forest outside of town, covering either side of the road and rolling down to the river. If he could get to the trees, it might at least slow the thing down some.

At least, he hoped so.

He had a few hours of fight left in him yet, but he needed an advantage of some sort to get the best of this thing. The demon seemed to absorb his bullets, however much they hurt it. He needed to trap it, if he could. At least then it couldn't hurt anyone else while he figured out how to kill it. He didn't have time to create a big enough trap in the dirt, but maybe the blanket would work.

Grimluk kept running down the street, leaving a blatant trail of prints in the soft layer of muck for the demon to follow. There was no sense in firing anymore, but he squeezed off a shot anyway, for good measure.

He pushed hard and managed to make it to the forest's edge. He stopped long enough to see how far behind the demon was. Too close for his liking. Grimluk practically dove into the forest.

"Best hurry on. You can't get your vengeance unless you catch me!" he shouted as he slipped between trees. Thick trunks blanketed the area, their empty arms stretching to the sky in silent supplication for sunlight. Trunks cracked behind him and the thing roared, a howling sound full of fury and bubbling with hate. Grimluk let out a roar of his own. Anything to keep the thing coming after him.

Grimluk made for the river. The thing slammed into trees behind him, wrapping around them like the trunks were cutting through that wretched, oozing body. He spun and fired once, catching part of the demon as it flowed around a particularly thick tree trunk. It didn't take him long to reach the water's edge. Cold River was flowing strong and sure, no doubt even colder in the winter than its name implied.

More branches cracked and snapped behind him, joined by the sound of groaning trunks, the branches crunching into the snow as some of them broke away in the creature's haste and effort. When it came into view, the shape of the horned demon pushed forward again, surging toward him before jerking back into itself with squelching howl of pain. Something had hurt the beast, and it wasn't Grimluk.

It stayed still for a moment, mouths gnashing out along the dead demon's form and the rest of its putrid surface. It cried out a second time and backed off into the trees, rolling away.

"Where do you think you're going?" Grimluk said with a grunt. He started back into the wood but stopped, throat rumbling in thought. What if it was trying to trap him? It seemed likely. The demon appeared at least somewhat intelligent, and, while his bullets didn't seem to be having a great effect, he was certain they were still having an effect.

He moved forward cautiously, taking deliberate steps, hoping to keep from crunching the snow more than he had to. He scanned ahead, looking for a trail, but there wasn't one. Grimluk remembered the thing nudging the snow on the roof. This demon seemed to have an aversion to touching the stuff. The snow here sat nearly to his ankle and Grimluk could clearly see his own prints, but nothing else. Not even packed banks from the pressure the thing would no doubt exude. Had the thing climbed across the trees?

Snow crunched ahead of him. Grimluk ducked into the shadow of an old oak and crouched, readying his revolver with a flick of the hammer. Something moved ahead of him. He could just make out the movement in between the trees.

Except it wasn't massive. Its shape and movements were more elvenoid.

"Grimluk?" a voice called from the direction of the shape.

Emerald? Grimluk wondered silently. The voice almost sounded like hers.

"Grimluk?" the voice called again, thick but mostly clear, moving closer, snow crunching underfoot.

He watched as it approached. Red and gold, muted by shadow, fluttered with each successive movement. The skin had a vague green tint but looked too dark, even in the dim light reflected from snow and trapped under cloud. Grimluk's eyes narrowed. The colors fell away for the briefest of moments, just long enough for him to see the eldritch darkness of the demon's wretched form.

He dropped the hammer back and stood, holstering his gun and sheathing his knife. Grimluk pulled the demon trap-embroidered blanket from its holding spot on his bag and then stepped forward.

"Here I am, Emerald," he called.

Her head snapped toward him and she started marching in his direction. "Grimluk!"

He moved slowly. "Reckon the demon's gone. I'm glad you're okay." He watched Emerald walk, each step stiff, her movements plainly different from what he'd seen over the past few days. He stopped and waited.

"My, but you're a vision of beauty. Quite a sight for sore eyes," he continued. "Look a mite cold, though. Care for a blanket?"

Emerald nodded, within arm's length now. He could clearly see the bruised-looking skin now in the moonlight, the lovely green of Emerald's skin distorted with darkness. Skin that looked too soft and puffy, as well. "Come, this will warm you up."

She nodded again and he stepped to her side, unfurling the blanket with a snap before laying it across her shoulders and back, making sure the trap side would be against her.

A shrill hiss filled the air as Emerald fell forward into the snow. A shrieking roar of pain followed it, making Grimluk wince and grunt from being so near the sound. Emerald's demon twin flopped and thrashed and rolled onto its back, shrieking like a massive, broken kettle boiling over with malice. Once flipped, its face and body bubbled and contorted in melting, roiling motions that almost turned Grimluk's stomach.

Something hit him, knocking him away and into a tree. He slid to the ground with a grunt and shook his head. Something slapped his leg. He looked down at the perfectly clean femur resting in his lap. When he looked up, the oozing monstrosity was pulling away from the trap, flailing upward with the desperate strokes of someone trying to escape drowning.

Grimluk watched in shock and horror as the grotesque, bloated form ripped away from the demon trap. A crackling, tearing sound followed and the thing flung itself at a tree and vanished, leaping away into the dark, screaming in abject pain. The screams soon died away, leaving an eldritch silence.

Grimluk tossed the leg bone aside and got to his feet, inching toward the blanket. A sheet of charring ooze sizzled and jerked against the blanket, stinking worse than any creature that he'd ever come across, dead or alive. The blobby flesh turned black as it reached into the air. It stiffened and cracked, suddenly still and unmoving. The whole of it started to diminish, crumbling into powder and burning away in a white flame that left the blanket untouched and clean.

The hunter looked at the blanket, now unmarred by any sign of what had just happened. "Gods-damn," Grimluk muttered.

CHAPTER 8

The walk back to town was agonizingly quiet. Grimluk's nerves felt like they'd turned to sharpened points as he attempted to have eyes in the back of his head. And the top. And the sides. He really hated the situations that pushed him to have zero blind spots. He could handle running for miles at a time if he needed to. He walked leagues every day he traveled, and that was fine, too, but trying to keep sense and sight in every direction was exhausting. He couldn't think of another hunter who could do it for long.

His efforts appeared for naught, though, at least for the moment. Grimluk wanted to feel grateful for a temporary reprieve but his instincts refused to quiet down. Maybe the demon would strike again, maybe it wouldn't. He was fairly certain it would be, at best, observational for the time being. The demon trap had hurt it badly, though Grimluk wasn't sure whether it had been the trap itself or the thing getting out of the trap that had done the damage. Nothing demonic had ever gotten out. Ever. If it had ever happened, no hunter had survived the encounter to talk about it.

There might be some other explanation, but

Grimluk lacked the time and information to figure it out. He had more pressing concerns at present. Chief among them was how to evacuate a town. In all his years, he'd never had to do it. A family or business, occasionally a tiny settlement, but never an actual population. A horde of ghouls usually ended up as a waiting game unless you had enough ammo to thin them out quickly.

Priorities. He could worry about the town as a whole after he checked on everyone from the Coming Conqueror. Especially Emerald. To his knowledge, the demon had eaten or possessed Amos and masqueraded as the halfling. If it had pretended to be Emerald, she could be dead or possessed. His pace quickened. Outside of staying alive and killing the demon, he needed to find the survivors.

Grimluk remembered glimpsing the crowd running away after they laid into each other. Someone had shouted at them and they'd bolted so he didn't have to go back and check the Conqueror again. The peacekeepers' office seemed like the most logical place for scared people to run to. That was usually how it went. He headed in that direction.

He hadn't been sure what he'd find when he arrived, but the block of ice in front of the building was definitely a surprise. It was a big block, all things considered. It glittered as he approached, covered in a thin layer of frost. His throat rumbled as he passed it, taking in what appeared to be an outstretched hand.

When he tried the door, it didn't move, probably bolted or barricaded. He heard quiet gasps from within, so he knocked gently and made himself known.

"It's Grimluk," he called. "The demon hunter. You folks all right?" He waited in silence, muffled words catching his ears.

"How do we know it's really you?" a deep voice replied.

"Because if I was that thing, I'd have squeezed through the cracks already. But I reckon I can offer somethin' a little more substantial." He unfurled the demon trap blanket again and laid it on the porch. "Ever heard of a demon trap?" He stepped into the circle. "Got one on a blanket and I'm standing in it. If I'm a demon, I'll be unable to get out."

The contradiction of that fact and what he'd just witnessed fluttered in his mind. It wasn't the time to start doubting everything he knew, though. Besides, the blanket trap had worked back in Arbortown, so it had to be something to do with this shapeshifting demon.

The door cracked a bit, showing most of the face of a man Grimluk recalled as one of the bartenders. The man looked out at him and down to the ground. Grimluk held up his hands, empty of weapons, and stepped to his right, out of the circle.

"Need to see it again, or you figure I'm true?" Grimluk asked.

The man visibly sighed, practically shrinking with the effort. "Just had to make sure," the bartender said as the door opened.

"A wise choice, partner." Grimluk gathered the blanket up and stepped inside. Someone closed and bolted the door behind him. "You folks seem to be in one piece. What's the story with the ice block?"

"Emerald did that. Hear tell from one of the magi-tell operators she froze Amos."

"She did that?"

"Ayup. Then she passed out with blood pourin' out her nose. We dragged her inside."

Grimluk nodded, his fears about Emerald being eaten were doused. "She all right?"

"I ain't no healer, but I reckon so. She's still out. We laid her down in a jail cot, back there in the middle. Tulip's been lookin' after her. Magi-tell ladies said they got word out to the rangers 'fore Em dragged 'em over here."

"Smart work," Grimluk said with another nod. "Here." He laid the blanket out again in front of the door. "This'll give the door a bit of protection at least. I'll check on Emerald."

The bartender nodded rapidly, letting out a long sigh as Grimluk walked toward the jail cells. He'd seen plenty like them before. A simple row of five, separated by iron bars. Each cell had a bucket and a cot with a wool blanket folded up on it, save for one. The middle cell was open, with Emerald inside on the cot, covered in the blanket, breathing steadily. Tulip was sitting next to her.

Grimluk touched the brim of his hat in greeting. "How is she?"

"Fine, mostly." Tulip paused. "I think. Looked like she just pushed herself too hard with the magic, but I ain't too sure. Never seen Em use it like that before. She was shoutin' and then I heard a thump and she was on the ground in front of a very frozen

Amos." Tulip looked up at Grimluk. "Why would she do that to him?"

"Wasn't him."

"But how—"

Grimluk held up a hand to silence the elf. "Shapeshifter, remember? And trust me, it wasn't him. She saved you folks."

Tulip nodded, looking down at Emerald and stroking her forehead. "You're here, so I guess that means its dead?"

"Gods-damn it, no." He let out a long sigh and rubbed at his face for a moment. "But I reckon, between the two of us, we hurt it. Hurt it bad, maybe. And that is a big damn deal at the moment."

Tulip didn't respond. They just went on stroking Emerald's forehead. Grimluk watched, running through the details of the night in his head as best he could. He could test Emerald for possession again. Her actions spoke against the need, but if he was wrong, it would spell their doom. Grimluk looked out at the crowd. A few of them watched him while the rest murmured and whispered to each other.

"So, now what, sai?" Tulip asked.

"Reckon I leave, make myself a target out of town. Or I get you folks away and come back for the rest of the town. Still thinkin' on it."

"Cold River," Emerald muttered.

Grimluk knelt next to her, pushing his hat up. "What about it?"

"Rangers comin'. We—" Emerald winced. "We could go meet them."

He frowned. "Rangers ain't gonna stop this thing. We managed to hurt it, you and I, but the rangers ain't equipped for this."

"Escort," she said. Her eyes rolled around dizzily for a moment before settling.

Grimluk's throat rumbled. "That might work better, provided it doesn't follow us. You gonna be able to make that right now?"

Emerald frowned. "I'll manage. Food?"

Tulip stood up quietly. "I'll go find some."

Grimluk looked at Emerald and reached out to take her hand, giving it a squeeze. "Heard you were a big damn hero. Mighty fine work with the ice. I'd even say it was a real gem of an idea."

Emerald looked at him in silence for a long moment, blinking rapidly. A smile cracked her lips. "Shut yer mouth with that."

"Multifaceted, even," he continued. "Definitely a crowning achievement."

Emerald sighed and very dramatically rolled her eyes. "I think I liked the demon better than this torture."

Tulip returned with an apple for Emerald and he left them to themselves. The crowd was restless, staring at Grimluk expectantly, no doubt hoping for answers or a plan. He could only think of the two options he'd given Tulip. He just didn't have enough information about the demon. Especially after what happened near the river. The scenarios played over and over in his mind.

Unfortunately, those thoughts were interrupted by someone speaking.

"Gobby bastard ain't got brains 'nuff to save

us." It was Roscoe, of course. The man wasn't speaking to Grimluk, naturally, but he wasn't trying to hide his words either.

Grimluk growled low in his throat. A sudden, bone-deep weariness rose in him. He was grateful there was only the one person to deal with this time. In the past, he hadn't been so lucky. Not that you were ever really lucky to be dealing with anyone who viewed you and your people as worthless monsters. Ironically, he tended to encounter such sentiments less in the Borderlands. Probably because real monsters tended to come rolling out of the Wastelands every so often. That sort of thing tends to kick your perspectives on people around just a bit.

Just one person to deal with, but it had to be done, especially now. Especially if Grimluk was going to escort them to meet the incoming rangers. He took a deep breath and turned toward Roscoe. Grimluk couldn't help but wonder if the man had any other expressions besides sneering.

"Reckon you and I oughta have us a palaver, friend," Grimluk said.

Roscoe lifted his chin, doing his best, and failing, to look down at Grimluk as he answered. "Ain't no one in the Mallaghan family what ever paylavered wit' no gods-damned goblin. So you take yer two-bilt word and go fuck yerself."

Grimluk nodded. "Say true, Roscoe? I'll make it real simple for you, then. If you got words for me, you say them to my face."

"Or what?" Roscoe asked, stepping forward with one fist balled. He walked up and jabbed his finger into Grimluk's chest. "You ain't shit here, goblin."

Grimluk loathed that word with everything in him. That single word that disregarded every orc as nothing but baby-eating monsters. As profoundly dimwitted and evil. It didn't matter that in a thousand years, the only stories of orcs stealing children and devouring them had turned out to be blatant lies, so far as he'd heard. It was one of the few things that made his blood boil.

The orcs did their best to pass down the stories, whether orally or in writing, to keep track of their history since they were freed; the truth of what they were, not the monsters they had been. The old implications had a fresh sting for him, too, after the events of the summer. After meeting a little girl with a prophetic spirit living in her. After adopting her as his sister when her family was killed. After having that fact twisted into lies and used against him, forcing a terrifying ordeal on the both of them because of a demon-worshiping bastard of a judge.

Grimluk hated that word.

The only warning he gave Roscoe that anything was about to happen was a growl, then he seized the man by the neck and skull and hoisted him into the air, letting Roscoe's body dangle helplessly. Shrieks and yelps filled the room around him. He ignored them, staring into Roscoe's eyes with every ounce of steel he had. He fought down a part of him that wanted to rip the squirming man in two. He had enough sense to know that was nothing but frayed nerves.

"I told you not to use that word. I asked

politely. Warned you somethin' bad would happen if you kept it up. Did I not?" His voice was iron and grit, practically growling the words, but he made sure he spoke clearly even through the anger. "Now, friend, I'm giving you one. More. Chance. Your last chance." Grimluk gave Roscoe's head a little squeeze for emphasis.

"You're free to choose otherwise. I can't stop you and nothing I say will ever turn your blind, pointless hatred away. But I would consider the consequences of that choice. I've been hunting a long time now. I've been all over New Gilead, trav- eled the Borderlands and the Wastelands. I've had demons in my head and fought them off. I know what goes bump in the dark and damned places of this world, Roscoe Mallaghan. And you know what else?"

Roscoe stared at him with eyes like saucers. "W–what?"

Slowly, Grimluk brought the man close to his own face. "I bump back. You wanna live, shut your gods-damned mouth until I'm out of earshot. Or better yet, out of town. Do you ken it?"

Silence filled the slight space between them. Roscoe's eyes watered like he was on the verge of crying.

"Do. You. Ken it?" Grimluk deliberately repeated.

Roscoe nodded slowly and then replied emphatically, "Y–yes!"

Another growl filled Grimluk's throat. An orc's growl was bestial to begin with, but Grimluk was mad enough that he let it color the sound, making it turn into something darker. He was putting on a bit of show, even if the feelings were sincere.

"Good. Because Roscoe, my friend," Grimluk set the man down and gently released his skull, "if I hear that word come out of your mouth again, I just might lose my temper. I just might forget we're two civilized folk. Say that word again, and I might hurt you."

Roscoe gulped and stepped away, knees all but clacking against each other. He never looked away from Grimluk as he did so. Grimluk held the man's eyes, hoping to make it as uncomfortable as possible. Hoping to make his point perfectly and completely clear so he wouldn't have to follow through. The part of him that was all frayed nerves hoped he would get to follow through, but he pushed that part away. It wouldn't help anything or anyone right now.

Roscoe finally looked away and turned from Grimluk's withering glare.

"I apologize for the outburst, folks. Now, I reckon you're wondering what the plan for our continued survival is. For those who don't know, Emerald got out a call to the rangers. Seems they're comin' from Cold River. Easiest plan would be to escort you folks to meet them and then I can come back and kill this thing for good." He surveyed the room. "I am open to suggestions, though."

"We don't have any suggestions," one of the dwarf twins said, "but we do want to offer our help, sai. These are our folk, after all."

"Much obliged," Grimluk said, bowing his head. "If you and your sibling, and maybe your peers, wouldn't mind, just watch over everyone as we travel. I know everyone's scared. That's perfectly fine and understandable. In fact," he turned in a slow circle, to speak to everyone in the room, "our best bet to make this as safe a journey as possible is to all work together. Take care of each other, keep each other movin', keep each other's spirits up. You've all made it this far. Keep your heads on right and you'll make it all the way."

He took the measure of anyone who looked at him, nodding his head in silent encouragement. "Tulip and I will get Emerald up and around. The rest of you, find whatever supplies you can and be prepared. We'll leave once she's ready."

His words seemed to catch with the frightened patrons and Companions alike. The preparations to leave were relatively calm and quick. Few of the Conqueror's patrons had anything beyond what was on them when they'd all fled. Though peacekeeper provisions were sparse, they managed to find a few bits of food, mostly jerky and hardtack, staples of travel. Someone even managed to find a lone bag of beans that was still reasonably full. After almost an hour, Grimluk and Tulip helped Emerald out of the cell.

"You ready?" Grimluk asked, leaving Emerald in Tulip's care for the moment.

"Ready as can be," Emerald replied.

He made his way toward the door. "If no one has any further business, we can set off. I'll give things a look first."

He stood on the demon trap blanket and looked over the street and the porch. Save for the block of ice, he saw nothing of note. He stepped out and motioned for the patrons to follow, pointing them toward Cold River. He watched each of them pass over the trap, each person who passed relieving some of the tension that had been building in him. He waited until Tulip and Emerald crossed the threshold before pulling the blanket back up and closing the door.

As Grimluk understood it, the journey to Cold River could take two to three days on foot for the average person. Alone, he probably could have made the trek in a day and a half. Most folks would have ridden a coach or a horse and traveled in far less time, but Grimluk preferred not to ride unless it was an emergency. While this was an emergency, there wasn't a coach or wagon or even enough horses, so the group did as he did and walked. Given there were rangers on the way, who tended to be mounted, it stood to reason that the survivors wouldn't have to walk more than a day at most before the rangers found them.

Grimluk stayed at the back, letting the blanket drape over his shoulders. If the demon came at him from behind, he hoped the blanket would deter it. Most any other direction meant he could see it and react.

As they traveled, he traced the grip of his revolver with an idle finger, wondering about the viability of the enchantment on the top of the barrel. He'd held off from using it thus far due to the surprise nature of the demon's attack, and the damned lack of information about the thing.

While either side of the barrel of his gun was etched in runes that allowed the bullets to harm, and thus kill, demons, the top runes were a new tool one of the smiths in Hunter's Hollow had found. He'd used the runes only once since acquiring the weapon over the summer. The new runes came at a strong price; they required blood. His, to be precise, and while they imbued the weapon with power that could outright cripple and kill a powerful demon with frightening immediacy, the tradeoff was that it would leave Grimluk weakened and practically defenseless.

Blood magic was inherently built on such trades, all varying in severity, and, while not necessarily unlawful, it was still incredibly taboo. Grimluk's boots were enchanted with a subtle spell that all hunters used, protecting themselves from getting lost, whether by demonic or spiritual trick or their own misjudgment. As long as the wearer knew where they were headed, and set their will to it, nothing could lead them astray. They could arrive, if not directly at their destination, close enough to find it.

That spell required a yearly renewal of blood from one's feet in a small ritual. A moment of pain for a year of protection. The runes on his gun would drain him for a time. His guild amulet required blood for its emergency purpose, allowing the user to open a portal back to a specified location. Reasonable purposes in a hunter's hands, but taboo because of how easily such magic could be used for ill.

Grimluk had met those instances frequently in his work, one which was more personal, thanks to the Hanging Judge. Blood magic could offer powerful defenses or it could rip your will away and corrupt your body. Demon hunters did not share this knowledge lightly. Apprentices had to earn it, even being sworn to secrecy among other apprentices.

Movement pulled Grimluk's attention away from his thoughts, though his instincts remained calm. Emerald had fallen back to join him. He gave her a nod and offered an arm. She smiled, slipping her arm through his and leaning into him slightly.

"Feelin' any better?" Grimluk asked after a few minutes.

"Ready to sleep for a few days, but yes, mostly. What about you?"

He thought about it, running his tongue over his gums and up one side of a tusk. "Reckon so, for the moment."

"Heard some of your confrontation with Roscoe. What about that?"

He grunted. "An unfortunate conversation that needed to be had. Would've preferred otherwise, but there wasn't much choice." A bitter smile crossed his lips. "Or maybe there was, but this was the better of them."

Emerald sighed at that. "Suppose you're right. Not like you could've left him to fend for himself."

It was Grimluk's turn to sigh, long and slow and through his nose. "Not as such, no. I have never left a mortal to a demon's mercy if I could help it. Even he doesn't deserve that fate."

Emerald gave his arm a little pat and said no more. They walked together in silence for some ways before she spoke again.

"You know, you never did answer my question the other day."

"Hm? Which was that?"

"About why you hunt."

"Mm," he replied as he chewed on the thought. There were a dozen potential reasons he could offer. Maybe the simplest reason would be his cenka having been a hunter right up through his conception, but he knew that wasn't it. If it was down to parents, he could have just as easily become a chef like his father. The man could flavor a dish in the same way Grimluk could shoot a gun.

Emerald was frowning lightly when he looked at her, maybe a hint of disappointment washing over her from his lack of answer. "Because it's what I chose," he said simply. "No one becomes a hunter for any other reason."

She scoffed lightly. "You really expect me to buy that as your sole reason? You chose it and that's that?"

His throat rumbled. "Why did you become a Companion?"

"I like people. I like sex," Emerald replied matter-of-factly, flourishing her free hand.

"Sex doesn't require a guild membership and training," Grimluk countered.

"Just seemed like a smart choice, I s'pose. Companions focus on people and pleasure."

Grimluk held up his free hand in a gesture of presentation. "Simple choice."

"Nope, I still don't buy it. You're being awfully..." She thought about it for a minute. "Well, you're acting like an old elf about it. Aloof and detached but I don't believe it."

He gave a little grunting chuckle of amusement. "Reckon that ain't too surprising considering an elf helped train me."

"Ooooh, you mean little shit," she said, giving him a teasing shove with one hand. "You're no fun."

"Occasionally," he said, grinning. Emerald met it with a sigh and another dramatic eye roll before silence fell upon them again. Some of the Companions and the Conqueror's patrons talked quietly among themselves. The bits of conversation Grimluk caught were inconsequential. Some talked about wanting a stiff drink. He heard mention of poker. The man Tulip had been with was chattering at the tall elf again, probably trying to get whatever else he could out of the money he'd paid. Tulip smiled and responded, maintaining a clear level of professionalism. All the Companions had gone above and beyond the usual duties expected of them. But then, only demon hunters were really expected to deal with demons.

Grimluk couldn't help but admire them for it. He thought about sending the Companion guild a few gluts for their trouble. Seemed right.

"Mighty impressed with all of you tonight," Grimluk said, looking at Emerald. "I'd almost have guessed you were apprentice hunters."

Emerald gave a small smile, touched with sadness. "If you hadn't been there, we'd…" She let out a sigh. "We'd have all ended up like Denny. Or worse."

"Everyone still reacted smartly."

"I trusted you, and we all trust each other. Never been scared like that, though." She looked off at nothing in particular. "I walked over a big snake once, as a young 'un. 'Bout jumped out of my damn skin. I think it'd just eaten, though. It looked fat and it just hissed at me, like it couldn't get up to bite. I'd gladly deal with that again over this."

Grimluk gave her hand a little squeeze of support but said nothing.

She squeezed back. "I don't guess you ever get so damned scared, do you?"

He grunted. "All the damn time."

"Grimluk, I am a grown woman. Don't you lie to me. I saw how calm you were."

He gave another rumbling chuckle at that. "I swear it. One of the first things we're taught is a healthy respect for fear and how to harness it."

"But you were so calm. You didn't show it a bit."

Grimluk shrugged. "Got a lot of experience. But you better believe I was afraid. There's basically two kinds of fear. Fear in the moment, which can be good and keep you safe. Rational, even. That kind of fear can make you sharper, more focused, set your will to making it out of whatever's happening as safe as possible, provided you learn how to wrangle it.

"Every time I take a contract, I tell them I can't guarantee success. That the demon could just as easily end me as me end it. The only thing I guarantee is that I'll fight it to the best of my ability, and if I can't take it down with me, I won't let it forget what happened. It keeps me grounded. Keeps the fear for survival real. Keeps me going to protect myself and the people I'm trying to help."

"What's the other kind of fear?" Emerald asked.

Grimluk grunted. "Reckon you could call it a baseless fear. I guess all fear stems from the unknown, but baseless fear is the kind that keeps some people convinced that, despite the War ending a thousand years ago, we're just monsters incapable of rational thought. Only concerned with violence. Only concerned with blood and death. The kind of fear that makes folks start fights over every little thing. Sometimes it just eats at you about everything. Maybe I don't quite know how to explain it. I do know there ain't no shame in bein' afraid – unless that fear only makes you hateful and mean for the sake of it."

"Mm, I s'pose that's true. Feels like it, anyhow."

"You know, I think I have a question for you," Grimluk said, rubbing at the scruff on his chin.

"If you ask me to marry you, it'll be the third time someone's done it this year," she replied with a half-grin.

Grimluk grinned back. "No, no, though I reckon you'd make a fine partner. Now, you don't have to answer, it's just a simple curiosity on my part. Is Emerald your given or chosen name?"

"Oh," a bit of laughter spilled out of her. "Given, actually. I was adopted when I was very young. No older than three, maybe four, I believe. A lovely pair of dwarves who were unable to have children of their own decided to take me from the orphanage in Dragon Tongue. I remember going home with them so clearly. I thought my name was 'Orc' before they took me home, but they said—" Emerald paused, "—they said, 'no, baby, orc is what you are, your people. Now you're ours. Our precious little jewel. Our little emerald.' And that was that. They named me Emerald and they gave me all the love in the world."

A smile tugged at Grimluk's lips. "That's lovely. And they clearly did a fine job of raisin' you."

"I certainly think so. Poppa and Daddy are such gentle souls. Poppa's a mason and Daddy's a chef."

"Well, ain't that somethin'. My dakka's a chef, too."

"Really?"

"Mm-hmm. He just cooks for the hunters and apprentices and anyone else in Hunter's Hollow but he refuses to let the meals be bland. Anytime he gets word of new spices or recipes, he'll order up the ingredients and put 'em to use. He told my sister he'd make her a feast that would make Governor Feely jealous for her adoption party."

"An adopted sister? My, my, you are full of surprises. What's she like?"

Grimluk's throat rumbled. "Little. Reckon she'll always be little surrounded by orcs, though. Turned eight a couple of months back. Human. Been through too much already for one so young. And she's a spirit caller and decided she wanted to be a hunter, as well. We make it out of this, I might tell you her story."

"I'll hold ya to it."

CHAPTER 9

In the dark hours of the night, a solitary ranger sat awake, cleaning her revolver at a little table next to a bunk. The bunkhouse was filled with such tables, where there was room for them. She cleaned her weapon less because it needed it and more because it served as a reasonable distraction from her current bout of insomnia. She'd learned to live with it. When she slept, she rested well and functioned well. When she didn't, a few cups of coffee helped bring her back for her daytime duties. She hoped when she finished her task she could get some sleep. As she slid the gun's cylinder back into place and started oiling the metal, a messenger interrupted her.

"Oh, Manyara, you're awake!"

She pulled her attention away, the clear, brown gun oil rolling down her brown skin. The messenger, a halfling man with tan skin, a mop of chestnut hair, and alert, hazel eyes, took in a breath to calm himself. Manyara waited. Better the messengers take a moment to compose themselves than deliver a flawed message.

"Sai, there's an emergency in Downingville. Magi-tell report says there's an attack. No drill."

"Much obliged, Bill," she replied with a nod. "Tell the stable to have the horses ready in an hour if they can manage it."

Bill nodded and departed as quickly as he'd come. Manyara splashed oil in her revolver's holster and stood, using her fingers to let out a shrill, piercing whistle that could be shockingly loud when she wanted it to be. It was loud tonight.

"Rangers, we got an attack to respond to! Wake up the marshal and get yer asses in gear!"

Groans of protest met her, but they were superficial at best. While Manyara was still technically the least senior ranger, she'd earned respect and authority enough to call out an emergency. Besides, the rangers worked best when rank was a touch lax. Chain of command could get in the way during emergencies. A new ranger might only be denied the first time they spoke up as such, depending on the details, but it was a formality.

Four fellow humans rolled out of their bunks, followed by a trio of elves. All dressed rapidly, brown trousers, shirts, and green vests hanging ready nearby off the bunks themselves, or nearby hooks on the walls, or on one of the little tables. Gun belts lay folded up underneath, as well. Two dwarves, beards braided tightly and intricately, rolled out of their bunks, half-dressed already, or maybe half-undressed when they got in. One rolled out of the top bunk and landed with a heavy thunk. A halfling rolled out next to them. Manyara exchanged nods with one of the dwarves as she donned her own vest. Her badge, a silver, rayed star in a circle, slapped her chest.

"Manyara!" a voice boomed.

"Marshal Bringar," she replied as she slipped her gun belt on.

An orc with three ragged scars across his left cheek walked in, suspenders hanging down at his side. He had skin the color of wet grass in spring and his exposed chest was covered in a thick layer of black hair. "Report." He slipped into his shirt and pulled the suspenders up.

"Downingville's been attacked." She slid into her own vest.

The orc grunted, adjusting his gun belt. "Sandsky! Copperspoon! Bring your rifles. Might not need sharpshooters, but be ready to set up all the same."

One of the dwarves and the halfling responded in unison. "Sai!"

Manyara's estimation had been true. By the end of the requested hour, around two o'clock, the posse of rangers, twelve in all, were saddled up and thundering off behind their marshal. Each was armed with at least one revolver and a variety of knives or cavalry sabers. Sandsky and Copperspoon had rifle holsters strapped to their saddles, dark stocks bouncing as they rode.

Marshall Bringar rode hard. He always did. Manyara always thought he looked like a thief or a drunk freed from a peacekeeper cell, bolting fast for fear his jailers would change their minds. She'd asked him about it once, out of curiosity. Being drunk had helped the matter for both of them. Bringar was generally a guarded, private man, but good whiskey would occasionally loosen his tongue.

"Ain't no other place for me but out there,"

he'd said after a long pull. "Fightin', or endin' a fight, or tryin' to keep one from happenin'. Much prefer the fight though. A good fuck don't even feel as good as victory."

She'd nodded. She understood that fairly well. Manyara liked a bloody scrap and she was good at it to boot. She'd been a peacekeeper for a time, but she wasn't very good at keeping things peaceful. At least, not that way. Peacekeepers were named aptly. Her temper had mellowed some since she'd joined the rangers, but she still liked being in the thick of things and rangers always got the dirty work. Always had, even since before the Five-Hundred Years War.

She guessed things were about to get pretty dirty. Downingville was a younger sister to Cold River. They were pretty similar, except for size and age, though Downingville was usually quieter. Since the rangers' fort in Cold River was so near the border between Westlynth and New Gilead, they were reasonably close by to patrol Downingville every so often. They'd been there not a week ago. Nothing had ever called them there in an actual emergency before now, though, and Manyara couldn't help but wonder just what in the world had happened. The curiosity gnawed at her as they rode. A touch of worry gnawed as well. She knew some good folks there, especially at the Coming Conqueror. Especially Em.

Dusk was fast approaching when they came upon a fairly large group of people on the road. Probably thirty or so by a quick head count. Manyara realized as she counted that a portion of the group were wearing red and gold clothing. Companions from the Coming Conqueror.

A huge orc – maybe bigger than Bringar; she couldn't tell with the marshal in the saddle – stepped forward. The orc was dressed all in black, with a wide-brimmed hat. His hat band was covered in what Manyara guessed were teeth. He touched the brim of the hat as he approached. Another orc stood close by him, dressed in the red and gold of the Companions.

"Emerald?" Manyara muttered to herself. A little wave of relief snaked through her guts despite her friend looking utterly exhausted.

"You made good time," the orc in black said.

"You got business with us?" Bringar said, tone curt as always.

"Name's Grimluk," the orc in black replied amiably. "Demon hunter. Escorting these folks after the attack."

"The fuck is a demon hunter doin' escortin' folk?" Bringar asked.

"Reckon I'm makin' sure the demon that hit the town can't jump any of these folks as they run. Reckon with you here now, you can take them on and I can go back and finish huntin' the gods-damned thing."

Manyara's brow furrowed. She rode up next to her marshal. "That true, Emerald?"

A smile touched Emerald's face for a moment before she answered. "Sure as shit is, Yar—um, Manyara. It was…big. A—and just horrifying. It made itself look like Amos! You remember him?"

Manyara chewed on the question for a moment

before nodding. "Reckon I do. Old halfling peace-keeper, right?"

Bringar regarded Manyara with a frosty look. "You done, Ranger?"

"Sai."

"A demon, eh? Ain't never killed me no demon," Bringar said, scratching his scars. "Bet that's a shitkicker of a fight."

"Mean no offense here, Marshal, but it slaugh-tered all the peacekeepers in town. I know the rangers are made of tougher stuff than the average peacekeeper, but," Grimluk crossed his arms, "you go after this thing yourselves and you will die, too."

Manyara couldn't help but register the author-ity the hunter spoke with. The conviction in his voice meant they'd be wise to heed his warning. There was a reason demon hunters still had work. Rangers weren't equipped to handle demons, except maybe imps, sometimes. A pack of trolls? Not even an issue. Though as of late, it seemed the move-ment to domesticate them might make that a non-issue in a few years. Maybe they'd stink less, too.

"Marshal, maybe we oughta listen to him," Manyara offered.

Bringar outright ignored her comment. "Mean no offense, demon hunter, but you ain't killed it. Maybe you ain't actually much for demon-killin'. Maybe we go in and clean up your mess. What say you to that, eh?"

Grimluk sighed, reaching up to rub his jaw idly. "The thing was…strange. Never took on anything like it before. Much prefer to go on back and set up some traps. Provided the rest of the town's still alive."

Bringar grunted and started forward. "Take the people on to Cold River, hunter. We'll handle things from here on."

Grimluk reached up and gently put one hand on the shoulder of Bringar's horse. The horse stopped. "I swear to you, Marshal, if you take your rangers to that town and hunt the thing yourselves, death is all that awaits. This thing damn near ripped a man's skin and muscle clean off his bones and I saw it pull the legs off another like mud on a stick."

"Sai, it's true," Emerald interjected. She stood defiantly but spoke gently. "He might've killed the thing outright if he hadn't had to help us get away from it. It crushed part of the Conqueror and killed a couple more people to boot. Listen to Grimluk. Please."

Manyara watched Bringar regard the hunter. She could just make out the sneer on his face. Marshal Bringar was upstanding for the most part. He led his band of rangers fairly, even if he was a little aloof at times. He always did his job to the best of his ability when they were responding to a crisis or being sent somewhere. But he was not a patient person. Or particularly intelligent at times, especially if he got it in his head that his view was the only correct one.

Not that Manyara would ever fault anyone for a lack of smarts. She could be pretty damn stubborn herself, and it'd bit her in the ass on plenty of occasions. Smarts were a subjective matter most of the time anyways. She couldn't do much math or reading, but she could gauge a fight and knew how to ride a horse well enough she could shoot with a gun in both hands if she wanted to. She'd heard someone call Bringar a brute once, though. He was a good man, whatever his faults, but "brute" was, however much she disliked it, an apt description at times.

She'd seen his reaction when that comment had hit him. It felt the same as what she was seeing now. Manyara wondered for a few seconds whether or not he would attack Emerald and Grimluk. Manyara looked at Emerald staring up at Bringar. Grimluk held his gaze as well but looked far more relaxed, his hand still resting against the horse's shoulder.

"Take your hand off my horse 'fore I take it off," Bringar said after the silence had stretched on for far too long. "Rangers! We ride!"

A sigh escaped Manyara's lips. The others pushed their horses on to follow their leader. Manyara hesitated for a moment before riding up to the two orcs.

"Sorry 'bout that, Em. And to you, sai. The marshal is…intense."

"Yara, don't go," Emerald said softly.

Emerald was looking at her with pleading, watery eyes. Manyara groaned without thinking about it.

"I can't disobey an order like that, Em, you know that." She looked away, her eyes landing on Grimluk's. The orc's eyes were dark, like two little lumps of coal. The lack of hardness aimed her way surprised her.

Grimluk reached into his coat and pulled out a

huge knife, gave it a little flip to hold it by the blade and held it out to her. "I'm gonna take these people on and come back. This might help you stay safe. If you can get your posse to listen to you, find a place to make a circle and put that symbol—" he tapped the strange twig symbol on the base of the blade, "—in the center and have everyone stand in it." He paused. "It should keep you safe."

Conflicting thoughts warred in Manyara's mind. A demon hunter was offering her one of his weapons and telling her a method of potential safety. Part of her was screaming to ignore Bringar, stick with this man, and keep herself alive. The other part of her couldn't bear the thought of abandoning her posse. They'd been through a lot together. She reached out and took the hilt of the knife. Grimluk's grip held.

"Safety above all," he said. "Watch yourself, Ranger."

The knife slid away from his fingers and she tucked it away. "Keep them safe, sai." She couldn't help but look at Emerald when she said it. Manyara clucked at her horse and took off after her posse. The part of her that wanted to run was screaming like a banshee. Manyara hoped it was just paranoia.

Emerald stood next to Grimluk, silently watching the ranger ride off. Fear knotted in her guts as she worried for her friend's safety. The survivors from the Conqueror had only escaped their fate thanks to

Grimluk. What hope did the rangers have against something so horrifying?

Weariness ate at Emerald. She wanted to just collapse and sleep. Maybe wake up to find that it had all been a nightmare.

Someone remarked that there was supposed to be a waystation not too much farther along, so the group started moving again. Emerald stood there, looking at the two parties moving in opposite directions. Grimluk watched her, a quiet sentinel.

"Thank you for trying to help," she said, sighing and following the crowd to Cold River.

"Seemed like she'd take the help. Friend of yours?"

"Mm. You remind me of her a bit. When she comes through, she just pays to spend time with me, too." Emerald smiled. "Though our first meetin' wasn't quite so...eventful as me and you."

Grimluk chuckled. "And what do you two do together?"

"We, um..."

"Yes?"

"Don't laugh, okay? We like, um, what's it called...geo–um–geomanciligy? Ah, shit. Rocks. We like to study rocks."

"Rocks," Grimluk said, just a hint of a drawl in his voice. "My sister likes rocks."

"They can be so interesting. Especially crystals. Sometimes we go visit the magician nearby. Yara's got some talent with magic as well, but she don't like it much. Magician once said she had a lot of potential, if she'd just settle down and study, but

Yara likes bein' a ranger. And she can't read so well. Says the letters jump around, trip her up."

A rumble emanated from Grimluk, deep in his throat. "Knew a couple of apprentices who had that problem. Loremaster had to figure out new ways to teach 'em. They'd get rowdy sometimes out of frustration but Vatris has the patience of a mountain. Reckon you have to as a loremaster and apprentice teacher."

"Yara gets that way, too, but mostly it doesn't seem to bother her."

"What about her marshal there? Bringar, wasn't it?"

"He's mostly a decent person but, as you saw, he's got a skull that needs thumpin' sometimes. He's gonna get them killed."

"Ayuh," Grimluk replied with what sounded like frustration. "Wasn't much more I could say than what I did. Sometimes you just say true as best you can and hope you're heard."

Emerald nodded. Sometimes that really was all you could do. She'd seen plenty of violent drunks ejected from the Conqueror after being warned politely, sometimes by her. They didn't listen, though. Threw punches and out they went, just like she and everyone else had to escape the demon. A flash of light and a thump to the ground.

She spun around, walking backward so she could watch the disappearing horses in the distance. "You're gonna go back, aren't you?" she asked.

"If I wasn't worried about the rest of you, I'd go now."

"I'm going, too," Emerald said, turning back around.

Grimluk's throat rumbled. "Reckon there's no way I can talk you out of it?"

"I stopped Amos. Maybe I can do it again if Yara needs me."

Grimluk let out a sigh. "You need some rest, first. Let's get to the station and let you sit for a spell."

She couldn't argue with that logic. She was still so tired, but she had to help her friend.

When they arrived, they found the station was barely big enough to hold them all. The attendants were amenable, having seen the rangers riding past. Emerald was given a rocking chair and allowed to rest, though it was a struggle. Her mind demanded that she stop wasting time and get on, but her body countered with bone-deep weariness. Eventually, the weariness won out and Emerald slipped into a dreamless sleep.

When she awoke, most of the patrons and Companions were asleep. Grimluk was still awake and watching over them. He nodded at her. She started to nod back but a yawn took over and, for a moment, she wondered if her face would split open from it. She stepped lightly over to the hunter.

"What time is it?"

"Midnight? One? Not quite sure. Never did get used to winter nights."

"Well, I'm ready when you are," she said through another yawn.

He looked down at her for a long moment. "You really sure?"

"I have to."

He just nodded before turning his gaze away. Emerald turned to follow it to find Tulip standing there. "I need you to take everyone on to Cold River. I'm gonna go with Grimluk, back to town," she informed her friend.

"Is that wise?" Tulip asked, their normally placid face shifting with furrowed brows.

"Maybe not, but I'd rather do what I can to help Yara and the others stay safe. Maybe...maybe I can do what I did to Amos again." Emerald reached out and hugged her friend tightly. "I promise I'll make it back."

"You better," Tulip replied. "You still owe me two bilts for last week," they said with a wry grin.

Emerald couldn't help but smile back.

The Companions separated, and Emerald followed Grimluk out. A sigh of effort escaped her as they set off. She was still dog tired, but this was her truth right now and she had to say it and had to listen.

Grimluk laid a blanket across her shoulders. "I'd really rather you didn't come with me, but I reckon you're as set as you can be. Just keep the blanket on you. Should keep the thing from sneakin' up on you at the very least. Probably make it think twice about going near you at all."

"Also, I'll freeze it again if I need to," Emerald replied, looking at him seriously.

"Also, you'll freeze it again," Grimluk said with a soft smile.

Emerald took a deep breath, shifted the blanket some and willed her feet to move.

Chapter 10

Had Grimluk been alone, he'd have moved quicker. He probably would have run the whole way back to Downingville. He never would have caught up with the riders even if he'd followed right after them, but the effort would have shaved some time off the journey. An hour, maybe two if he'd pushed himself. Emerald was in no shape to run, though, so he kept pace with her. It was clear from her occasional grunts and stumbles that she was pushing herself.

He allowed her to go like that for maybe an hour before he stopped her. "You're no good to your friend if you collapse from exhaustion."

"We don't have time to—"

He held up his hand. "Time or not, you still haven't recovered from last night. Here." He handed over his waterskin. Emerald took it and drank. "You need some food in you, too," he added, digging his jerky from his bag.

She sighed but took it. "Thank you."

Once he was satisfied, they continued on. He kept the jerky out and ready, making her stop every hour or so. It frustrated the both of them. Part of Grimluk wanted to beg Emerald to go back to the waystation, to continue on to Cold River. He found the idea of dragging someone else into a fight distasteful, but he also couldn't argue with her. Emerald knew the risks. She'd fended part of the creature off already, seen it up close. He could respect, even admire that. So he did what he could. He recognized that either he'd keep her close or she'd get away from him and get herself killed.

He hoped the ranger, Manyara, managed to get her compatriots into the protection circle. Or that maybe the demon would ignore them without Grimluk there. That was a rookie's naivete, though. He knew most, if not all of them would die. Especially their damn fool marshal, unless he had a spirit of luck on his side.

The two of them made it back to Downingville sometime in around midday. The clouds had cleared by then, letting the sun shine bright as it crept through the sky, taking some of the cold away. Emerald had the blanket with the demon trap wrapped tightly around herself. Grimluk had given her his scarf as well. The wind hadn't been bad enough to bother him.

The entrance to Downingville greeted them with a total, unnerving silence. As they'd neared town, what few birds remained at this time of year had become scarce. The town should have had some life in it. Some sign of mortal activity. Only silence made its presence known – except for the rubble from a building nearby, wood and bits of iron scattered in a dazed semi-circle a few feet from the porch.

And the Preacher as he stepped out of the shadows of the building, standing clear and true for all to see.

The black-clad Preacher with his collar of bleached white, stark in contrast against the clothing and the tanned skin. The Preacher, whose morose smile somehow assaulted Grimluk's eyes, feeling casually obscene. The Preacher, whose eyes bored toward them with an unsettling intensity. He still held the massive, leather-bound tome against his chest with one arm.

Grimluk started to address the man but the Preacher spoke first.

"Lone Rangers the lot of them, wouldn't you say? Tempting such a fate in their childlike ignorance. Though only one was marked, mind. Oh, but my manners! Do join us for supper!"

The hairs at the base of Grimluk's skull prickled. Something wasn't right about this man. He'd felt it the first time they'd laid eyes on each other and Grimluk had heard the man's supposed message of truth and ignorance. Maybe the man was just touched by some sickness. Some retired hunters, orcs who were all too familiar with the effects and signs of demonic oppression and possession, and the rigors of being an object of fear, had begun studying cases. They'd discovered that sometimes, people weren't besieged by demons. Sometimes, they were just sick. The mind was occasionally an insurmountable enemy in various ways, some more violent than others.

Maybe the Preacher's mind was sour like that. Deep down. Grimluk doubted it. but the life of a demon hunter never lacked its mysteries.

"How do you do, sir?" Grimluk said to the man, erring on the side of caution. "Reckon you saw the rangers ride through. You should probably head on out quick. It's not safe around here."

"No, no, of course not," the Preacher replied conversationally. "Far, far too early. Have you heard the Truth? What am I saying? I can smell it on you." He paused. "Hmmm, part of it, anyhow. No matter! The time is now! The feast, the feast!"

Abruptly, the Preacher stepped away, around the broken wall and back into shadow. Something in the air nudged Grimluk and he knew the man had vanished just as sure as he was breathing.

Definitely not just sick, he thought. But not the shapeshifter. He filed the man away in his mind for later. His hand went to his revolver and slid it free.

"Keep that blanket tight," he reminded Emerald. It might have come out harder than he meant it, but under the circumstances he doubted she'd be upset.

They moved on. Around the corner of the smashed building lay half of a horse. Its skin was shredded in parts, revealing bits of bone. Grimluk was astonished at the lack of viscera hanging out of the poor creature's gaping abdomen. There was even less blood than he would expect. Emerald gasped but kept on moving with him.

When they got to the market square, the stalls were all strewn about in piles of crushed or shattered wood. A horse skull and a partially dissolved arm covered in blood and leather lay in a heap of broken wood.

A low, rumbling groan caught Grimluk's ear, like a large animal in pain. Cautiously, he moved toward the sound. He moved to the back corner of the square. Another pained rumble met them as they approached. Words followed it this time.

"Help," the voice rumbled. "Help...help." It didn't sound like a request.

Heavy steps thumped slowly out to meet them. Bart the troll limped from behind the building, one massive arm clutched to his chest. Part of his face was covered in blood and his bulbous, dangling nose was missing, showing gore-glittered bone. Likewise, Bart's other arm was missing. There were chunks of flesh torn out of his left foot, provoking the limp.

Bart grimaced at them in what might have been a smile. "Emmy-rald, Barty try to help. Barty try. No goodsies. Mucky muck hurt Barty. Try to hurt Margy. Barty fight." The troll gave a heavy sigh as he collapsed to his butt. "Barty strong. Mucky strongest. Emmy-rald help now?"

Emerald gulped audibly. "Yes, Bart. We're here to help."

The troll nodded as it slumped to its side. "Good, good. Barty sleeps now. Barty tiredses."

Emerald knelt next to the troll as his arm unclenched and let go of the bloody thing it'd been holding. "No..."

Grimluk gently pulled her back up and away from Margy's severed head. Emerald spun and buried her face in his chest, sobs racking her. Grimluk held her and did his best to keep watch around them. He just let her cry for a minute or two before speaking up.

"I know it hurts, but we have to keep moving." He kept his voice low.

"I know," Emerald whispered back. She stepped away, sliding her hand down to take his free hand, and waited for his lead.

He gave her hand a light squeeze.

Several more buildings were damaged along the way. Mostly buckled walls or smashed corners, like someone or something had been thrown with great force. As they passed the street that led to the Coming Conqueror, Grimluk looked toward the building. The front had been torn apart. Beams were splintered and glass lay strewn about in the dirt, large shards sticking up like translucent teeth along with other pieces of debris. One of the batwing doors that led into the saloon was sticking out of the ground. The saloon entrance was now a gaping hole of jagged wood.

Emerald let out a weary sigh beside him as they passed the sight. Grimluk frowned, wanting to give her time to look over the wreckage, but he pressed on. She didn't hesitate or slow.

The peacekeeper building was an even more ruined sight to behold. Something had smashed through it. The one positive Grimluk could see was standing right where it'd been when they left. The pillar of ice stood tall, glittering in the afternoon sun. It was too thick to melt yet, but the sun's glow was working on that as fast as it could. Winter would hold tight a few more weeks, at least, before the new year ushered in spring. When midnight rolled around, the top layer would be frozen again.

Emerald gripped his hand more tightly as they passed the ice block. Grimluk couldn't blame her. She'd been more than impressive with her calm in the Conqueror, in light of what he assumed was her first encounter with a demon of real power. Most folks in New Gilead had dealt with an imp or two, at least in his experience. He imagined that was the case in Westlynth and Redaggia, as well, if at all.

Imps were the weakest of demons, more like pests, provided they were alone or in small groups. An infestation was cause for alarm. They tended to be simple-minded and easily trapped. The same could be said of ghouls, the spirit demons who, if allowed, by negligence or wicked influence, inhabited corpses and fed on the flesh of living beings. Unlike ghouls, imps were far more mobile. Most of them had wings and the rare specimens who lacked wings could still use claws and muscle to scale surfaces and move as they liked.

But they did not have power. Sensitivity to magic was a given, considering their nature, but you would never have to worry about an imp shifting its shape, or hurling fireballs at you or trying to possess you or trick your mind. Grimluk was glad he'd finally taken on a means of defense against the latter two methods of attack. Even if imps could possess or confound, the tattoo on the crown of his skull would protect him from it.

They walked on in silence toward the other end of town while Grimluk racked his brain on the details of the demon. The more he thought on it, the odder it seemed. It projected a form like the demon he'd killed in Arbortown, but it was so much more than that. He flipped through pages in his mind. The closest details he could recall were mostly speculation and half-truths about the true form of Shub-Niggurath, a being said to be the mother of demons and monsters alike. But even then, the facets Grimluk recalled gave the loathsome abomination more substance and form than the blobby, oozing thing he was hunting now.

And none of that ever mentioned shapeshifting. The need to test identities flickered in his mind.

Emerald had made one thing clear and certain, though, and he'd seen it for himself, too, albeit in less spectacular fashion. This demon, whatever it was, hated severe cold. That could be enough to deal with it. Maybe. It was a start, at least. Something to hope for. Whether Emerald could repeat her performance on the whole creature was another matter entirely.

There were a couple more mangled horse carcasses as they walked on. The huge bodies were broken and painted in scarlet, along with the walls and ground around them. Grimluk grimaced at the look of clear terror that had been frozen on the animals' faces. Their eyes were practically rolled all the way back and several of their mouths were open in a rictus scream.

There were weapons on the ground as well. Grimluk counted five revolvers as he went. Each appeared to be the standard, long-barreled Peacemaker model carried by peacekeepers and rangers alike. Compared to his revolver, they looked delicate. One of the pistols stuck out of the ground, buried up to the trigger guard, butt up, displaying the unmarred cylinder, decorated with etchings. The rayed-star of the Ranger badge had been burned into the pale wood of the grips. A rifle also lay nearby. Grimluk thought he recognized it as a modified Verington, a sharpshooter's rifle. A frighteningly accurate weapon.

As they passed the little peacekeeper shack at the other entrance of Downingville proper, Grimluk looked at it. He'd left Amos there and, to his knowledge, the gray-haired halfling had met his end there, too. Grimluk was fairly certain the demon had split itself, given that Emerald had frozen the Amos lookalike before he put the demon trap blanket on Not-Emerald. He wondered for a moment if maybe the demon had worked Amos like a puppet. If maybe it hadn't actually taken his form.

It didn't matter though. At least, not yet. He put the thought away with a bit of effort. He could reflect on the dead later.

The pair walked out of the town and into the Downingville residential area. Grimluk was unsure whether the lack of destruction here was truly a good sign, but he held out hope for the people of Downingville. Maybe they ran while the rangers had their losing battle. Maybe the lot of them had escaped once he'd given them the opportunity after getting the demon's attention.

"What's that?" Emerald asked in a hushed voice. She nodded to their right, toward a little park Grimluk hadn't noticed when he'd come to town. Something was sitting there, unmoving, partially obscured by a young oak not yet massive with age.

Grimluk looked around, shifting his revolver as he did. He grunted in acknowledgment and headed for the park. "Forgive the repeat, but keep the blanket close."

Emerald let go of his arm and pulled the blanket tighter to herself. When they got closer, and out of the tree's way, Grimluk could see another horse, on its side but whole. Something was lying across the beast's body. It was Bringar. His clothes were torn to shreds, along with some of the flesh underneath. Blood dripped down, running across the horse's body.

Someone screamed and a tall form sprang up from behind the prone horse, pointing a gun at them. Grimluk stepped nimbly in front of Emerald before he had much time to think about it. His own gun rose, but the other gun barked first and something slammed into his chest. He let out a sharp hiss, a mix of pain and frustration, while Emerald let out a strangled shriek.

Ranger Manyara stood there, a shaking revolver barrel bobbing in front of her. Grimluk's knife was in her other hand. Her eyes were wide and bloodshot. She just stared at him, daring him to move again.

Hesitantly, he held the barrel of his gun toward the ranger. "Emerald, do you see a circle in the dirt?"

"I think so."

"That's good. We're gonna circle her and I want you to make sure it goes all the way around, unbroken." He stepped slowly around Manyara, neither of them taking their eyes or their guns away from the other.

"It's unbroken," Emerald whispered from behind him.

"Sign in the middle?"

"Looks like a twig."

Grimluk let out a long sigh and holstered his gun. "Seems you're really you, Ranger. Reckon we're at a bit of an impasse now."

Manyara kept on staring at him. Her hand glistened with blood.

"Promise," Grimluk added, holding his hands up, "hard as you try, you won't put a second hole in me by lookin' at me. And I'd really prefer not to have a second hole in me."

That broke her steely gaze. The ranger's eyebrows rose. "You're you?"

Grimluk gave her a friendly grin. "Still not a holy man, despite your efforts." A snort came from behind him while Manyara's jaw hung open.

"What—" Manyara started to say before her eyes got big again. "Get in the circle! Quick!"

Grimluk turned and pulled Emerald from behind him, pushing her toward the ranger insistently.

"Did you just shoot him, Yara?" Emerald asked as Grimluk pushed her forward.

"I'm fine," he replied, following closely behind. "Not the first time. Doubt it'll be the last, either."

"You shot him!" Emerald said in utter surprise. "You fuckin' shot him, Yara!"

"Um. I'm sorry?"

"Just help me get the bullet out right fast and we'll call it square." Grimluk slipped his elk-skin bag from over his head, dropping it to the ground. "And maybe tell me what happened. The marshal there dead?"

"Not that I could tell, but he ain't exactly in a great condition, is he?" Manyara said, her voice quieter.

Grimluk knelt as he dug into his bag and pulled out a leather roll tied with a simple cord. "You say true. And smart thinkin' makin' the circle in the dirt like this. Harder to disrupt." He spread the roll open. "You know how to use any of this?"

"Sure, required ranger training. Can't be one without knowing your way around a field dress kit."

"Reckon you know what to do then, Ranger."

"Okay, but you shot him," Emerald said for the third time.

"And now she's gonna take the bullet out. Really, I'm fine. It just smarts a bit. Always does."

"You've been shot before?" Emerald asked incredulously.

"This makes, uh, let's see." He held up a hand and counted his fingers. "Fifteen? Sixteen? Something like that. Had a necklace with the slugs strung on it but I lost it over the summer." Manyara and Emerald both stared at him, jaws agape. "What?"

"Never met anyone but corpses shot that many times," Manyara said, looking him up and down.

"Hazards of the job," Grimluk replied with a shrug.

The ranger shook her head and retrieved one of the tools from the roll, a little metal stick with a tiny claw on the end. It took her all of a moment to jab the little thing in and pull the bullet out. They never got in very far, but it was still a hassle to do on his own.

"Much obliged. Always easier when someone else can do that. Just set everything down there. I'll bandage myself."

Manyara looked slightly flustered but shrugged and set the tool and the slug down. Grimluk knelt and gathered up a bandage and a bottle of green salve and set them aside.

"Reckon you got quite the story, Ranger." He popped the cork on the little bottle and dumped it over, rubbing the bandage across the mouth of the bottle as he shook the liquid free. It was thick and made a slight smacking sound.

"Reckon so," Manyara said with a sigh. She'd put away her gun but still held Grimluk's knife tightly.

Grimluk waited for her to get the words out. When he was satisfied with the salve's coverage on the bandage, he pulled his shirt open and slid the bandage up over the wound. He pressed it flat and hard and ran a finger along the edges and then dug his fingertip very slightly into the wound, working the substance into the hole.

He'd been using this salve since before he'd finished his training. It was powerful and sticky, adhering tightly to skin once applied. Normally, he'd have sewn his wound closed to help the healing process, but considering the circumstances, it seemed best to let it go this time. It'd be a bigger scar because of it, but that was hardly news. Grimluk knew Death would meet him eventually and find a body covered in scars. That was life and he was just fine with it.

Manyara rubbed the bridge of her nose and let out a sigh. "Went like this."

CHAPTER 11

"We come into town and it was quiet. Ghost town in the Borderlands quiet, ya know?" Manyara paused for a moment, seeming to consider something. "I guess you would know, bein' a demon hunter and all. Anyways, it wasn't quite dark yet, but there was no one around. 'Cept..."

"The strange human with the white collar?" Grimluk asked, sliding everything back into its place in his dressing kit.

"We took to callin' him the Preacher," Emerald offered to Manyara. "Showed up sometime after your last visit. Always preachin' about truth and ignorance or some such."

"The Preacher, then, yeah." Manyara squatted down, glanced behind herself, and then dropped to her butt with a grunt. "He was just...laughin' real hard. Like someone told him a real gut-buster of a joke. A mighty big one. Says some of the rabbits slipped the snare but here's some hounds ready and good. At least, I think that's what he was sayin'. Maybe I don't remember it right.

"Anyhow, that's when Maurn started hollerin'. I was in back and I saw somethin'. I don't know what it was. It looked like an arm, but it wasn't an arm. It was dark and slick and...and..."

"And it had eyes on it?" Grimluk asked.

"Gods, and a mouth came out of one of the eyes. It grabbed Maurn's horse and flung it aside. But the horse tore in half! I don't...it was so strong. Everyone scattered and then the arm thing came out of hiding." Manyara groaned and a little sob spilled out of her. "Gods, it hurts just to recall the thing. You told us, sai. You told us true, and we came ridin' in behind the marshal unprepared."

Emerald knelt beside Manyara and reached for her hand. The ranger flinched at first, still refusing to let go of Grimluk's knife, so Emerald settled for her wrist. After a moment, Manyara reached over with her other hand and rested it over Emerald's.

"I didn't see everything, mind. I saw Maurn. I heard Sandsky scream and then wood breaking. Everyone started shooting. I took some shots, too, but mostly I pulled out your knife. All I could think about was what you said. Someone rode toward the Conqueror and I heard more wood and screams. It threw them around and tore 'em up like Maurn's horse.

"Preacher man just laughed more and then the demon chased Bringar and me. He'd managed to keep clear of it and I'd just stayed away. Couldn't do nothin' but watch. But it came at us, flingin' bits of the others at us. Guns and guts flyin' at us instead of bullets. Copperspoon had gotten up on a roof and started on the thing with his rifle but it didn't pay his shots no mind." Manyara went quiet for a moment, memories all but dancing across her face.

Grimluk just waited quietly. These kinds of massacres were never easy to listen to, much less recount.

Manyara looked at the prone marshal. "Figure you saw all that comin' in, though. Marshal followed me. Reckon he thought I was gonna try and set up an ambush. We done it before, plenty of times, matter o' fact. I ran over here and did like you said. Sent my horse off and started to circle up the dirt. The marshal got real confused and started shoutin' at me before I could get the circle really started."

Grimluk looked down at the Elder Sign in the dirt between them as he listened. It was clean, if a little stubby compared to how he was accustomed to seeing it. Worked all the same, though.

"Bringar's horse got pushed away. That big fucker got his horse knocked plum out from under him. Damnedest sight. Landed on its neck. Too hard not to kill it outright, so I put the circle around it. Seemed smart. Bringar was screamin'. Demon had his leg and he was danglin' while it seemed to just be lookin' at him. If I didn't know better, I'd think it looked..."

A rumble filled Grimluk's throat. "Looked...?"

Manyara hesitated, looking at Grimluk for a minute. "Reckon it's not like you'll call me mad given the situation. It seemed addled by him. The eyes looked the marshal over. Some of 'em even blinked, and then it just...set him down on his feet and stared him down some more.

"So Bringar did what Bringar does. He drew and shot it. Six shots, neat as you please. Popped a few of those eyes. Another demon, – or maybe the actual demon, I don't fuckin' know – came out of it and slapped Bringar away. He rolled into the horse, so I hauled him up quick as I could and made the sign. Fortune smiled, 'cause when I looked up, the thing was spreadin' out like a blanket to smother us but it couldn't do it. Least not completely."

Grimluk's brow furrowed deeply at that. He couldn't say he was surprised by that but it was still troubling to hear. "How's that?" he asked.

She thought for a moment. "Sorta like it was trying to force through. It pushed down close but couldn't quite do it. So I stabbed it. Seemed to hurt it enough that it backed off and disappeared back into town. Been sittin' here since. The marshal ain't dead, but I can't get him woke up and his leg and belly are all tore up from where it touched him."

"I think it eats the flesh off things," Grimluk said. "It took out the peacekeepers here. You see any bodies?"

Manyara's eyes went wide and her nostrils flared. "Gods-damn."

"I'm glad you're safe, Yara," Emerald said, resting her forehead on the ranger's shoulder.

Manyara laid her head against Emerald's and sighed. She looked at Grimluk, doubt swimming in her eyes. Grimluk guessed she was probably wondering how much longer that safety would last but didn't want to upset Emerald. He stood back up.

"Reckon I oughta get to huntin', then. If I could have my knife back, Ranger?"

Emerald moved away from Manyara. The ranger looked at the massive blade. She took in a deep breath through her nose and held it up, her hand trembling slightly.

"Kick its ass, sai."

Grimluk took the blade from her and gave her a confident nod. "That's the plan. Blanket, please, Emerald. This thing likes surprises more than most, it seems."

Emerald pulled the blanket from her shoulders and handed it over. "Good luck, Grim."

"Stay in the circle until I get back. And just to be safe, Em, ask me what's on my back. To make sure it's me."

"What's..." she started to ask before realization dawned on her. "Right."

The winter sun grew lower, casting its afternoon light over the town as Grimluk stepped out of the protective circle. He looked at Emerald and Manyara for a moment and then decided to do one last thing before he went hunting. He enclosed the circle in a triangle. From each point, he dragged a line to the circle's edge. While the circle had held, he didn't want to take any chances. The added triangle would bolster the circle's power. As an apprentice, he'd heard it called a Great Circle. If he'd added a square around that, it'd have been a Grand Circle.

Those same concepts could work for summonings as well, with some alterations. The use of geometry had a long history few demon hunters ever learned outright, but the loremasters always gave them the basics as apprentices. It was enough to know that they worked.

Grimluk headed back into town, hoping maybe

this time he could find and pin the thing long enough to end it. At the very least, he could burn it with the trap. He slung the blanket over his left shoulder and unholstered his gun. He hoped he could do it before dark, too. The town was either dead or abandoned, even temporarily, so no one would be around to light the lamps. Not that they'd helped him much the first time.

He moved silently down the empty main street of Downingville, not bothering to move with a hunter's stealth. He wondered as he walked whether the oozing monstrosity was trailing him or waiting somewhere or maybe moving with him. Grimluk couldn't help but wonder why the demon hadn't summoned any imps or lesser demons, either. Its strength seemed blatant enough that there should have been a small swarm of the little beasts, if not something bigger.

As he passed the peacekeeper building, he glanced at the glistening block of ice vaguely shaped like a person. It seemed to be a little wetter on the surface than when they'd come into town. The thought nagged him, so Grimluk indulged it. He reached into his coat, to the pocket where he kept his chalk, and pulled out a thin, folding knife. He flicked the short, slender blade out.

Grimluk brushed a hand over the top of the ice, where Not-Amos's head would've been, flinging the thin layer of water away. Blade met ice as Grimluk began to carve out a circle. Carving into ice wasn't something he had much practice with, but he tried to take his time, forming the rough shape. It didn't have to be perfect, just clear. The five-pointed star came easier and quicker.

He stopped for a moment to check his surroundings. Still quiet. He didn't see anything approaching. Even so, he did his best to set the runes quickly. In the space between each arm of the star, he carved the runes of the demon trap. When he finished, he brushed off the knife and put it back in his pocket.

Grimluk watched the ice for longer than he'd have liked, but nothing happened. Maybe nothing could happen through the ice. He didn't know. It would have to be enough.

When he approached the street that led to the Conqueror, the Preacher stepped around the corner and motioned for him.

Given everything Grimluk had seen, it didn't take much thought to conclude the man was probably leading him toward a trap. Grimluk's revolver slid back out of its holster, ready to work.

The Preacher spun in a circle and shook his book above his head. Grimluk headed toward him. For the second time he'd seen, the Preacher stepped out of sight and vanished. The street ahead was completely empty save for a few bits of debris, allowing him to keep to the center as he went. The shadows were growing longer, but he doubted it mattered now.

The massive form of the Coming Conqueror loomed at the end of the street. Everything in him said to avoid the place. Only misery awaited there, only anguish. Only death.

Grimluk set the fear aside and moved on, his steps swift and deliberate. His eyes were hard and focused. His hands were ready.

He heard the harsh squeaks as he approached. That seemed to answer his question about the imps. The sound shifted and rolled into chittering squawks. A moment later, Grimluk was in front of the building, the chittering demons crawling out to greet him. They weren't exactly imps, though; not completely. Flabby, glistening bodies the color of deep, dark bruises crawled out of windows and out of the saloon-side entrance, scurrying across the awning roof. Their bodies were shaped like imps, with small talons and sagging, chubby wings. However, they had no faces. No eyes or sharp little mouths full of wicked teeth, just nubby little horns. Had they been sleeker and blacker, they'd have passed for miniature nightgaunts.

Grimluk didn't wait on the creatures to advance. His gun went up to his hip in a pseudo-draw and roared. Bullets ripped through six of the little imp-like bodies, splattering them across the building as globules of the bruise-colored flesh exploded everywhere.

The Coming Conqueror roared its disapproval. The rumbling cry rattled every window. The imp things chittered wildly and started flinging themselves at Grimluk. A dozen of them hurled at him like fleshy cannonballs. His fingers were faster though, and the revolver was reloaded before they could get too close.

He caught two with one shot and waited for another to come screaming in close, where he met it with his knife in a downward slice that split the creature in two. The flabby flesh split like jelly, part of which slammed down in front of his boots with a sickening squelch. He kicked the bits away and focused on the rest coming toward him.

His revolver spoke up again, condemning the things with its power. More of the imp-shaped blobs exploded. The gun dropped into its holster as Grimluk pulled the blanket off of his shoulder. With a twist, he gathered the corners and used it like a net. Four more of the imps slammed into the blanket and into the demon trap within. The creatures screamed. The sound would've hurt his ears if not for the muffling layer of cloth that separated them. A great, burbling roar filled the Conqueror.

It only took a moment before the bag lost the scrambling weight of the imps. Grimluk flicked the blanket out, scattering the clumps of burnt flesh made black and hard. That meant these things were part of the demon. Real imps would've been trapped like any other demon.

"Come on, then!" Grimluk roared. "I'm game!"

The imp things hesitated but it was a ruse. The entrance to the Conqueror's saloon exploded in a shower of wood. The whole bar followed after it, right at Grimluk.

He flung himself into a twisting drop on sheer instinct, barely dodging the bar. The bar rushed past him, cutting through the air to crash through one of the buildings behind him. The slightest hesitation and the thing might have ripped his shoulder out, if not worse. Grimluk rolled to a crouch and his gun came back up in a flash, spending his last two shots. Two more of the chittering imp things exploded, staining the Conqueror with oozing fluids.

The revolver's cylinder flipped out, spilling its spent guts into the dirt. Fresh shells found their way back into the chambers, ready to deal death. The imp-shapes just screeched at him and retreated. Something skittered out of the building in their place. The same glistening, oily, bruise-colored flesh appeared, probably as long as the bar had been. Bones protruded from all over it as it used them to propel itself forward like a monstrous centipede covered in mouths.

Grimluk shuddered. He'd seen insectoid demons before. Killed plenty of them. Those beasts looked wrong in their bug shapes, but this thing made them look normal.

Then it looked at him. The motion made clear the pile of skulls atop what could loosely be described as a head. Every skull was perfectly clean and smooth, with glowing eyes shining from every hole. Bone pincers rolled out from beneath the skulls, curved and just as smooth-looking as the skulls. The tips were jagged though. They looked like broken rib bones.

The pincers clacked together before the voice he'd heard the night before rolled out. "Grimluk," it growled from every mouth on the thing's body.

"I'm your huckleberry, demon," Grimluk said with his own growl as he rose, drawing the blanket across his shoulder again. "We gonna play for keeps this time?"

The bones along its body quivered in an undulating wave. But it didn't move any closer. It just moved slowly to the side, toward the Conqueror's hotel entrance. Grimluk watched it, waiting for the demon to make its move. He spared a quick glance to his rear, making sure the thing hadn't split apart to come at him from behind as well.

The Preacher was watching, once more staring at Grimluk with unnerving concentration and a smile to match, still clutching the book to his chest all the while.

Two more shapes joined the centipede as Grimluk watched, trying to keep track of the Preacher, too. The horned demon of Arbortown rolled out, looking like it was floating with the motion. An elvenoid shape followed it. The body was perfectly smooth but grotesquely large, with stubby legs and arms, and a belly that shook too loosely, like a puddle of congealed blood. It had a head but no face, like the imps. No ears either, just perfect, glistening smoothness. The stomach split open vertically into a wide maw lined with jagged bone teeth and a spiral of horrendous eyes all aimed at Grimluk. He growled low in his throat at the sight of it all. The two new forms felt like grotesque mockeries of life.

Running wouldn't matter, now. The thing had been fast when it was a gigantic ball of eyes and teeth. Split into three like this, it would outmaneuver him easily. All he could do was make a stand, maybe his last, and hope he hurt it enough to let Emerald and Manyara run.

"You might kill me, you sorry sack of shit, but I'll make you remember it. And I'll make gods-damned sure you fuckin' choke on me." Grimluk squared up and aimed his gun at the horned demon shape before thumbing the hammer back. "You want me? Come and claim me."

He was prepared for the demon to strike, for

each form to come at him in its own way. He wasn't prepared for the slow applause from behind him. For the lone laugh from the Preacher.

"Delightful!" the man called, the clapping growing closer. "Simply marvelous! Wonderful!"

The Preacher walked into view, ending his applause. Grimluk did his best to watch all four beings in front of him, staring ahead but letting his eyes relax enough to keep track of them all. He didn't reply to the man.

"What a show! What. A. Show! But I think we can end it now, yes? For the time being? There's business to discuss, though not just yet. Not just yet at all."

The three forms of the demon all moved their heads in unison. It almost reminded Grimluk of a puppy. Almost. But their bodies didn't move from where they stood. Grimluk's revolver didn't move either.

The Preacher sighed. "Children. So prone to stubbornness. Settle down, the lot of you!" The man waved the book in a horizontal arc from Grimluk toward the demon.

Something pushed on Grimluk's mind. He could feel it as sure as a stiff gust of wind, but it rolled off him, sending a shiver down his spine. The feeling made him utterly certain the Preacher had tried to influence his thoughts. The tattoo on his skull held the man at bay with ease but it still made Grimluk bristle. Anger rolled through him.

The demon, on the other hand, seemed to lose control of its shapes. The three forms splattered to the ground in a puddle while the Preacher kept his eyes on Grimluk.

"Be smart, whelp, and lower the gun. The battle is over, but if you want to push it, I feel obliged to inform you that while our friend here cannot get to your women, I do not heed such barriers."

"You summoned this thing?" Grimluk asked. It was a valid question. It could also provide him with a few moments to think.

"Don't be such an addle-headed mule," the Preacher replied sharply. "Does this magnificent creature look like something to just be summoned on a whim? I mean, really."

Like the question, this, too, was valid by Grimluk's reckoning. He still couldn't recall a single demon that looked or behaved like this thing.

"Why should I believe you at all? What if it's beyond my ken to do so?"

The Preacher gave him a contemptuous look. "Then you're no use to anyone, and the remaining living things in this town will die. Horribly, I might add."

Grimluk lowered his gun slowly, letting the hammer move forward again. Response enough to the Preacher.

"Excellent," the man said, nodding his approval. "What is it the card sharps say? 'Aces'? Never kept up with cards. Never saw the point. Ah, but you're wondering about what to do now, am I right? I can't touch your mind, but I can see the thought on your face."

"Reckon so."

The Preacher held up a hand in a placating gesture. "Settle, boy. Now, as I said, this battle's done. Go on and collect your women. You've nothing else to fear. For now, at least. I'll even leave a coach ready for you, if you'd like! Or would you prefer a wagon? I like coaches so much better. So comfortable. Ah, maybe I'll just leave it as a surprise. How does that strike you, hunter?"

None of this made a lick of sense to Grimluk, but he held his tongue for the moment.

"Shoo, off with you."

"Why?" Grimluk asked.

The Preacher seemed to consider his answer. "Mayhaps it's an opportunity to open your eyes to the gospel. Mayhaps it's a lesson. Then again, it could just be benevolence. Or it's everything! That seems a touch more accurate. Any other reason isn't your business, and I'd thank you to respect that."

Grimluk took a step back. Just one, to test the veracity of the Preacher's word. And to see if the demon would remain where it was. It did, so Grimluk took a few more steps back. When nothing happened, he turned and moved off. He'd just stared Death in the eyes and been released, or so it seemed. Might as well ride it out as far as he could. Even if it made his skin crawl and set off every instinctive warning in him.

Sooner or later, he'd learn the nature of this trap. He just hoped he'd know how to escape it by then.

Chapter 12

The puddle of oozing malice and hunger watched as the orc walked away. Watched the human in black looking at it with his teeth showing. Watched, unmoving from underneath a house, the two women it couldn't get to for some reason. It let out frustrated burbles and a low growl. One eye, red and slit-pupiled, rolled up and glared at the human man.

The man looked back toward Grimluk and when the orc was out of sight, he walked over to the blob and knelt next to it. The blob could feel something pressing it to the ground. Something pushing on its thoughts. It could move enough to rejoin itself, though. The part of its body that had been watching the women slithered slowly back to the whole.

"I must beg your pardon for the invasive influence," the man said to it. "Seeing you and he in action brought a realization upon me."

"Why?" it asked through three mouths. The distraction the human was presenting had ruined its concentration. The eyes and mouths bubbled and burst across its prone flesh again. It liked being smooth, but the sensation wasn't unpleasant.

"Aaaah, I see wisdom buds in you. Wonderful." The man seemed to regard the object in his hand, running his other hand down the front of it. "As I said, an opportunity presented itself. You, my beautiful creature, have much to learn. The hunter might yet have similar lessons. I have use for him still, too. Though that use hardly concerns you."

It bubbled in thought, combing through new thoughts and information. Though a fair amount of the town's residents had fled, the ones called "rangers" had contained a wealth of concepts and knowledge. Its missing chunk finally neared as it sifted through that new information. Even during this momentary reflection, its implacable hunger burned.

The moment made the blob realize it didn't know whether the hunger was for sustenance or vengeance. The feelings were bound so tightly together, swirling with other things it still didn't understand.

"What lesson?" it asked the man.

"For the time being? You can be more than you are. You've tried and done well so far. Succeeded wonderfully, I might add, but there is more yet. Tell me—oh, manners. Do you have a name, dear thing?"

The slime thought about that. What had it said before? It had, in its initial attack and rage, tried to claim the demon's name, but it had come out wrong. Or had it? It didn't understand, but it knew things had names, and this man wanted its name.

"Shoggoth," it said in its bubbling voice.

"Really?" the man said, showing his teeth again

before looking away. "How…interesting. So it shall be. As I was saying; tell me, when you took the halfling's shape and waded among this place's patrons, and when you confronted the hunter in the forest as the orc woman, did you take their shapes and make their clothes from your body or did you fill clothes with your shape?"

The presence on its mind and body loosened and it used its regained freedom to curl into a pulsing ball of darkness. It had taken the halfling and pressed the clothes into the man's shape. It had done both things at once. Pretending to be the orc woman had been slightly harder, as it had no clothes to model the shape. It thought about how to speak the words.

"Both. Then…shapes," it said.

The man nodded. "A smart effort, indeed. Indeed. I would hardly deprive you of the glorious exploration of yourself, but might I make a suggestion?"

It grumbled but made no movement, a loose indication that it was listening.

"Make use of the garments you see to make your shapes easier to hold. For instance, if you were to find, say, a magician, or a monk, especially a plump one, you could hide yourself beneath their robes. Or several of them, if you wish. I've no fathom for how it might work for you to stay split like that. I could help you find such a person, if you like."

Splitting itself into multiples pieces was no challenge at all. It had done so with ease. The idea had merit. Shoggoth could inhabit the clothing and not worry about changing the tones of its body. Just the parts that could be seen.

"Why...help?" Shoggoth asked, a streak of suspicion filling it. Sheogorath had claimed it wanted to help but then attacked it and attempted to force it to help dole out its vengeance.

"Many reasons, but chief among them is your glorious uniqueness. I can feel Sheogorath within you. A clever creature in its own right, though it clung to its sibling so strangely. Devouring the demon has made you something greater altogether. Is that why you made the imps?"

Shoggoth thought this over. "Felt...right."

"Fascinating. The pair of them were practically glorified imps themselves. Especially Bashuurga." He stood. "Come, come. There's a magician nearby, alone and ripe for your use. Call it a gift for your birth. I have more questions, if you'll grant them."

Shoggoth mulled the offer over. "Sheogorath helped," it began, focusing on speech. "Until I wanted new food. Then it attacked. If you do that, I will eat you as well." The remaining pressure on its mind vanished. It twisted into the air for a long moment, enjoying the sensation, the sudden release of restrictions.

The man bowed his head. "Aside from this momentary lapse in your autonomy, I dream only to help you achieve greatness. Ah, but first," the man waved the book behind himself without looking.

"What did you do?" Shoggoth asked.

"I did offer the coach to the hunter. That should satisfy him."

Shoggoth bubbled in sudden anger. The strangeness of the conversation had distracted it well enough but now the reminder of the demon hunter surged forward. It was strong and hot, but the blob tried to keep it at bay. To regard it with detachment. The hunger roared from deep within.

"Will have him…" it said, taking the large elvenoid shape again, now a bit larger from the collected girth of itself.

"I've no doubt about it, but not yet. Not just yet." The man in black waved the book again, to the side, and a dark, shimmering light suddenly poured out over them. "After you, dear Shoggoth."

Shoggoth took a lumbering step forward and looked at the light. A shack lay beyond it, obscured slightly and wavering faintly. The great body stepped through what it realized was a portal. The man followed and the light winked out.

"There now. We'll pick you up a nice outfit and then you can make your way out to Cold River to do what you will. Shall we?" The man inclined his head and held his free arm out.

Shoggoth gave what the swirling pool of knowledge in its mind indicated was a polite, if curt, nod. It didn't quite understand the purpose of the gesture. The motion was an echo from one in its mind, from one or maybe many of the people it had devoured. "Verily," it said, heading for the shack.

"Do you trust him?" Manyara asked Emerald after Grimluk was out of sight.

"Hasn't given me a reason not to," she replied with a yawn. The pair of them were attempting to treat Bringar's wounds, where they could get to them easily. "Especially after the night before."

Manyara nodded. "Was just wonderin'. He seems a trustworthy sort, but you know what people say about demon hunters."

Emerald frowned. Her brow hardened and she looked at her friend. "And you know half that shit is from most of the hunters being orcs. If I didn't know you better, Yara, I might consider poppin' you in the mouth for that."

Manyara's head jerked up. Her eyes were big, like Emerald had slapped her. "Gods, Em, that's—no, that's not..." She ran a hand over her head. "You're right. You're right, beg yer pardon. I didn't think."

"That man did everything in his power to get as many of us to safety as he could. I watched the gods-damned thing chase after him, Yara. He even warned you and gave you his knife. And..."

"Yeah?"

"He reminded me of you," Emerald said quietly as she finished wrapping Bringar's mangled leg. She twisted the bandage around to tie it down and sat back with a sigh. "Sorry for snappin'. Roscoe's been at me again. Was takin' swipes at Grimluk, too. Kept it up even while the damn demon was wrigglin' all about us."

"Fucking Roscoe," Manyara said sharply, scorn dripping in her voice. "Why ain't he learned yet?"

Emerald let out a soft laugh. "He might've for the time being. I heard Grimluk shouting at him before we set off to meet you. When we were comin' back after y'all, he said he grabbed Roscoe by the head and held him up to make his point."

Manyara let out a quiet laugh. "No! I bet that scared the bastard worse than the time Bringar rung his bell."

Manyara had such a beautiful laugh, when she allowed herself to show it. Emerald liked trying to make her laugh in quiet moments, hoping to catch her off guard like she just had. She smiled at her friend.

"Definitely worse. He kept his face shut the rest of the night and the whole way down the road. No doubt he started moanin' again as soon as Grimluk was out of sight."

Manyara wiped away dried blood from Bringar's eye. "So he's trustworthy and he scares the piss out of Roscoe. Sounds like a keeper to me, Em." The words had a playful tone to them.

"Said his sister likes rocks, too. Might even know a thing or two."

"Say true?" Manyara said, holding her hand to her chest in a sarcastic gesture. "Well, shit, now he's poachin' on me. Can't have that."

"Ya don't say. And what are you gonna do about it, huh?"

"Gotta duel him. Only way. Pistols at high—"

Gunfire rang out like booming thunder, commanding their attention. Emerald looked toward the sound, her strained ease quickly replaced with a fear that snaked through her heart.

Grimluk.

It sounded like he'd fired several shots but she wasn't good at recognizing the sounds of battle. Manyara would know. She reached back for the woman's hand and found it. Manyara's fingers were calloused, her palms scuffed softly from her duties as a ranger, but she held Emerald's hand with a gentle fierceness that helped calm her heart some.

They listened. Something big crashed and splintered a building, a sound Emerald found immensely disconcerting in the otherwise silent town. Roars and screeches met their ears. Someone was shouting, probably Grimluk. It sounded like him, and she'd heard him shouting at the thing already. It all happened so fast and then there was silence. It drew out like a blade, sharp and painful in its suddenness. Part of Emerald wanted to run off and make sure Grimluk was all right. He'd said to stay in the circle, though. They were safe here.

They just sat, holding each other's hands, and waited. It felt like years passed before Grimluk appeared again, walking slowly toward them. Emerald thought he looked worried, or maybe confused. Maybe both. Maybe neither. For someone so friendly and plain-spoken, he could be incredibly hard to read from under the wide hat he wore.

He stopped a few feet away, looking at them. He shifted his weight and grunted. Did he want something?

"Oh!" Emerald said as the memory struck her. "Um, what's on your back?"

"My ass," he said with a deceptively charming

smirk. "And a whole mess of scars." He stepped into the circle.

Emerald watched him, relief washing through her. He was here. It had to be over. She hoped it was.

Grimluk dropped to his butt and pulled his hat away for a moment, running his hand across his face. He pulled his bag around and started digging in it. A roll of paper appeared and he opened it up, revealing the fat pile of jerky he'd shared with her earlier. He offered them some. Emerald took a piece and stuck one end in her mouth. Goat. Whoever he got it from, Emerald was still surprised at how good the stuff was.

Grimluk mirrored Emerald, chewing lightly on one end of the jerky. "So," he said over the meat. "How's the marshal?"

"You saw his leg," Manyara started. "Em wrapped it and we tried to clean him up a touch elsewhere. Pretty sure his wrist is broken. Ribs, probably. Maybe that thick skull of his, too. No idea how long he'll be out."

Grimluk nodded.

"So," Emerald said, holding her jerky, "how did...we heard your gun. How did it go?"

He let a sigh out through his nose, following that with a low growl. "Didn't get far. Would've been a shitkicker for sure if the Preacher hadn't showed up."

"What?" Emerald and Manyara asked at the same time.

He slid the jerky to the side of his mouth. "Reckon the thing's gotten smarter since last night.

It seemed more confident. Split itself up into three parts, all different. Preacher showed up. He is definitely a wizard of some sort, not no town magician. Damned powerful, too. Commanded us to stop. Seemed to push the demon down when he did it. Reckon some sort of psychic control. Couldn't get in my head, though. I got protection from that sort of thing."

Emerald looked at him, her jaw hanging open while she tried to find the words. "How? No, wait, so...so the Preacher's on our side? Did he kill it?"

A rumble came from Grimluk's throat. "I'm not convinced he's even human, much less mortal, so I reckon his intervention was as much for the demon's benefit as mine. Probably more so."

"So we're trapped," Manyara said softly. "We're gonna die here."

Grimluk shook his head, pushing the brim of his hat up. "No. He...basically guaranteed safe passage out of town."

Manyara scoffed. "And you trust the bastard?"

"Not even a little bit. But I do believe him. I think he wants something from me and it requires my continued existence. He seemed to understand that also required letting you two be, as well."

"What do we do, then?" Emerald asked.

"Go on to Cold River, I reckon. Only thing we can do." He paused for a moment, swapping sides with his jerky. "Said he'd have a coach or wagon ready for us, too, so we can get Bringar loaded up. Worst case, I can carry the man on my shoulders."

Emerald looked at Grimluk, trying to wrap her mind around his words and the situation at hand.

He still looked too calm to be scared. She wondered if she looked as scared as she felt. She was sure it was etched on her face, as plain to see as her tusks.

"I–I guess we should go," Emerald muttered. Her eyes fell to her hands. The jerky between her fingers suddenly felt very interesting.

"Reckon so," Manyara agreed sullenly.

Paper crinkled. Emerald looked up to see Grimluk wrapping the jerky back up. He stood and offered his hand, gently smiling at her. She took his hand and, with his assistance, rose swiftly to her feet. Grimluk wrapped the blanket back around her. It was still warm from his body. Considering how she felt, the warmth was divine.

"I'll let you hold on to the jerky. And the water," he said, handing her the jerky before untying a waterskin from his bag and handing it over as well. "Might need to pop by the river and refill them. I don't trust the well here."

"Smart thinkin'," Manyara said, standing as well.

Emerald looked at her. Her friend gave her a strange look she couldn't quite place, but she took a guess.

"Um, could...could Yara have your knife again? I have your blanket and you'd have your gun still."

Grimluk's tongue rolled behind his lip and up one tusk briefly. An errant thought rose in her mind as she watched the gesture, making the blood rush to her cheeks. She pushed it away. It was hardly the time for such ideas.

"More smart thinkin'," he said. He slipped his

hand behind his back. A dull, clicking snap followed and he pulled the knife out, still in its sheath. "Here you are, Ranger. Stay sharp."

He winked.

Emerald groaned but couldn't help smiling.

Manyara stared at him for a long moment. "Not the most appropriate time to cut loose, is it?"

Emerald snorted.

"Mm, I get your point, Ranger."

"Oh my gods," Emerald said, rolling her eyes in lieu of throwing up her hands. She walked out of the circle of protection. "I'm gonna go throw myself at the demon before you two get worse."

Manyara made a pained sound. "Oh, Em, you wound me," Manyara continued.

"Gods-damn it, Yara," Emerald replied with another groan. "You are a villain."

"Agreed," Grimluk said with a grunt.

When Emerald turned to look, he was in the middle of standing Bringar up. Once the marshal was on his feet, propped against Grimluk, the hunter twisted and bent, hauling Bringar up onto his shoulders.

"Your displeasure is like a razor," he finished.

Emerald stomped away, growling loudly to stifle her laughter. "I hate you both."

They found a coach at the edge of town with a horse grazing to the side, off the road. Grimluk, with Manyara's help, got Bringar inside. There wasn't enough room to lay the man down, so Grimluk did his best to settle the Ranger as flat as he could. He hoped the man just stayed unconscious for the time being. Until they could get him to a healer's clinic.

Manyara opted to stay inside with her marshal. Grimluk nodded in affirmation and then went to coax the horse into its harness. He didn't have to do much in the way of actual coaxing, though. The beast was a massive draft horse, covered in thick muscle and a nearly white coat. It snorted idly as Grimluk secured it. He was fairly certain coaches needed two horses usually, but considering the size of the horse, and the nature of its arrival, he wasn't terribly worried about its ability to pull them. It reminded him of his fallen friend Eagle's horse. Eagle and his partner, Beast, rode steeds that could only be described as war horses.

Emerald watched Grimluk, wrapped in the demon trap blanket. He imagined she'd want a change of clothes once they arrived in Cold River. She'd asked if they could stop at the Coming Conqueror first so she could get some but, in truth, he didn't trust the building. It'd taken a lot of damage from the demon and could have held more traps to boot. Mostly it was that last part that concerned him.

"You can load up with the rangers," Grimluk told her, finishing with the horse's harness. "We'll be pullin' out momentarily. Reckon you've had your fill of the cold. Oughta be warmer in there."

"Truth be told, I'm not sure she and I can fit in

there with Bringar, too. I'm not exactly small, am I?"

Grimluk chuckled. "Course not. You're an orc."

"Exactly. I'll ride up front with you for the time being. If you'll have me, I mean."

Grimluk laid the reins where he could get to them and offered his hand to help Emerald up. "If you're sure, then I'm more than happy to oblige. You're fine company."

Emerald smiled softly and took his hand as she climbed up onto the box. Grimluk followed her a moment later, once she was seated. The box was a touch cramped with the two of them, but he didn't mind. He could think of worse people to be so close to. He gathered the reins and turned his head.

"Ready, Ranger?" he asked loudly. Manyara replied with two confident thumps on the roof. "All right. Now, let's see if I can remember how to do this."

Grimluk released the brake, clucked at the horse, and shook the reins. The huge horse just snorted and stood where it was. "Let's see...yah?"

"May I?" Emerald asked.

"By all means," Grimluk replied, handing her the reins.

"Yip-yip!" Emerald called and snapped the reins lightly. The coach started forward with a heavy jolt, slow at first, but gradually picking up to a smooth pace as the horse gained momentum. The steady *clop-clop-clop* of its hooves gradually settled into a brisk refrain.

Grimluk grunted in approval. The afternoon

sun hung low in the sky. In another hour or so, dusk would roll in, bringing shadow. He grunted and looked to the sky, crossing his arms as he did. Maybe they'd just ride through the night, after a stop at the waystation. Might be the safest choice.

"You really think we'll make it?" Emerald asked.

"Reckon so. Like I said back there, since I could resist his sway, I'll bet he could piece together that hurtin' you three would guarantee real fast him not gettin' whatever he wants." He still couldn't fathom what that might be, but it didn't matter. Yet. One crisis at a time.

And I'll be prepared next time, he thought. It was his job to be prepared, after all.

"I'm glad it didn't hurt you," Emerald said. "Besides us not dyin' as well, I mean. I'm mighty glad for that, too."

"You, me, and the ranger makes three."

"Mhm. Maybe Bringar, too, when he wakes up. Maybe."

"Have my doubts there. Man's got a death wish."

"I know it wasn't too smart of him to ignore you, but you really think it's as bad as that?"

Grimluk let out a sigh through his nose as he thought about how to phrase it. "Even rangers don't rush off to deal with the aftermath of a demon, much less a live one, with a hunter tellin' them 'don't go.' Reckon he's hurtin'. Or maybe just eat up with fightin'. Battle lust. Happens some-times, even among hunters."

Emerald didn't say anything to that. Grimluk

looked over at her. She looked like she was contemplating what he'd said. Her tusks bobbed slightly as she worked her mouth in thought.

"Guess you might be right. Yara said he'd been leadin' their crew for years before she joined."

A grin tugged lightly at the corner of Grimluk's lip. "She's pretty loyal from what I've seen."

"Shit, that's an understatement. She's a long way from her family, so she likes to keep folks close if she can. When she cares and they earned it."

"Reckon you two keep pretty close then, too, huh?"

"Well, no, not like that," Emerald replied with a little laugh. "We're friends, sure, but I'm no ranger. I just help her unwind on time off, that's all."

Grimluk let out a lone chuckle. "Say true?"

"Well, yeah. I do. Not like she don't pay me like you did. Just part of the job."

He considered that for a moment, scratching his chin. "I figure it wouldn't rightly be my business, but considerin' the circumstances, I reckon it'll be okay."

"How's that?" Emerald asked, trying to pull the blanket tight again.

Grimluk took the reins to let her bundle up better.

"Oh, thank you," she said, pulling the blanket tighter.

"Way I see it, you nearly die with some folks, you get a different view of things. True?"

"Seems a fair point."

He leaned toward her. "She's sweet on you, Em."

"What? No, no."

"Mhm. Plain as tusks," he said. "And I reckon you're sweet on her, too."

"W–what? No, no, that's–"

"Emerald, I hunt demons. You think I haven't learned to see what's around me? Pay attention to folks? Not my place to get into your relationship, but I reckon you two feel mighty good when you're together."

Emerald huffed. "I get paid for sex. I feel good a lot. A lot."

Grimluk shrugged. "Rocks and magic."

"I–she–that is..."

He nodded. "Just think on it. Maybe it wouldn't work, but maybe it would. Just maybe it would. No sense tossin' that away on assumptions unsaid, right? Better to know and be secure in the knowin', wouldn't it? If you two are as close as you seem, nothin' would really change."

Grimluk gave her a glance as he leaned back. She was looking at him, her mouth hanging open and her brow furrowed deeply. She just blinked and then turned away slowly. They rode on in silence while Emerald stared at the road. He'd clearly given her something to think about, and it was an important something, so he left her to it.

CHAPTER 13

Whether the horse was supernatural or not, the trip to Cold River was faster than Grimluk expected. Through the dimness of predawn, Grimluk could see the town twinkling with street lamps. Cold River appeared to be a bustling town on the verge of becoming a small city. Unlike Downingville, it had been built hugging the river it took its name from. Along the river were modest warehouses, docks of all shapes, and small cranes for unloading river boats. The river was wide here, stretching out well over a mile. There were already several boats lined up along the docks as they rode in.

"I've never actually been over here," Emerald said.

"Mm," came Grimluk's reply. He'd never been far enough east to get into the Westlynth province until now. He'd spent most of his travels along the Borderlands and in west and central New Gilead, with one notable trip along the New Gilead border of the Wildlands to the north. He'd taken a job to kill a huge, hairy creature his employer had sworn was a demon. The job had not gone at all the way he or his employer had expected. He still occasionally wondered how the creature was doing.

Grimluk held the reins out to Emerald. "Reckon we can stop for a moment. Manyara should probably direct us where to go. And she and I will both need to make reports."

"Oh, uh, right," she said, taking the reins. "Hup hup!"

The horse slowed its pace before coming to a stop that bucked the coach lightly. The horse snorted and shook its head as Grimluk climbed down to open the door to the coach. Manyara stirred, looking like she'd been dozing, and let out a long yawn.

"We there?" she asked through the yawn.

"We are. Why don't you hop up with Emerald and tell her where to go? Neither of us have ever been here."

"Right, yeah." She looked at Bringar before climbing out. "He's still unconscious. Watch him for me?"

Grimluk nodded as he moved out of the way. "Wouldn't be the first time I've looked after a wounded person."

"Much obliged."

Grimluk hauled himself into the coach interior, trying to move delicately to avoid jostling Bringar. A few moments later, he jerked slightly as the carriage started moving again. He closed his eyes and half dozed as they went wherever they were going.

Grimluk had been awake for the better part of two days now. While he could push himself a few days without sleep, he didn't normally do so except as a last resort, usually to stay on the trail of something that didn't need to sleep at all. He'd walked, run, fought, escorted, and investigated nearly constantly since the demon had initially attacked. He hoped very much that he could get at least a few hours of real sleep.

His stomach grumbled loudly. And a big damn meal, he thought.

He had a sudden craving for a nice bit of liver – buffalo, if he could get it. He wasn't sure if there were any buffalo out this way. As far as he knew, they tended to stay within the Sapphire Plains, which didn't reach out to the southeast like this, but he wasn't an animal scholar.

He sighed and put his thoughts aside for the time being, allowing himself to drift off. In what felt like a blink of his eye, the coach stopped again. As he climbed out, he saw Manyara had taken them to the rangers' fort. He nodded to her as she climbed down from the box.

"Wait here a moment," she said, helping Emerald down. "I'll get the doc out here. We got sleds or cots we can put Bringar on."

She didn't wait for a reply, and Grimluk didn't feel one was warranted anyhow. He leaned against the carriage and waited. Emerald handed him the blanket for a moment and stretched, raising her arms toward the night sky. Without the blanket covering her, he could see more of her curves as the fabric of her dress pulled taut against her. A little flush of heat hit his cheeks and he looked to the sky as well. The stars glittered.

"They're beautiful, don't ya think?" Emerald asked, covering herself with the blanket again.

His throat rumbled. "Mm. Sometimes I wonder what's up there."

"Some folks say the gods live up there."

"Maybe. Supposed to be vast like an ocean from what the loremaster told us once. They call it the 'cosmos.'"

"How do folks know that?"

Grimluk shrugged. "Ancient elves, maybe. Outside of the important constellations, we never learned much about all that. I'm sure Vatris could've taught us more, but it's not somethin' you need as a hunter. But I still get curious sometimes." He looked down at Emerald again.

"Guess someone oughta know a lot then, if your loremaster knew." She stepped closer. "Um, Grim, do...do you really think—"

"Out here," Manyara called. "He's in the carriage."

"Yeah, I do," he said, guessing what Emerald was going to ask by the surprise on her face when Manyara came back out. Two gray-bearded dwarves followed Manyara out. They wore white aprons over their clothes and carried a cot between them.

Despite his offer to help, the two dwarves retrieved Bringar on their own and carried the cot swiftly, like there wasn't an unconscious, and probably quite heavy, orc lying in it. Manyara motioned for him and Emerald to follow. The dwarves led them to the building that housed the clinic. Grimluk felt a similar enchantment to the one upon the Coming Conqueror as they entered. Once inside, he could see the room stretched far enough around to house a dozen partitions with beds and little tables.

Off to the left was an open door, revealing what looked like an alchemist's lab. Aside from the grunts of the dwarves and the scuff of boots, the clinic was quiet. The duo positioned Bringar over a bed and slid him as gently as they could off the cot onto the mattress.

A halfling, also in a white apron, came padding out of the lab, bare feet slapping against the floor lightly. Grimluk couldn't help but notice the lack of hair on their feet and knuckles.

"Good evenin'," the halfling said. "I'm Dr. Gamgee. Ranger Arendse has given a brief explanation of the situation. We thank the both of y'all for yer help, sais. If you would, I'd like to look y'all over as well, along with the rangers."

"I'm mostly just cold and exhausted," Emerald said wearily. Her stomach gave an audible roar that made her giggle a bit. "Oh, and maybe a touch famished."

"Outside of the good ranger shooting me, I'm fine. I took care of that already. Some food and a bed would be mighty fine, though."

The healer nodded. "Quite understandable. If you'll foll—wait, you were shot?"

A little chuckle escaped Grimluk. "I know, I know, but trust me, I'm all patched up. It's a semi-regular occurrence, unfortunately, but I have some elvish salve I use."

Dr. Gamgee's brow furrowed. "I see. Well, uh, I'd still prefer to look y'all over. Professional responsibility. You are welcome to the mess hall first, however. Manyara can show ya the way."

Grimluk shrugged. "Fair enough. Before we

go, if you don't mind my asking, you ain't a saw-
bones, are you? Only doctors I've met were pretty
quick to lop off a limb instead of working in
potions or poultices and wraps."

"Mm, an unfortunate history for the title. No,
you'll find most doctors, at least in Westlynth, are
trying new methods of healin' along with more tried
and true alchemical practices. Less of the traditional
elven methods, as well. Frankly, those ways are
being taught less and less as the old elves are
retirin'. I swear, yer limbs will remain intact under
my care, my friend."

Grimluk nodded. "Good enough. Let's get
some grub. Feel like I could eat a whole buffalo and
still want seconds." Manyara led them across the
yard into the main building of the fort, also forti-
fied with the same enchantment, which,
presumably, housed the mess hall.

"The cooks are probably just wakin' up," Manyara informed them, "but due to our occasionally
strange hours, the fort's open as we please. Pantry
should be quite accommodating."

The mess hall was simple, just a few scattered
tables and an open kitchen. The pantry stood near
the kitchen, behind slatted doors. A range of cured
meats hung on strings in the back with a shelf of
tightly wrapped shapes under it, labeled with
stamps. Wheels of cheese lined one shelf; underneath was a shelf with baskets of vegetables, and
below that was a shelf covered in cans and jars.
Grimluk felt it safe to assume that the prevalence of
vegetables meant Cold River had at least one talented alchemist or magician, allowing for year-
round growing, if only for the rangers.

Grimluk's mouth watered at the sight of the meats. Emerald must have been thinking the same thing, no doubt just as ravenous as he was. She rushed forward and seized something that looked like a long sausage. She tore it free and bit into it. She let out a sigh of pleasure and just stood there for a moment.

Grimluk bent to inspect the cans and jars and found a jar of peaches. It'd been a long time since he'd had peaches. They were hard to get in the Borderlands. Or maybe he'd just never been lucky. It didn't matter, though; he had some now. Manyara slipped past him to grab a few things with Emerald.

"Got any salted beef over there?" he asked, grabbing a small cheese wheel.

"Sure do. Small slab, anyhow," Manyara replied, taking the paper-covered meat down for him.

They each gathered a little pile of food and took it to a table. Emerald collapsed into a chair, gnawing on the sausage stick contentedly. Manyara disappeared back into the kitchen and returned with a few knives and forks before collapsing as well. The three of them devoured their meals with zeal. There was no speaking, no eye contact, little in the way of acknowledging each other. They just ate and sighed and burped and relished the opportunity to do so.

Once Manyara finished eating, she went back to the kitchen and returned with three brown bottles of sarsaparilla.

"Gods-damn that's good," he declared.

"Mmmmm!" came Emerald's agreement, bottle tipped back.

"Brewer in town bottles it himself," Manyara said, taking a pull. "Has a few different flavors, too. Calls this one 'Sunset'."

"Damn good," Grimluk repeated, looking at the bottle approvingly.

Once they were full, Manyara led them to the guest barracks, usually reserved for commanding officers in town for inspections and the occasional errant rangers. Instead of a communal bunk room, it was several small bedrooms, allowing for privacy. Emerald stumbled into the room Manyara offered her and started to close the door. She turned suddenly.

"Will you be up here, too, Yara?" she asked.

Manyara seemed to consider it. "Reckon so. I'm...I–I don't want..." She looked down and sighed.

"If you'd like, you can sleep with me," Emerald offered. Even with exhaustion tugging at her, it couldn't diminish the sincerity in her smile. "I'd be just fine with the company."

Manyara looked up and nodded. "You sure?"

Emerald bowed her head. "Absolutely. You come on in when you're ready," she replied before closing the door.

Manyara showed Grimluk to the next room. "This one should be big enough for ya."

"Much obliged," he said. "You go on and get some rest. Tell Emerald good night for me."

"Sure," she replied, heading for Emerald's room.

After shutting the door, Grimluk took enough time to hang up his hat, coat, and gun belt up before kicking off his boots and shedding his clothes in a trail behind him. He pulled back the bedding and crawled in. If he hadn't known better, he'd have sworn he heard his muscles sigh in relief. It didn't take long for sleep to find him, swallowing him hungrily.

Grimluk woke sometime in the early evening feeling leagues better. After redressing, he headed to see Dr. Gamgee, to let the doctor look him over.

"How's the marshal?" he asked, sitting on one of the beds.

"Hm? Well, I'd bet this demon o' yers cracked his head pretty good. We'll keep watch, though. You orcs are mighty stout, so for all we know at the moment, he could wake up somewhere between now or next week and be fine. To know anything deeper, we'd have to find a proper mystic healer to come take a look at him."

"I'd recommend our guild's healer, but he's the only one we got and it'd take him probably a month at best to get out here."

"Well, for now, we'll handle it. If his condition changes, we'll go from there. Let's look at that bullet wound."

Grimluk shrugged and pulled his shirt open. "Reckon by now it'll be closed up."

"So soon?" Dr. Gamgee asked as he pulled the dressing away. "Oh…so soon, indeed."

Grimluk ran a finger over the spot. It still had a bit of an indention, but was otherwise whole.

"How?"

"Salve made by the aforementioned healer," Grimluk replied, closing his shirt and buttoning it. "He's mighty talented, as you can see."

"Quite. Well, I can find nothing wrong with you, sai. If you would, send Emerald on in when you can. I know she was quite tired, but the sooner the better."

Grimluk stood up. "Will do, doc."

He found Manyara and Emerald in the mess hall. Emerald had changed out of her dress, and was now clad in clothing similar to Manyara's. The clothes hung loosely on her, just a bit too big. Her makeup had all been washed off and her hair braided. The two women sat sipping mugs of something steaming, maybe coffee or tea. Emerald waved and smiled when she saw him.

"Looks like some sleep did you a world of good," Grimluk remarked as he joined them. "Doc asked me to send you his way when you can spare a minute."

"I'll get to him in a bit, then." She sighed. "I have never been so tired before. That normal for you?"

"Not if I can help it. I can go without if I have to but it's not a wise practice."

"Mhm," Manyara replied. "Couple of years ago we had to ride down some rustlers. Real big gang, too. We couldn't make camp for two days. By the time we caught up, fought 'em, and cuffed 'em, everyone, including them fellas in the cuffs, just slept for a day."

Grimluk grunted. "Hunted down a pack of death hounds once in a similar fashion. That was a long gods-damned week."

"What's a death hound?" Emerald asked.

"Ever heard about huge black dogs attackin' folks?"

"Mm, once. Also heard once about one that just followed folks along a road up north."

"Former would likely be death hounds. Latter might've been a grim, though you don't see them much anymore. Anyways, death hounds get pretty nasty if they ain't put down quick. You ever see one, make sure it doesn't bite you." He paused for a moment, thinking something over. "Now that I think on it, I reckon it's pretty solid advice to say don't ever get bit by a demon at all. A fair number of them have undesirable effects. Ghouls mostly just won't stop chewin', but vampires, death hounds, werewolves in their wolf form, that's another matter. At least with vampires, it's not the bite that turns you. And thank the gods werewolf claws can't pass on the curse. Damn hard to heal, though."

Manyara and Emerald looked at him, eyes a little wide and their eyebrows raised.

"What?"

"Uh, we'll, uh, keep that in mind," Manyara said.

"I sincerely hope you never have to deal with any more demons. Though if you come upon ghouls, just aim for the head. Crack the fucker's skull like an egg and it's done. Folks get scared 'cause of the rot or the blood but ghouls are, quite frankly, just tedious. Ghouls would be a holiday right about now."

"So, wait, ghouls are demons?" Emerald asked. "I thought they was just a, what's it called...necromander thing?"

"Necromancer," he corrected. "And that's a bit different. Necromancers can raise corpses to serve them, but they're just mindless. Like a flesh puppet, I guess. Or bone puppets. Ghouls have some smarts to them. Ghouls want flesh and death; thralls just serve."

"Anyone ever tell you demon huntin' is fucked up?" Manyara asked.

Grimluk gave a grunting laugh. "Regularly and enthusiastically. And that's just among ourselves."

"Long as ya know it," the ranger replied, tilting her mug to him.

"Be hard to miss it at this point, what with that thing eatin' everyone. Reckon we oughta change subjects, eh? I'd wager you two have had more than enough talk of demons."

"Ain't that the all-fired truth," Manyara said with a nod. Emerald sighed in agreement. "Still gotta report to the captain, too. Get somethin' in ya and we can go do that."

He sighed and nodded. "Reckon your captain can see to informing the peacekeepers, too. I'll need to find the magi-tell office and post a notice either way."

"Captian's office is nearby. Cooks might have some leftover bacon and biscuits."

"Don't suppose they got any liver ready?"

"You'd have to ask."

He nodded. "Pardon, then." Grimluk rose and went to see what was left from earlier. As he walked away, he heard Emerald's voice.

"Will you be okay makin' your report?"

His throat rumbled. The very same worry sat at the edge of his mind. Surviving an attack had its own set of difficulties. Grimluk suffered nightmares at times; a common ailment among hunters. The memory of the one he'd woken from before the attack drifted through his mind like a ghost. He pushed it away. At least some of the people in Downingville had gotten away. That had weighed on him heavily.

The lack of liver disappointed Grimluk, but the biscuits were buttery and soft, and the bacon was thick and fatty. It all worked to settle his growling stomach. He washed it down with water from one of his skins and then he and Manyara were off to speak to the captain of the fort, Emerald following them with her mug.

Manyara entered first, Grimluk following close behind while Emerald stayed outside. The captain was a human man, hatchet-faced and hook-nosed with dark hair, a mustache and a stubbly beard. He was leaning back in his chair behind a huge oak desk, reading through some papers and puffing on a black pipe. The space in front of the desk was bare, lacking any chairs or rugs. The room itself was sparsely decorated as well, with a single painting of some wilderness scene behind the desk.

Manyara gave a formal bow. "Cap'n Van Cleef."

The man's eyes rose to meet them, brown and full of piercing steel. Grimluk recognized the look all too well. He'd seen it on rangers he'd met, as well as some peacekeepers and more than a few demon hunters. It was a look he saw in himself on the occasions he could look at a mirror. It was the look of someone who knew death well.

"Ranger," he said, setting his papers down. "Back so soon? Where's Bringar?"

"He's infirm at the moment, so I'm here to report on Downingville. This is Grimluk, a demon hunter."

Captain Van Cleef gave his pipe one more puff before pulling it from his mouth. "Am I to understand Downingville was attacked by a demon?"

"That's right," Grimluk replied. "Left a mess of casualties, too."

"Well, shit," Van Cleef said. "Which one of you needs to go first?"

"I can recount the whole story, if you wouldn't mind," Grimluk said. "It would be the fastest."

Van Cleef nodded and waved his pipe. He stood and walked to a window, hands crossed behind his back as Grimluk recounted events as succinctly as he could, hoping to spare Manyara the pain so soon after everything. She stood silently next to him, staring at the floor as he spoke.

"Damn it, Bringar," the captain grumbled at the window as Grimluk recounted their conversation. He stayed silent as Grimluk relayed Manyara's portion of the story. As Grimluk told of his fight with the demon, the man just grunted at him. When he finished, the captain pulled his pipe free and turned.

"In the first, I appreciate your attempts at helping my rangers, successful or not. In the second, I must apologize for Bringar. He's a fierce and loyal soldier, but, as you saw, he has his flaws."

"Reckon so. Hope your man pulls through."

"I suspect that tough bastard will need that hope. In the third, if I remember protocol right, you'll need to post a notice. I'll send word to the peacekeepers to let them know of the situation. Their captain will help you with your notice if you've need of it."

"Much appreciated, sir."

Van Cleef waved his hand dismissively. "Prefer 'sai' around these parts. You got two of my rangers out of there safely. I assume the group that wandered by recently was your doing as well?"

"Companions and patrons from the Coming Conqueror," Manyara added.

Van Cleef nodded. "That explains why they went to the Horned Court. Guild's probably gonna have a fit, but there was no helpin' it from what you said."

"Place might still be salvageable," Grimluk said. "Once this thing's dead, anyhow. Reckon I could lend a hand. Maybe even two."

"Call that an official word from your guild?" Van Cleef asked.

"Official word from myself at the very least, but I'd be surprised if anyone argued it."

The captain nodded. "I'll include that in my

notes, then. I'd make a fair wager that will calm the Companions down nicely. For the time bein', Fort Alisde is at your disposal. You're free to make use of our facilities if you so wish or else find a room at a hotel. Hear tell Rothwilde's is a fair stay."

"Cap'n?" Manyara spoke up.

"Arendse?"

"Sai, if you'd allow it, I'd like to help Grimluk with anything he might need. I owe him."

"To be frank, Ranger, I would much prefer to keep my last officer close, but I ain't yer pappy and such a debt is well within my ken. Consider it your new assignment until all this is over."

Manyara gave another formal bow. "Sai."

Captain Van Cleef looked between Manyara and Grimluk for a moment. "Got two orders, though, Ranger."

"Sai?"

"For the first, you seem to be missin' your hat. Best see about a new un'. As for the second," he paused for a long moment, staring at Manyara. "Second, keep yourself safe," he said with a wink, "or I'll take it out of your hide."

She gave a single gut laugh and took in a deep breath. "You kiddin' me, Cap? Damn thing couldn't even kill Bringar."

Van Cleef gave Manyara a wolfish grin filled with low laughter and capped it with his pipe. His eyes, however piercing and hard when they entered, softened a touch with his laugh. Amusement and smoke flowed in equal measure.

"Dismissed, Ranger."

"Sai," Manyara said, bowing quickly before leaving.

Grimluk touched the brim of his hat and gave a respectful nod to the man before following Manyara out of his office. Emerald stood a little ways from the office, next to a window, a smile spread across her face. Grimluk smiled back as he approached and then looked to Manyara, serious again.

"Reckon we oughta get somethin' straight, Ranger."

"What's that?" she said, a bit of an edge to her voice.

He looked her in the eyes. "You...do not owe me a damn thing. Far as I'm concerned, there was never any debt and never will be." Manyara's eyebrows rose a little and what tension had started to build seemed to drain from her. His own face softened again. "Would welcome your help all the same, though. Perhaps not just yet, but my gut says I'll need it."

He offered his hand to her. Manyara smiled and took it, giving it a solid squeeze as she did. Emerald, possibly feeling left out, threw an arm around both of their necks and pulled them in for a hug.

"So what do we do?" Emerald asked when she pulled away.

"Ranger—" he started.

"Manyara," she corrected.

He bowed his head lightly. "Get me back to the road, if you would. For the time being, I'll head back to Downingville and do some further investigatin'."

"A-alright," she replied, walking ahead.

"Don't be ridiculous, you big green ass," Emerald spat.

Grimluk couldn't help but laugh.

"What the fuck is so funny?" she asked incredulously. "Just don't want you disappearin' and gettin' yourself killed!"

"You sound like my dakka," he said as the laughter died away. "I'm fairly certain I won't find anything new. At the very least, I doubt there'll be another fight just yet. Preacher ain't got whatever he wants yet."

"Oh," Emerald said dourly. "Still think it's a damn fool idea."

"Wouldn't be the first time," he said with a shrug. "I'm a demon hunter, Emerald. This is what I do. Besides, don't you have somethin' that needs doin', too?"

Her tusks sank a little as she frowned. Her arms slipped across her chest. "Shut up."

Manyara looked at them, confusion on her face, her mouth pulled to one side. "That's right. Doc wants to see you still."

"Not quite what I meant, but there is that," Grimluk said. "Lead on."

Manyara looked at him with a tilt of her head before shrugging and moving on. Grimluk looked at Emerald and tilted his head toward Manyara. Emerald stuck her tongue out at him and walked off after her friend. Grimluk rolled his eyes but grinned a little.

The coach and horse were both gone when they got to the yard, vanished at some point after they'd arrived, according to the stable hands. Grimluk just grunted. He'd planned on walking back to Downingville anyways.

"Don't need the coach. Just point me to the road."

"We have a few extra horses still," Manyara informed him. "Why wouldn't you ride?"

"I have my reasons," he said. "It'll work out. I'll just be a little longer because of it."

Emerald and Manyara looked at each other doubtfully, but didn't argue the point.

"Is it a straight shot to the road?" he asked Manyara.

"Go right from out of the gate, mosey on and you'll come to it. There's an alchemy shop on the corner and Rothwilde's across the street."

"And the magi-tell?"

"Left at the alchemy shop, second street on the left. You'll see it. Has a full courier service attached, too."

Grimluk touched the brim of his hat and nodded to them. "Enjoy yourselves, ladies." He started to walk away and stopped at the gate. The two women were watching him.

"Think about what I said, Emerald," he called. He didn't wait on her to reply, just held up his hand in a lax wave and headed down the street.

Chapter 14

Fort Alisde was relatively isolated at what amounted to the edge of town. Wood-and-stone walls stretched out on either side, wrapping around in what appeared to be a loose square. On the other side of the street was the greenhouse Grimluk had wondered about, surrounded by an orchard of some kind. Whatever the trees grew wasn't around for him to see. Maybe apples. Maybe the peaches he'd eaten.

Grimluk followed Manyara's instructions, heading down the road toward the river. At the end of the road, at the corner to his left sat the alchemy shop. As he followed the road to the magi-tell, he took in the sights of Cold River. The street was speckled with various little clothing shops, some selling finery, others leather, along with a small smithy and a general store. To his right stood a tall hotel, an elegant sign over the entrance informing him it was the Rothwilde's that Captain Van Cleef had mentioned. It looked a comfortable sort of place, like the captain had said. Decorated well but not lavishly so, with four stories and a well maintained exterior.

As Grimluk walked, he saw more elves than

he'd seen in one place in a long while, and a fair portion of them had dark skin like Arbortown's sheriff. The rest were a mix of white and various shades of brown. More than a few wore buckskin, while the rest wore the latest fashions, or simple work clothes. Most of them ignored him, or tried to, but a few watched him. Grimluk would've had to make an effort to miss it. Elven eyes tended to be the colors of bright plants or sunsets or other such arresting sights of the natural world. If an elf was watching you, and you could see their face, you knew it. He nodded to some of them as he passed.

Aside from the elves, he mostly saw humans and halflings. He saw few dwarves and only one other orc, hauling lumber for an elf with long golden hair tied in a simple braid. The elf regarded Grimluk with eyes the color of sunflowers. The orc was heavier set than Grimluk, with deep blue eyes that he met with a smile and a nod. The orc grunted, abstaining from a smile, but gave his own nod in return. Wasn't often he saw that kind of blue in an orc's eyes. The rare color was considered a mark of beauty among his people, and he found the fellow striking and pleasant.

"Thulsk!" the elf snapped.

"Sai?" the orc replied.

"Tarry not, ye fool!"

He sighed. "Sai."

Grimluk's throat rumbled as they crossed paths, the elf quickening their pace. He passed the first street to his left and continued on. After the hotel, there wasn't anything else to block the view of the river. Down the way, Grimluk could see a large boat of a make he didn't recognize, though that hardly meant anything considering he could only name a rowboat and a raft by sight. Sailboats, too, but only by virtue of knowing what a sail was. The boat appeared to be a ferry of some kind, painted white with two black pipes rising from the back above some sort of red waterwheel-looking contraption. People were walking around on it and leaning against the railings lining its edges.

A few minutes later, he found the second street to his left. It was short, leading directly to the magi-tell and courier office like Manyara had told him. A dwarf with a wild shock of red hair and a beard to match slung a bag over his pony's rump as Grimluk passed. The bag bulged and crinkled with letters and packages.

The office was mostly empty, though a few halflings were over by the bounty board, looking it over. Grimluk found a clerk behind a desk that seemed a little too big for the pale-skinned, plain-faced human.

"Welcome to Cold River Courier Services. How may I help you, sai?" she asked.

"Need to put out a demon warning on the board. Captain Van Cleef's sending a report to the peacekeepers with all the major details. No citizen or city bounty has been put on the beast. It attacked in the middle of the night a few days ago. I've taken the job."

"O—oh...um." She blinked in surprise. "I...that is, um, just a moment, please." She dug around in her desk and then pulled out a little journal. After a few minutes of poring over it, she stopped and looked back up at him. "You're a demon hunter, sai?"

"I am."

"Um, from which guild? Oh, I mean, are you a guild member or a freelancer?" She took a piece of paper and readied a pen.

He sighed. Cold River hadn't had a situation like this in some time, if at all. "My name is Grimluk. I'm with the Hunter's Hollow Guild in New Gilead. The demon attacked in Downingville. It's an unknown type with shapeshiftin' abilities and is extremely dangerous. Any other hunters within a few days' ride would be more than welcome to assist."

She finished scribbling a few moments later and consulted the journal again, mumbling what she read to herself. "We will post the advisory as soon as the peacekeepers have verified it. Is there anything else I can help you with today, sai?"

He thought about it. "Do you have any policies about delayed letter sending?"

"We do indeed, sai. We are able to hold letters and parcels for up to three weeks at most, for a fee of up to ten pence for a letter and fifteen for a parcel."

He nodded. "I'd like paper and a pen, if you would."

"Paper is a penny for two pages," she said, handing over two sheets. "You may write at the standing desk behind you if you wish, or bring the letter back when you're ready."

"Thank you," he said, moving to the desk. He sighed and wrote "Little one" at the top of the page. He had to have some sort of letter waiting in case he didn't make it back from Downingville. Something to let Gwen know it would be okay, that he loved her and was sorry he wouldn't see her again. He sighed again as a lance of pain pierced his heart at that thought. He missed his sister. He'd tried to send her messages after jobs when he'd left her in Hunter's Hollow. He'd had to miss her birthday two months prior, and the Festival of the Dead after it due to hunting a demon knight. And now here he was, planning a possible death letter.

He wrote out what he hoped wouldn't happen, telling her to show their parents immediately. He wrote out his feelings and how proud of her he was. Asked her not to rush her training now that he was gone. Told her to remember his face and the faces of her mother and father. On the second sheet he wrote details to their parents, telling them where he'd been, what he knew about the demon, and whatever else came to mind that seemed relevant.

Once finished, Grimluk signed it and took it back to the clerk, dropping eleven pennies into her hand. She folded up the letter into an envelope and sealed it.

"What are your instructions, sai?"

"If I don't retrieve it within two weeks, send it to Gwen Quinn in Eagle Point, New Gilead. That'll be more than enough time."

She frowned as she wrote everything down, maybe guessing the purpose of the letter. Maybe she was just concentrating.

"Thank you for business, sai. We'll take care of

it," she said, putting the coins away. "Is there any-thing else I can help you with?"

"No, thank you. Reckon that's everything."

"Very good. Have a—" she stopped, stifling a nervous laugh, "—pleasant day." Her brows were knit with concern.

Grimluk simply nodded at her and made his way out. He had a long walk ahead of him and it'd be noon tomorrow before he arrived at best. After writing that letter, he was a little too aware of how much time he would have to think as he went.

His thoughts had grown a touch jumbled as he made his way out of Cold River. They faded when he felt eyes on him, though. He looked for the source, hoping to see someone gaping at him or glaring with disdain, but Grimluk knew it was not the usual curious or judgmental looks he was accus-tomed to. He couldn't find whoever it was, though the encroaching dark of the evening made that a chore in itself. The feeling persisted as he walked, dragging his attention with it. The back of his head itched.

The distraction was so heavy, pushed on his mind so badly, that he walked right into someone without realizing it. He looked at them, putting a hand on their shoulder in reflex to keep from knocking them over. The brown-robed figure, fat and on the low end of tall for a human or an elf, jerked away from his hand with a hiss and glared at him from under a hood.

"Pardon, friend," Grimluk offered. "Seems my mind was elsewhere. Didn't hurt you none, did I?"

The figure didn't move save to shift their

weight, like maybe they still hadn't quite regained their balance. Grimluk couldn't quite read their body language to tell whether they were hostile or just surprised.

"No," came the response. The voice was raspy and a little high, tinged with a measure of discomfort.

Grimluk stayed wary but made no threatening move. "Glad to hear it. Right sorry about that. Haven't bumped into anyone like that in a long time. You sure you're all right? Didn't feel like I bumped you too hard, but it's not always easy to tell when you're my size."

The figure seemed to relax, if only a bit. "It is...fine. You reminded me of someone who hurt me once."

Grimluk nodded. "I understand. If you're unhurt then I'll leave you to your day, friend."

He touched the brim of his hat and started for Downingville again. The sense of being watched had faded with the interruption, which both relieved and frustrated him. A part of him wondered if he was just jumpy after writing the letter to Gwen but his instincts said otherwise. They'd served him well up to now, so he didn't feel much inclination to ignore them. Still, he hadn't seen anyone.

He quickened his pace, taking long strides. He'd deal with the issue when it arose again. In the meantime, he could move faster on his own. Downingville waited, though he hoped it would be silent and uneventful. Maybe, just maybe, he could find something to help him fight the shapeshifting demon.

Manyara frowned in curiosity at Grimluk's parting words, telling Emerald to think about what he'd said. She gave a small shrug and shivered. The cold was trying to break as spring approached, but it remained for the time being. The cold ran down her scalp and tried to tear through her clothes. Emerald shivered beside her. Manyara was missing her hat and coat, and Emerald only had a baggy set of Bringar's clothes at the moment.

"Let's go get warm, Em," she said.

"That would be lovely. I'd really rather not freeze my tits off." She turned and slipped back inside quickly.

"That would be a damn shame," Manyara agreed as she followed. "Big damn shame."

"Probably lose half my clients, too."

She chuckled at that as Emerald headed back toward her room. Manyara was glad for the warming enchantment on the building. Before they'd had it done two years past, it was drafty at best and frigid at worst. The bureaucrats hadn't made room in the rangers' budget for it so they'd all chipped in a few months' pay and called in an enchanter. It was strong work and kept the fort interior comfortable, allowed them to relax between winter patrols and assignments. Bringar had said they'd have had the proper funds if they'd been in a bigger city.

Manyara reckoned if Cold River got any bigger, they'd see that change.

Emerald stopped just inside her room. "It occurs to me I should really head to the brothel and check in with everyone once the doc's checked me over. They're worried, I'm sure." She wandered over to the bed and picked up her dress, folded and dirty. "I can get this washed, too."

"Reckon so. You want me to come with you?"

Emerald smiled at her. Some people said orcs were ugly. Manyara always thought that was the biggest crock of shit she'd heard. Tusks and beastly eyes and green skin had a beauty of their own. And besides that, Manyara knew Emerald and it made her all the more lovely. Tusks or not, a genuine smile from Emerald made her feel lighter.

"You don't have to," Emerald replied, "if you have somethin' that needs doin.'"

Manyara shook her head. "You heard the captain. We'll get you a coat and a scarf and me a hat, and head on after we talk to the doc."

"Rather have that stupid blanket, but I know he needs it. Gods, Yara, missin' a blanket like I'm a babe. Ridiculous." Emerald huffed before letting out a tired sigh.

"Reckon it's understandable. I'm missin' his pig-sticker. I ain't never seen no demons before. Not even them little ones."

"Imps?"

"Imps, yeah." She led Emerald to the barracks to retrieve her coat and scarves and see if there was a spare hat anywhere. "Not even ridin' on patrols."

"Mm. I saw one once, but it was dead already. Gave me the shivers."

Manyara opened up her trunk and pulled out two scarves, one gray and thick and the other a faded green that was thinning with age. She handed Emerald the gray one. She looked around the room for a hat and found two. She wasn't sure whose they were. Her heart sank all the same. Atticus's? Kel's? Maybe Rancher's?

It didn't matter anymore. They were all dead, except her and maybe Bringar. Seeing the empty bunk room hurt. Emerald's hand was soft and warm on her shoulder, though. She must have sighed and not realized it. Or maybe her friend just knew her that well.

"Years runnin' with all o' them and all I got left is hats." Her face felt hot and wet all of a sudden. Tears splashed on one of the hats. "We shoulda listened to Grimluk," she whispered. "We shoulda listened and—and..."

Emerald hugged her tight from behind, wrapping her arms around Manyara's body. She always forgot how strong those arms actually were. Emerald had such a soft body, but her arms could turn to steel. She always squeezed Manyara when they parted ways. Emerald squeezed now and leaned her face against the back of Manyara's head, tusks brushing lightly against her neck.

Manyara shook with silent sobs, holding one of Emerald's arms in her hand. She shut her eyes tight and let herself cry even though it felt ugly and weak. She knew Emerald would never say that, though. Rangers didn't cry; leastways, Bringar preferred it that way. She wasn't really sure. She was sure that rangers didn't usually survive a demon attack like she had, though. Manyara thought maybe that allowed for it this one time. Just this once. So she cried and sank to the floor, Emerald following her down, and just leaned into her friend's arms. Grief rolled out of her in strong, boiling waves.

When the crying passed, Manyara kept leaning against Emerald. She felt so heavy and tired. In the face of survival, of something she couldn't fight or shoot, she felt frail. They sat there in silence, Manyara taking whatever comfort she could for the time being. Emerald moved her head a little and one of her tusks brushed against Manyara's cheek.

"I'm sorry," Emerald whispered.

Manyara let out a long sigh. Her eyes hurt and her nose was full of snot so she pulled out a handkerchief. She sat up and blew hard. "Cryin's fuckin' ugly, ain't it? Snot and tears pourin' outta yer face."

"Maybe, but I've had more than snot and tears on me before."

Manyara let out a bark of laughter that rolled into low belly laughs. She shifted around to lean against a bed and look at Emerald. "Reckon ya have, Em. Thanks for that."

Emerald shifted over to sit opposite Manyara, waving her hand dismissively. "I'm still upset about Denny and Amos. Cindy, too, but we weren't close like y'all. You always said your posse was family."

Manyara snorted and smiled. "The assholes."

Emerald let out a chuckle. "I'll drink to that once we get to the Horned Court."

"Gods," Manyara drawled, "I ain't had a drink

in a few days. Whiskey oughta put this down some."

"It's on me, Yara."

"Prolly a li'l of me on ya right now, too," she said with a laugh.

"Just a little," Emerald replied after a long pause. She smiled again. "Whenever you want. To go, I mean."

"Sure, sure." She looked at the hats again. She groaned lightly, letting the pain roll out a little with it. She handed one of the hats to Emerald. It was black with silver trim and a wide, flat brim under a simple, flat-topped crown. "Try this on."

Emerald took the hat gingerly and looked it over. She donned it and looked at Manyara, dragging a finger across the brim. "What do ya think? Pretty cunning, right?"

"Cunning as aces, Em. It's yours, if ya want it." She stood, slowly, and tried the other hat on. This one was brown. Just brown all over. Brown trim, brown band, brown hat. It mostly fit. She could let her hair come in a little thicker and it'd fit just right. She held out her hand for Emerald and helped her up.

Manyara gave a squeeze, letting her fingers linger before pulling away. "Mighty thirsty. How 'bout you?"

"I could drink," Emerald replied solemnly.

It didn't take long for Manyara to lead the way to the brothel and saloon known as the Horned Court. Unlike the Coming Conqueror, the place didn't have a hotel built into it as well. The Horned Court was a simpler place built for drink and pleasure. The outside was unpainted save for the sign bearing its name, which was decorated in a slew of thorny floral reliefs, painted with greens and pinks and reds and purples. The name itself was painted in simple, clean white.

Manyara pushed through the batwing doors, Emerald following. She looked around at the place. She'd never been in the Horned Court. If she wasn't visiting Emerald, she was drinking with her fellow rangers in the barracks. Occasionally she'd wander the riverside, but the only other saloons were farther on, in the newer parts of town built near the residential areas and on the other side of town altogether. It seemed a nice enough place as she took it in. Large area for games of chance and tables to watch; bar in the back with a selection of alcohol she found downright glorious to behold. Labels of fancy whiskeys, bourbons, and scotches stared back at her, glittering with golds and reds.

A staircase snaked up to her right leading to a hallway and a walkway with three rooms connected to it. Three Companions in greens and whites stood on the walkway, waving and waggling suggestively at them. Manyara looked up at them: a chubby human man with bronze skin and short hair in a vest and pants, and two elves whose appearances were ethereal enough she didn't bother guessing at their genders. One wore a dress with a vest over a loose white shirt, the other was in pants and a corset covered in floral patterns.

Maybe they were like Tulip and didn't bother. Plenty of elves didn't care about such things, especially the older they got. It didn't matter, anyways. She wasn't there for them.

Emerald gasped and stepped forward. "Rose?"

The elf in the pants stopped and looked down. "Emerald? Oh gods, hun, I didn't even realize it was you! Hold yourself there, darlin'." The elf descended the stairs, long blond hair bouncing as they went and wrapped Emerald in a tight hug. "You're safe! Tulip has been worried sick."

"I'm sure they have. Where is everyone?"

"I'll send Carlos to fetch your people! The twins are over there watching a faro game." The elf took Emerald's hand in theirs and gave it a quick kiss before disappearing into a back room.

"Didn't know Companions knew each other so well," Manyara observed.

"We don't, really," Emerald replied, "but Rose and Tulip and me went to school together, learned all our manners and whatnot. He stopped here while Tulip and I went on to Downingville. I think that was a year or so before you started comin' around."

Manyara replied with a grunt of affirmation before heading to the bar. "Reckon I'll have that drink now. You?"

"Gods, yes."

The bartender was a human with dark, slicked-back hair, a clean face, and wire-rim spectacles over pale eyes. He nodded to them both. "Am I to understand you're a Companion, sai?" he asked Emerald.

"I am."

He pulled out two glasses. "Standard rates for off-hours Companions, then. What'll y'all have?"

"Whiskey for the both of us," Manyara said,

setting her hat aside. "Try the house label if ya got one, or else a good Cimmerian."

"Got a fresh crate of our bottles in last night, in fact," the bartender replied, pulling a bottle with a thorned rose on the label off the shelf. "Bottle's half a bilt, glasses are three pence for the Companion."

"Bottle can stay," Emerald said, "though I'll have to start a tab until I can get back to Downingville and get my things."

The bartender set the opened bottle in front of them. "I heard 'bout all that. We can settle up when you're able. Ain't like I gotta worry 'bout a Companion payin' their tab."

Manyara poured a bit of the amber liquid into each of their glasses and held it up in acknowledgment. The bartender nodded and went back to cleaning glasses. Manyara downed her drink in a smooth gulp. There was a slight prickle to the burn that felt oddly pleasant. She usually preferred a more straightforward whiskey, but the pleasantness felt right at the moment. She poured another glass and looked to Emerald, who held out her glass for the same.

Manyara turned to lean against the bar, looking toward the door. She took smaller sips, enjoying the sensation. There was no rush and the bottle was plenty affordable.

When Rose returned, a group trailed behind him, led by Tulip. They all rushed forward when they saw Emerald, with Tulip getting the first hug. Manyara smiled and scooted aside a few steps to let Emerald's friends get closer. The lot of them hugged on Emerald or took her hand in turn. Rebecca wiped away tears as she stepped away.

"Reckon they missed ya, Em," Manyara offered.

"Oh, pish, Yara. Who could ever tell under all this bluster?" Emerald replied playfully, a smile so big it lifted her tusks. The twins joined the group in time to hear the comment, laughing in unison.

Tulip took Emerald's hand anew as they spoke. "Don't keep us in suspense, hun. What happened? Where's the hunter?"

Emerald looked at Manyara, who just motioned with her free hand for Emerald to tell the story. After another quick drink, Emerald sighed and began.

"Gods, it seems almost a lifetime ago now. Let me see if I can piece it all together."

One of the twins huffed; Manyara could never remember who was who. "Bah, Emerald. You stop all that balderdash, now, and get on with it."

Emerald's smile faltered as she started in earnest. Describing the walk back to town, following the rangers, was easy enough, but Manyara could see and feel the shift as Emerald started talking about the return to town proper. It weighed on the others as well. Rebecca gasped first when Emerald told about the troll and Margy. The telling paused then, a moment of silence for the dead. Manyara sighed and waited, her mind slipping away slightly. She didn't want to live it all again so soon, but Emerald's people had a right to know. She couldn't begrudge them that, and she wouldn't leave Emerald to tell it alone.

When she finished, everyone was silent and grim, tears in their eyes or jaws clenched and quivering. Manyara poured another glass and held it up, tears rolling down her own cheeks again.

"To fallen friends," she said hoarsely.

"Hear, hear," the rest of them mumbled in agreement. The bottle began to pass between them, each pulling a swig and letting out a heavy sigh.

"So the demon hunter is off lookin' to finish it, then?" Tulip asked.

"Seems so," Emerald replied, wiping her nostrils with a handkerchief. "I just hope he comes back. He seemed sure, but..."

"Big fucker like that ain't so easy to kill," Manyara offered.

Emerald gave a throaty chuckle. "Certainly looks it."

Manyara finished what was left in her glass and set it back down. "Well, who wants to play a hand and lose a bit of their purse?"

CHAPTER 15

It was into the next afternoon by the time Grimluk returned to Downingville. Sunlight glittered off snow on the side of the road as he passed, his steps deliberate and sure. He kept his senses open. At worst, the Preacher would hold the demon at bay again. At least until the man got what he wanted, whatever it was. The best-case scenario was a quiet investigation in the solitude of the abandoned town, but even still, relying on the supposed kindness of a man who was clearly demon-touched could prove hazardous.

Grimluk marched down the main street, coat pulled back, gun ready to draw. He'd moved his knife out to a loop on his coat, likewise waiting to be called to action. His breath steamed out in puffs as he walked but he paid the cold no mind.

He did pay the Coming Conqueror's bar mind when he came upon it, cracked but seemingly still whole. Grimluk approached the shattered building the bar currently resided in after being hurled at him. The floor creaked at the addition of his weight, but held. He ran a hand lightly across the bar's surface, looking over the room. The shattered wall and busted windows let in enough afternoon light for him to tell he was in a ruined office. There probably wouldn't be anything to find here, but it was better to be thorough. There were plenty of times when the key to answering a question was in plain view.

Paper crunched underfoot as he searched the dim space. A small lamp dangled on a hook over a desk, shaking unsteadily as the wind swept through every so often, throwing gusts through the street and into the broken building. He guessed it might have been a solicitor's office. Along with the scattered paper, he saw books and a fallen bookcase. Grimluk circled around the bar, looking it over. As he suspected, it showed him little except for a rough handprint and a reminder of how close he'd come to losing his head.

He grunted. "Probably won't be the last time, either," he mumbled, leaving the bar behind. He plucked the small lantern from its hook, just in case he'd need it, before taking to the street once more. Maybe there would be something to find at the Coming Conqueror.

He doubted that as well, but he could always find the cornerstone and leave the expulsion circle on it. The symbolism of marking the cornerstone might be able to guarantee the barring of any demonic entity from setting foot in the building again. Grimluk's throat rumbled. The circle had spit the abominable thing out of the boiler easy enough. Given the strangeness surrounding this beast, he felt confident that the act could ward the Conqueror from other demons. Might be something to send back to Kort and Archel to teach the apprentices, too.

The stink of a corpse wafted out to greet him as Grimluk approached the saloon. He supposed that was Denny, the poor cook who had been half-devoured and forgotten in all the panic. Grimluk let out a long sigh. "Shit."

More than likely, Denny had passed while they'd all escaped, but he couldn't be sure. At the very least, if the man had come back a ghoul it'd be a simple matter to dispose of him. You could always trust ghouls like that. As tedious as he found large groups of them, they were reliable that way. Get enough of them lined up right and you could split several of their skulls with one bullet.

Denny's body was, of course, no longer on the bar where they'd left it. The body had rolled off and lay against the wall in even worse shape than before. The blood was long dry but there were chunks missing out of the legs. The building's enchantment must have held longer than he'd thought after the demon had cracked the walls because the stink was strong. The cold would have slowed the process down quite a bit.

Grimluk gave the corpse a tap with his boot. It made no movement. If it had been a ghoul, it would have moved by now; growled, blinked glow-ing eyes, even taken a slow swipe. They were most effective with ambushes and weren't known for restraint when a potential meal wandered close. Grimluk grunted, glad he wouldn't have to cave the dead man's skull in, adding further insult to an already messy death.

That just left a further search of the place. The boiler and pipes would remain clear. Even residue from the demon, ectoplasmic or bodily, would be unable to remain. Ectoplasm, the substance left behind by spirits and some demons interacting with the physical world, evaporated within hours of manifestation anyway, unless whatever made it continued its activities.

Grimluk decided to start with the kitchen and work his way through to the hotel and up to the top floors. The place was dark and empty when he entered through the single batwing door, so he held up the lantern and flicked its little door open. He focused his will to flame and spoke a quick rendition of his campfire spell, sending a small flame out to the wick. Orange light filled the kitchen.

He checked the pantry first, pulling his chalk out to draw on the bottles and wrappers as he went. He was hungry, and the food would go to waste otherwise. He prepared a cold meal and ate as he searched, not entirely sure what he was even looking for.

Time moved slowly as he tread the Conqueror, leaving a trail of demon traps and Elder Signs in his wake. He searched the headless corpse of the dead patron again, likewise stinking and foul and bloated like Denny's. The bits of the demon that had been on the pillow when Grimluk had found it were gone now, too. If there was anything else to find, it was covered in dried blood and probably useless. Aside from the corpse and some luggage, the rooms of the first two floors were empty.

The third floor was likewise empty, though the last room was locked. Like the others, it had a number on the door, so he knew it was a guest room. Grimluk took the doorknob and gave it a solid tug. A crack and the bending of metal called out, signifying the lock's destruction. The door swung open with a creak, the lantern's orange light cutting through the curtained darkness of the room. It was silent and bare like the others, but something glinted on the wall directly across from him.

Words were scrawled across the wall in blood that appeared fresh. He held the lamp up to read them.

"Tick-tock, it's time to talk. Let us lift your mind to the cosmos and find the truth."

His brow furrowed as Grimluk puzzled on the words. He looked around more as he thought, but nothing of substance presented itself – except another set of bloody letters on a mirror.

"Stop being such a bore. Come outside and we'll palaver."

Grimluk growled. The last letters formed as he read them. Something was waiting on him and he took a guess at who it was.

"Fine," he practically growled. "We'll have us a talk, then."

Night had descended as he'd searched, making the flashing lights filling the windows of the hotel lobby hard to miss. Yellows and blues and greens swirled slowly along the glass while someone sang, the colors changing in time with the strange melody. To Grimluk's ears, whoever it was couldn't hold a tune worth a damn. Or maybe they just refused to.

He stepped slowly outside, hand on his gun, nerves keyed up and ready. Out in the yard, twirling among the flashing lights, singing his strange song, was the Preacher. Some part of Grimluk said to shoot the man here and now. He didn't completely disagree with that part of himself, but he needed something from the man, too. Needed to be sure of a few things first.

"Yeah. Figured it was you," he called to the Preacher. "You mean to talk, fine. Let's talk."

The singing died away. The Preacher stopped twirling, taking to lightly swaying instead. "Didn't much like havin' to follow up that first message, but I should have guessed. You, my green friend, are a lesson in stubbornness." The lights flashed slowly around him.

Grimluk saw no source for the lights. "So my dear dakka used to say. Reckon I'll go first, if that is quite all right with you."

"Mmmmm, by all means, good hunter. You are the star—" one of the lights flashed bright, "—of this little story, are you not?"

Grimluk grunted. "Who are you? You actually human? Mortal?"

The Preacher let out a sharp laugh. "Right to the point, then? Right to the point point point." He turned to face Grimluk, smile wide and eyes wild. The big book pressed over his heart as he bowed low. "My name, good hunter, is Marlowe Jakobs. You may address me as Marlowe or Jakobs or His Loyal Emissary and Servant to the Truth. A pleasure to properly introduce myself at long last.

"As for this cage of meat, yes, I'm human. At least I was, once. And mortality? Well, let's just keep that simple, shall we? No grave exists that could hold my body down."

"Right," Grimluk said, fingers drumming on

the butt of his gun. "And where do I fit in to all this, preacher man? You're real chummy with that demon and that don't exactly sit right with me."

"My, oh my, but aren't you the direct one, sir? Or is it sai in these parts?" Jakobs's head lulled to one side, dragging his body into a slow circle. "Can we not share a friendly moment? Discuss the stars? Do you not see how close they come? I feel their touch on you. Do you not see the time will arrive? Soon, so soon, the stars will be right!"

Grimluk watched the man, refusing to take his eyes away for an instant. "Stars mean nothin' to me right now. Only answers. Only my duty to put down a damned abomination."

Jakobs was suddenly in Grimluk's face, screaming. "Do not talk to me as such, child! I am the vessel of Truth! Were you free of that cursed seal, I would make you look upon the cosmic sights this instant! I would free that child's ignorance that clings to your wretched little mind. You are nothing."

A growl rolled out of Grimluk's throat. "I would step away now before something unfortunate happens to you. You say I can't kill you, but I'll bet you still feel pain."

Jakobs sighed and turned away. "Manners, right you are, right you are. I requested this meeting, yes, yes indeed. One cannot render an invite knowing the one they'll host and act surprised at their behavior."

"You gonna get to making some gods-damned sense now, or shall I go?" The urge to draw his gun pressed acutely on Grimluk's mind. He could feel

Marlowe Jakobs probing as well, like he had before. Greasy, insubstantial fingers pressed against his mind, seeking some way in.

"The stars move toward their rightful places and the whelp wants sense. Oh, but I suppose I'm to blame for not recognizing you sooner. Truly, I apologize for such an error. I was...preoccupied. Yes, fine, the demon is not just a demon. Is that satisfactory?"

"Meaning?"

A loud sigh filled the air. "Meaning you'll have to try harder. But no matter...no matter. I have answered questions, now it's time I had my fill, as well."

The gun slid free of its holster and met the Preacher's forehead as he turned to face Grimluk again. "In my years as a demon hunter I have never taken the life of another mortal. If I put a bullet through your skull, that'd still be true, right?" The hammer fell back under his thumb. "Answers."

"Indeed," Jakobs said in a low voice, staring straight into Grimluk's eyes, a new smile spreading slowly across his face. The lights danced gently around them, flashing dimly. "Answers are what I mean to get, sai, for you have stolen my property!"

The lights flashed as bright as sunlight, startling Grimluk and burning his eyes, making them water in irritation. He let out a rumbling growl, snatching his knife up. When his eyes settled a moment later, Marlowe Jakobs was standing out of arm's reach, book clenched against his chest with both hands.

"Return what is mine now, whelp. There will

be consequences otherwise, you can set your watch and warrant on it."

"Go fuck yourself," Grimluk growled. "I have nothing of yours unless you put it there."

"Oh, but you did," he said, walking casually around Grimluk. "I cannot feel it on you anymore, but you had it once. I can feel its touch on you from using it. I did not loan it to you, hunter. Though it's hardly a surprise. That old fool, so obsessed with immortality, was bound to lose." Jakobs bent forward in a mock conspiratorial gesture. "And just between us, the failure with the vampire was rather amusing. You heard about that, I'm sure."

Grimluk stood staring at the black-clad figure. An old man obsessed with immortality. A vampire. A loan. "Name the piece, preacher." His voice was iron. He knew the answer but he wanted to hear the words spoken.

"My. Amulet," Jakobs practically shrieked.

The gun rose again and barked thunder, its owner thundering with it, voicing the font of rage that had risen. The amulet he'd taken from Kenton Selbie. The thing that resurrected the dead into immortal, conscious puppets. The man who had helped set events into motion to rob Gwen of her parents. Who had colluded with a demon in hopes of cheating Death.

Jakobs took a shot to the shoulder while another bounced off his book, and he somehow dodged two more. The book waved at Grimluk and a wall of force hurled him into the Coming Conqueror. The impact nearly drove the wind out of him as he fired twice more, catching the Preacher in the leg this time.

"You will return what's mine, thief, or you will suffer!"

Grimluk's practiced hands set to reloading, dumping out the spent shells for fresh. He laughed as he did it. "'Fraid you're too late, preacher. By now the thing's been ruined or contained. Either way, you'll never see it again."

The flickering lights lit up the yard in a solid white glow, illuminating the courtyard like it was high noon in the summer. Marlowe Jakobs strode forward, face contorted in rage. "Then you will suffer! And you will fail! I will give you one last chance, though. Just one. Hurry back to Cold River, demon hunter! Hurry back for your lesson in humility and ponder on my generosity. I would see you atone, but the decision lies within. Consider the Truth."

Fire erupted around the man in a spiraling tower, radiating heat as it did. The fire twisted into the air, thin as a needle before slamming into the ground and exploding with a furious crackle. Everything fell to darkness and Grimluk knew he was alone again even before his vision readjusted.

His breath came out ragged as his emotions surged. Grimluk threw his head back and let out a sound no orc dared to voice near another non-orc. The pure, bestial fury of an orc's roar filled the air.

The heat of Grimluk's rage had only just begun to cool when he got back to Cold River. The thought of how things would have been different if not for the amulet Jakobs had sent the mayor of Green-reach Bluffs played through his mind. Peter Quinn, Gwen's father, wouldn't have been charred by the fire of an undead dragon. On the other hand, Gwen's mother, Cassie, probably still would've died. Gwen's brother, Nicholas, for whatever reason, possession or choice, had murdered their mother in a ritual that had bound the demon Priskus to the boy. But maybe if Selbie hadn't had the amulet, it wouldn't have happened when it did. Maybe, just maybe, it could've been avoided altogether. While he was happy to call Gwen family and knew his own parents were treating her just as if she was blood, Grimluk still wished she'd been spared the loss, even if growing up in the Wastelands was less than ideal. Maybe her brother wouldn't have put the prophetic spirit in her, either.

These thoughts twisted and turned as Grimluk walked through town, not really paying attention to where he was going. He tried to remind himself it was all done and there was no changing the past, but it didn't help. Only time would calm his mind. Time, and maybe a dead demon. So he walked, cold and frustrated and desperate to burn some of that time and anger away.

The other part of Jakobs's words echoed in the back of his mind, too. The man could control the demon. He was clearly powerful, so Grimluk wholly believed the threats leveled against him. The real problem was the how of it. Though given Jakobs's ability to flit in and out of shadows, Grimluk supposed that the when of it could prove just as troublesome. As he wandered past a small saloon on the edge of town, someone called after him.

"Hold tight, goblin!"

Grimluk bristled at the word, heat flushing through him with rekindled anger. His fists clenched and his teeth ground, making his tusks twitch back and forth. He stopped and looked to the voice. On the porch of the saloon stood Roscoe and two other humans, holding bottles of liquor in one hand and thick tree branches in the other.

"Yeah, that's the one I told ya 'bout, boys. That's the piece o' shit what laid his filthy fuckin' hands on me. Ain't he just as ugly as I said?"

One of the other men spit a stream of tobacco into the dirt. "Yar, Roscoe, just as ugly as ya says. Reckon as dumb as he looks, too."

"Ain't no goblin alive got a lick a sense in their heads, fellas," the third man said. "Y'all know that."

Grimluk took in the faces of each man, his glare like steel. "Reckon you three are lookin' to brawl. I'll give you one last warning, Roscoe. Ain't in the mood to brook your shit so whatever happens after this is on your head."

"Gobby bastard," Roscoe said with a sneer. "What did I say, boys? Uppity fucker, ain't he?"

A growl rumbled in Grimluk's throat, threatening to turn into another roar. With a shrug, he slipped his elk-skin bag from his shoulder and let it tumble to the ground. He turned to face the trio in full. "Anyone ever told you you're an infuriating piece of shit, Roscoe?"

Roscoe tipped his bottle back and finished it

off. "Time to teach this gobby fucker a lesson, boys. A big damned lesson."

A moment later, Roscoe hurled his bottle at Grimluk, drunkenness skewing his aim and sending the bottle into the ground at Grimluk's feet. The three men rushed him with murder in their eyes and alcohol on their breath. The tobacco-chewing man got to him first, gray-haired and whip thin, with a messy beard. He swung his branch at Grimluk's head.

Grimluk batted the man's arm away, sending him into a spin before shoving him into Roscoe, toppling them over. The other man, young and red-headed, took two swings, which Grimluk dodged effortlessly, catching a third swing in his hand. He wrenched the man's arm behind his back with ease before seizing him at the shoulder, near the man's neck, with one meaty hand. Grimluk squeezed with his thumb and first two fingers, pinching with practiced precision. Almost instantly, the man collapsed to his knees before flopping face first into the cold dirt, unconscious.

Roscoe and his remaining ally got to their feet by the time their friend passed out. They still didn't hesitate. Grimluk didn't care. As the unknown man came at him again, Grimluk moved out of the way, dragging his foot to trip the man and emphasizing the fall with a sudden elbow to the back of the head.

A branch slammed into Grimluk's head a moment later.

"Gotcha, ya fuckin' goblin bastard!" Roscoe bellowed.

Grimluk took Roscoe's wrist in a vice grip and pulled it away from his face. The branch dragged his hat away from his head as he did. Cold wind raked across Grimluk's scalp, but it was a dim sensation from miles away.

Roscoe tried to pull away from Grimluk's iron grip, panicking at each unsuccessful attempt to wrench himself free. Grimluk planted a hand around Roscoe's throat, causing the man to give a choked yelp. He stepped forward, pushing Roscoe back with little effort. The man muttered drunken gibberish and toothless threats in equal measure, eyes wide.

Grimluk shook Roscoe's wrist hard enough to hurl the branch away before he hauled Roscoe high into the air by the throat and slammed him into the dirt. The sound of the impact mixed with the sound of Roscoe's body expelling his supply of air.

"I'd tell you I hope this teaches you the lesson, Roscoe," Grimluk said, reclaiming his bag and hat, "but frankly, I'd be surprised if you could put two thoughts together after that." He adjusted his bag for a moment and then gingerly pulled the other two men each onto his shoulders. Once steady, he took hold of Roscoe's ankle and stood. "Reckon I'll just drop you three off at the peacekeepers'."

Grimluk circled back the way he'd come and found a pair of halfling deputies patrolling the street. He called out to them, his voice still gruff with annoyance.

"Evening," he said as they approached, eyes wide as they looked at him. "Name's Grimluk. Reckon your sheriff probably got a letter about me yesterday."

"That's right," one of the peacekeepers said. "What, uh, what happened here?"

"These three attacked me just now. Seemed best to get them to you. The two on my shoulders will be out for a while. The one on the ground is likely to be dazed for just as long." Grimluk squeezed Roscoe's ankle. "Might have some broken ribs, but he'll survive."

"Uh, right. This way, sai," the Peacekeeper said, blinking rapidly before leading Grimluk to the peacekeepers' building. Roscoe and his cohorts were dumped into a jail cell. The sheriff insisted on getting the story from Grimluk. Despite the letter from Captain Van Cleef, and the circumstances around it, the sheriff's tone felt more than a little accusatory. More than once, he threatened to lock Grimluk up, too, if he wasn't completely honest with the events.

Grimluk wondered for a moment if the sheriff was being thorough or just outright hostile. He wanted to hope it was just a thorough job as a peacekeeper, so, with a shrug and sigh, he went with that view for his own peace of mind and swore to his honesty, offering to sign his name to it.

The ordeal finally ended when the sheriff seemed satisfied with Grimluk's answers about his self–defense. More questions followed about the demon, however, and Grimluk was greeted with further frustration for himself and the sheriff. He related some of the details of his return to Down-ingville and the lack of any sign of the demon. He considered telling the sheriff about Marlowe Jakobs but opted against it, settling on the less personal details.

"Listen here, demon hunter," the sheriff said wearily, "we got a few thousand people to protect in this town, you understand me? My first priority are the people of Cold River. So, you find this thing and you fuckin' kill it and you kill it good, ya hear?"

"That's the plan, Sheriff."

"So you've said. Get on outta here. I don't wanna see you again 'less you're bringin' me proof of a dead demon. Am I understood?"

Grimluk grunted. He was tired and drained and hungry. Might be best just to head back to Fort Alisde. He could get some food, update Manyara and Emerald, and get some gods-damned sleep. He'd need that rest if he hoped to get this job settled.

Chapter 16

After Grimluk left, Emerald and Manyara spent the afternoon and that evening with Emerald's friends, waiting on Grimluk to return. Tonight had been more of the same. When the Horned Court began to fill up with the evening crowd, the pair decided to head back to the fort. Emerald said her goodbyes for the night, giving her fellow Companions each a hug, and then she and Manyara wandered out into the soft dark of the budding night and back to the fort. A gentle warmth lingered in Emerald from the whiskey. Manyara's smile reflected the feeling, which made Emerald smile all the more.

"What you grinnin' at?" Manyara asked as they walked.

Emerald giggled and just took her friend's hand. Manyara rolled her eyes but gave Emerald's hand a squeeze.

As they approached the fort's gate, Emerald gasped and pulled away from Manyara. Grimluk approached them with a slow gait, but he didn't seem to notice them.

"You're back!" she called as she rushed toward him, throwing her arms around the hunter's neck. "Did you just get here? What did you find?"

He wobbled lightly but steadied himself and returned the hug. "Couple of hours ago. I'll tell you everything inside. I'm starvin'."

Emerald stepped back and nodded. "We were just comin' back for supper, too."

Grimluk looked past Emerald and nodded. "Manyara. Been keepin' Emerald out of trouble?"

Emerald looked at her. "Shit, she is the trouble."

"She says true. I drank a dwarf under the table once for five bilts. Easiest money I ever made. 'Course, I was sick as a dog the next day."

"I did that once," Grimluk replied, opening the gate. "Was twins, though, and they liked to switch out while you had your mug tipped back."

"How on Arkod did you out-drink two dwarves like that?" Emerald asked incredulously, stepping past him. Manyara followed close behind.

"Didn't. But at some point, they were drunk enough they messed up their switch. I thought I had double vision and tried to put 'em back together. Knocked 'em out and started a brawl."

Manyara let out a loud burst of laughter that tapered off into a snort.

Emerald started giggling again as she led the way to the mess hall.

"You laugh, but three of their buddies each gave me a shot to my gut. I puked harder than anyone should ever puke." He let out a long sigh. "Still get a little spasm when I remember it."

The cooks were still in the kitchen when the three of them came in. Despite a dozen dead rangers, they still had plenty of mouths to feed. As

Emerald learned, the fort was still run by local volunteers that outnumbered the soldiers on a regular basis. The staff waved them over.

"Usin' up the last of the open beans tonight. Got some pork needs eatin', too," the cook informed them. "Few loaves of bread will be out shortly."

"Thank ya, Cooky," Manyara replied. "Load us up, then. Any coffee?"

"It hurts me you would ask such a thing, Manyara."

"Meant nothin' by it. Had a lot to drink this afternoon."

Cooky snorted. "Tea first, then coffee." He handed over a big bowl of pork and beans.

"Tea first? I oughta thump you, Cooky," Manyara replied as she took the bowl and handed it to Grimluk.

Emerald took the next bowl, grinning at Manyara and the cook's banter. She hoped it helped Manyara feel some sense of normalcy again. While the bowl warmed her hands up, the smell of the pork hit her nose and set her mouth to watering. Cooky followed them to a table with a pitcher of tea and three glasses and it didn't take long for the three of them to fall silent as they filled their bellies and went back for seconds. Grimluk went back for thirds and, so he said, would've had fourths if his third bowl hadn't finished off what was left. Cooky announced there would be pie in an hour or so if they wanted any and left them alone. Emerald sighed and sipped her tea. Almost in unison, the three of them belched, provoking a round of laughter, though Emerald couldn't help but notice Grim-luk's face was still hard.

"So," Emerald began, "now that we got some food in us, you gonna tell us what happened back home?"

Grimluk's brows furrowed deeper and a rumble filled his throat. "Reckon so." He tipped back his tea and finished it.

He started slowly, eyes on his cup at first. Emerald guessed he was walking through it in his mind again. He told them of Denny's body, the stink of death on the place from Denny and the headless patron. When he got to the message waiting for him in the last room, Emerald shivered. The bastard preacher was something else entirely and it scared her as much as the demon had, maybe more now. She couldn't forget Grimluk telling her the man had shown control over the abomination. Another shiver rippled through her and she sighed a little pathetically.

"What did he want to talk about?" Manyara asked.

"That is a touch complicated, but he demanded I return a piece of property to him." A low growl filled his throat and he closed his eyes and let out a long breath through his nose.

"How would you have had his property?" Emerald asked skeptically.

"As I said, it's complicated. I had it, but I don't anymore. And he sure as fuck won't be getting it back as long as I have anything to say about it."

"So he wants whatever this thing back. And?" Manyara continued.

"And if I don't return it, I'll suffer. Under normal circumstances, I'd call it bluster and troll shit, but…"

Emerald looked at Manyara. The ranger returned her gaze. "But he's powerful."

"You say true, Em. Said his name was Marlowe Jakobs. Sound familiar to either of you?"

"Don't know any Jakobs, Marlowe or otherwise," Manyara replied.

"Can't say I do, either. And I'd sure as shit remember the Preacher comin' into the Conqueror." As the three of them fell silent, Emerald thought about the situation. A moan of fear threatened to escape her throat as she did, but she clamped down on it. Everything in her agreed with Grimluk. That this Marlowe Jakobs could and would absolutely hold true to his word. And that could mean…

Flashes of Not-Amos filled her mind. Emerald hugged herself and closed her eyes. It was one thing to handle a rowdy drunk, or Roscoe's stubborn ass, but it'd put her down for a while just pulling up enough magic to freeze Not-Amos. She wasn't sure she could do that again. And if she couldn't – if Grimluk couldn't stop the demon and the Preacher – it would mean death.

"To be quite honest," Manyara started, "I would love nothin' more than to get on a horse and ride the fuck away. I can handle gangs and rustlers and huntin' down killers, but this? Gods, it's so beyond me. Trolls was the worst we had, and you saw Bart. Trolls are bein'—what's it called—made domestic." She took a deep breath. "But I still mean to help ya if you'll have it."

Emerald watched Manyara wide-eyed. She knew her friend was just as terrified as she was, but she still wanted to help. Emerald looked at Grim-luk. His words about fear rolled through her mind. Fear was healthy. What she felt was natural and good. She swallowed hard. "Y–yeah. Yeah. I'd probably be dead without you, and—" She paused. "And it sounds like we might all be dead if we don't help you beat this."

Grimluk looked at them both in turn and smiled. "I do appreciate it. I prefer to keep non-hunters away from the fight if I can help it, but it seems like that's less of an option as of late. Not the first time. Doubt it'll be the last. Reckon I need to ponder a few things. Get my thoughts together. When Cooky brings the pie, we'll have us a slice and then we can all get some rest."

Emerald let out another long sigh and felt like she was deflating a little as she did so. Pie and sleep sounded absolutely divine.

Emerald woke an hour or so after dawn the next morning. It'd been a bit of a challenge to get to sleep. She kept wondering about everything. Impending doom clouded her mind, but so did her time with Manyara lately. So did her happiness at seeing Grimluk safe and returned. And he had been the one to encourage her to think about how she really felt about Manyara. She still wasn't entirely sure. She knew she'd always felt an attraction to the ranger, but that was hardly strange for her. Emerald was a Companion. It was certainly true – and important – that Companions were more than just their work. As much as Emerald enjoyed sex, she also liked being around people. She liked making people feel good, and Manyara had been on a very small list of clients who readily returned the favor in some fashion.

The two of them had never shared a bed – until recently at least, and that was still platonic. They had shared a lot of time together, though. After a few months and the two of them getting to know each other better, Manyara turned from client to friend, and now here Emerald was wondering if she wanted more than that and whether Manyara did as well.

Grimluk was there in the middle of it all, their defender and potentially their advocate. Like Manyara, Grimluk had quickly felt like a friend, and he seemed more than willing to listen. So Emerald decided she would let him listen. Once she dressed, she wandered over to his room and knocked on the door. It didn't take long for him to answer.

"Mornin'. What can I do for you?" he asked as he finished buttoning his shirt.

"Mornin'," she echoed. "I was just wonderin' if you'd mind talkin'. Thought we could go down by the river. Yara said there's a little park and a dock near where we came in at."

Grimluk nodded. "Sure, come in for a moment. I just need to grab my gun belt."

"Oh, all right." Emerald took a step inside and looked around. The room was arranged a little differently from her own, but she was willing to bet the other rooms were made similarly.

Grimluk looked at her as he buckled his gun belt to his waist. "Good. You're you."

"What? Who else—" She looked down. She stood inside a chalk circle she recognized as the demon trap from Grimluk's blanket. "Oh. I see."

He let out a sigh. "I'm reasonably certain it's in town. Before I left for Downingville, I could feel somethin' watchin' me. And it came at me lookin' like you once already."

Emerald blinked rapidly. "Oh." Everything started to feel a little numb, but she took a deep breath and tried to steady herself. "Suddenly, what I want to talk about doesn't seem so important."

"Bah," he said, waving a hand dismissively and checking the chambers of his gun. "Get my coat and we'll head on."

Emerald took the heavy canvas coat from the rack in the corner and handed it to him. He slid it on swiftly and then donned his scarf and hat. He stepped toward her, slinging his bag over his shoulder and motioned to the door.

"Shall we?"

"Would you rather eat first or—"

"I'll be fine," he said with gentle reassurance. "We can eat when we come back. Looks like somethin's weighin' on you."

Emerald nodded. "Right. Right. Off we go, then."

She tried to get her thoughts in order as they headed toward the river, which proved a little difficult. Grimluk walked quietly, a strong, calm presence beside her. His demeanor gave her a little comfort and her thoughts started to align. The riverside was quiet and mostly empty. A few fishers wandered about, either coming or going for a morning catch.

The dock, a little piece of public space along with the grassy park, was intricately and beautifully carved in a flowing elven style that reflected the river and the flora and fauna therein. Emerald walked to the edge, tracing her hands along the well-maintained carvings along the railing. Part of the railing was in the shape of a long trout.

As Grimluk stood next to her, she realized she was procrastinating voicing her thoughts to him. She took in a breath and looked up at him. His eyes were so dark, but so kind and patient. She'd never met another orc with eyes like his.

He smiled softly. "So," he said.

Emerald smiled back and looked down for a moment. "I…think you were right. About Manyara, I mean."

A low, rumbling laugh sounded in his throat. "Started figuring it out, then? Obvious as the tusks on my face."

She let out a dramatic sigh and rolled her eyes at him. "Yeah, yeah, ya big green ass."

"You actually said anything to her?"

Emerald turned to the railing and the river. "Not exactly."

"Will you?" he asked, bracing against the railing.

It was almost too short for her to lean against.

She imagined it was probably on well into the uncomfortable side for him, but he didn't show it.

"I want to, I think. But this ain't exactly the best time, is it?"

He shrugged. "Maybe not. Maybe it is. I won't pretend to be an expert on relationships, Emerald. Never really had an eye for the romantic, even if the inclination struck, but my parents were a pretty damn good example of it."

"Yeah? How so?"

"Seems like the best relationships work on a foundation of friendship. You two got that. Got that in spades, it seems. And maybe that don't mean romance and closeness and all that. I can't say for sure, but that's how it seems to me. What about your folks?"

Emerald thought on that for a moment. "I think so. I know Poppa and Daddy love each other immensely. Never saw 'em fight. They always did their best to work together where I was concerned."

"And Manyara?"

"Said her parents parted when she was still young, but got along. Her daddy said they just weren't right for each other."

Grimluk's throat rumbled. "Sometimes that's the case. Can't always be helped."

Emerald thought on that, too, and remained silent.

"Tell you what I think?" Grimluk asked.

"Please?"

"I reckon it's better to put it out there, if you think the other person might feel the same. Might be wrong, but at least you'll know. Then you can continue on. Reckon you'd rather have Manyara as a friend than not at all if she doesn't share your feelings. Would I be correct?"

"Tulip's the only other person I couldn't do without," she said softly.

"Sounds like an answer to me, Em."

A smile spread across Emerald's lips. She reached over and took Grimluk's hand, giving it a little squeeze. "Thank you for listening."

He squeezed it back and gave her a soft nod.

"You really never been with anyone?" she asked after a silent spell.

"Was always focused on training. Apprentices would bed each other on occasion, and I followed suit a time or two, but becoming a demon hunter is intense. Being one's even more so, and I'm always travelin'." He looked out at the river with a long stare. "Maybe one day."

Emerald watched him. She couldn't tell if he was a little sad or just distracted. Maybe both. "Grim?"

"Hm?"

"I'd like to give you a little kiss, if that's all right."

He grunted, a little smile tugging at the corner of his mouth. "Sure."

She reached up behind his head and motioned him down to plant the kiss on his cheek, clacking their tusks together softly. "I hope you'll find love, if you want it. Anyone would be lucky to have you."

He just looked at her, blinking in surprise. "I—

uh, thank you." He grinned sheepishly, but as he looked out at the river it faded quickly.

"Thinkin' about the demon again?"

"Haven't really stopped. Even before I left, I was worried I'd get back and you two wouldn't be you anymore. When you hugged me, I was ready to pull my gun. Worried anyone in town could be the thing. It could be anyone, maybe anything, and unlike at the Conqueror, I can't test thousands of people easily or in such a way to satisfy that fear." He sighed. "So, here I am, tryin' to figure out how to track a demon that can look like anyone and hide anywhere. I know two things for sure, though."

Emerald perked up. "Yeah?"

Grimluk turned to face her once more. "Between what happened with you and it chasing me into the woods, the gods-damned thing clearly hates ice. Strong cold seems to hurt it. When you froze the fake Amos, it reacted, screamed in pain. And it sure as shit hates demon traps. I think," he paused, "if we could freeze it, I could trap it and destroy it. And right now, you're the only person I know who has that ability."

Emerald hugged herself and thought hard about that. She'd offered her help, but freezing Not–Amos had almost been too much for her. She didn't know if she could freeze the whole of the monstrosity, as massive as it was.

"I know," he said. "It's a lot to ask of you. I'll ask the peacekeepers if there's a strong enough magician nearby, too. Doubtful there'd be a full-blown wizard down this way, but you never know. They are a mite unpredictable at times." He sighed.

"And they're so hard to get out of their studies anyways. Never did understand what the point was of learnin' all that and becomin' that powerful if you weren't gonna do anything with it."

"Merle didn't have that kind of power. Oh, gods. Merle. I hope he's safe."

Grimluk let out a sharp sigh and then put a hand on Emerald's shoulder. "Come on. Let's go get some food, check on Manyara."

Emerald nodded silently and followed Grimluk back to the fort. She tried to keep her fear down, but after Grimluk shared his fears, she found it hard not to look at everyone in town with suspicion. It could be anyone and they wouldn't know until it was on them. And then they'd be eaten.

Shoggoth was still getting used to having its body compacted and concealed under the heavy robe of the magician the man in black had taken it to. With that concealment came a dimming of its awareness, a fact that contributed to it and Grimluk bumping into each other in the middle of the street of Cold River. It briefly considered shredding the robe and diving on the hunter, but it knew now that devouring the orc would never be so easy. Besides that, it reasoned, he had that horrible blanket that had hurt so badly. Shoggoth wanted to avoid the biting touch of that thing desperately. Instead, it did its best to control the voice it projected, trying to sound as much like a person as the orc and the man in black. It could not control the sneer that rolled across the single mouth it wore for its disguise.

Grimluk's apology caught it off guard. It had expected a fight, despite the man in black's assurances that it could maintain a basic elvenoid shape in the robe. The demon hunter seemed distracted, though, and after Shoggoth replied with its slight bend of the truth – that Grimluk reminded it of someone who had hurt it once – he apologized once more and went on his way toward Downingville. Shoggoth just waited for a moment, watching the demon hunter walk away in silence. If he had suspected its true identity, he'd made no sign of it.

Cautiously, it stretched a thin tendril of itself to the back of the hood and jammed it through the fabric to make a small hole. It left the tendril hanging on the hole and walked on, watching the demon hunter. It reasoned, from the man in black's lessons, that a small hole in its hood would not be noticed. If it needed to, it could always pull the eye-stalk away and feign normalcy again. Shoggoth was far less concerned about other creatures, though. Those it learned were called "mortals". Grimluk had cunning, had weapons. Grimluk had hurt it.

Grimluk had killed its sibling. Grimluk must die.

It hissed at the sudden rise of that thought. Not yet. The man in black had told Shoggoth that those thoughts were Sheogorath's, not its own. It wondered, for just a moment, why only the demon's mind was capable of doing that when it could absorb so much information from the devoured mortals. Not all of it held, but after eating so many of them, it had learned enough to better pretend to be one.

Still, Shoggoth only felt the thoughts of the mortals in such an intense way as it digested them. Dimly, it recalled the final desires of the dwarves it had taken after it first woke up. Sheogorath and the mortal creatures had similar shapes, similar thoughts, but the demon's essence screamed furiously from deep inside whereas humans, dwarves, and halflings faded. The few elves it had tasted lasted longer, but they still faded, too. Maybe orcs lasted longer as well, but it had not eaten an orc yet.

Walking quietly down the street, it looked around, trying to take in the sights of the buildings around it. Of the river, the hotel, the huge boat, the people walking around it. No one seemed to pay it any mind. A person here or there held up their hands to it, or nodded their heads and gave a greeting. Shoggoth nodded slowly back but refrained from speech. Speaking as the mortals did was taxing. It could hold the shape. Maintaining human-looking hands and a human-looking face were reasonably simple, though occasionally it had to shift a new eye to the back of its head, or let a mouth form on its back and nip the fabric gently. Mostly, though, it just felt frustrated at the confines of the robe, having to experience the world directly in front of it only. At least the hands it wore could remain bare. It was small comfort.

The man in black had told it to move among the people unknown. Learn to hunt silently, carefully, deliberately. People, the man had told it, have a habit of disappearing as individuals. Whether getting lost or kidnapped or running away, it didn't always matter. But groups of people disappearing were hard to miss. More importantly, they were harder to ignore.

"A massive ball of slime with teeth tends to stick with you, eh?" he'd said as Shoggoth devoured the magician, a human man named Merle. It could not fault the man's logic, though it had trouble caring.

After being made aware of Sheogorath's influence on its mind, it hadn't been sure whether that indifference was its own or the demon's. It also couldn't seem to entirely care about that, either.

What it did suddenly care about was seeing a familiar orc and human not far away, heading into a place called the Horned Court. It had learned the human's name, Manyara, from the rangers, and already knew the orc as Emerald. And like Grimluk, Emerald had hurt it, too. The woman had frozen a part of itself in a solid block that had left the split-off form ruined and trapped. Something had happened in that ice that had destroyed that part of it altogether. Shoggoth suspected Grimluk had done that before their brief fight.

Of the three orcs it had dealt with so far, two of them had hurt it, but it had hurt the other. Orcs, Shoggoth decided, were the most dangerous of the mortal creatures.

Bubbles rippled down its body at the remembered feeling of ice biting into its flesh, razor sharp and piercing cold. It had to focus to keep a flurry of mouths from spilling out in horrific gnashing. It took a few minutes but Shoggoth steadied itself, following the orc and human toward the Horned

Court. It could hear the orc talking not far inside and decided to try something.

The tip of one of its fingers dropped to the ground, no bigger than a pebble, and rolled forward along the dirt to the building. Shoggoth walked on, calmly, idly, nowhere in particular, and let the small piece of itself find a spot to watch and listen.

The pair reunited with the survivors from Downingville. They recounted their side of the story. Shoggoth felt a slight curiosity at hearing about itself like that. About how it had been wrong and terrifying and how they had escaped death. It didn't comprehend being called wrong, but it did understand terror, if only a little bit. Grimluk pro-voked a certain measure of terror in Shoggoth. Especially the blanket, though his gun hurt as well.

Shoggoth's hunger reared up as it walked and watched. The hunger was so hard to resist but Shoggoth held itself back. It wanted to learn. That was one thing so many absorbed mortals had given it: curiosity. The man in black had encouraged this interest. So it continued waiting, learning the lay of the town and listening to the orc and her group carry on.

Eventually, the two of them left the others. The piece of Shoggoth that watched slithered after them. It wondered where they would go. It fol-lowed the pair into the walled-off building, sliding under the gate, rolling across the dirt with ease. The human was leading the orc to a smaller building from the one ahead of the gate. Inside was a well-lit room with beds all around and white sheets hang-ing between them. On one bed was the other orc, the one who had come with the human after Grimluk's escape. Bringar. The little piece of ooze rolled into the shadows underneath the orc's bed. Outside, Shoggoth stood in front of the gate, silent and still.

The human woman asked one of the other people in the room how the orc was doing. Shoggoth hadn't fed on the orc out of confusion and frustration that he hadn't been Grimluk. When he had attacked, it had swatted him away, an act that allowed the woman to drag him behind the strange force that had kept it away, kept it from devouring them. It hated her, too, but she had only repelled it.

The creature's hunger roared once again, pounding through it like the blood of the things it had eaten. It could find itself again later. Or maybe it would curl up inside Bringar, to listen and wait. Yes. While the rest of it explored and fed, the little piece of itself could listen and learn, almost like it had with Maisy. It could sate itself a little at a time inside the orc and learn.

After Emerald and Manyara left, and the care-takers of the orc disappeared, the little blob rolled up the bed. It slid smoothly into Bringar's mouth, nipping bits of the moist flesh as it did, before rolling down the man's throat.

The robed body moved on, ready to find itself a meal. It wandered back down to where it had bumped into Grimluk and looked at the tall build-ing called Rothwilde's. It circled the building, looking at the windows and noticing the balconies on the top floor behind it. Two figures stood out on one of them, embracing. Most of the other win-dows were dark. The other balconies were empty. Shoggoth clung to the building, staying in the shadows. Its hands spread out and flattened before dragging its clothed and booted form up the wall effortlessly, noiselessly. It crept across the roof, stretching a finger out over the edge to watch the mortals.

One of them giggled while the other slid its lips down their arm. They moaned and cooed and it wasn't long before they wandered back inside. Shoggoth stretched the digit farther to see what was happening.

As the balcony door closed, one of them spoke. "Reckon maybe we should get warmed back up, don't you?"

Shoggoth glided down to the balcony and dropped its rotund elvenoid shape, sinking to the balcony floor. It hissed and bubbled lightly at the cold of the stone before flattening itself and hastily sliding through the cracks in the door.

Inside, the pair of mortals were removing their own clothes as well, dragging their lips across each other's flesh again, together and in turns. Shoggoth kept its form compact, easier to hide in the dim light of the room, and watched.

The mortals stood bare before each other, parts of them dangling and bobbing about. It took in the similarities of their bodies. It understood those better now, and the differences. Shoggoth reasoned that knowing these things could help it blend in better.

The pair shifted onto the bed. Shoggoth watched, feeding its curiosity as the hunger urged it on. It looked like they were devouring each other. Would Shoggoth be denied its meal in such a way?

One of the bodies climbed on top of the other, pressing against the one below. More of the soft giggling and moaning filled the room as the blob slithered up onto the ceiling to see better.

From the new vantage point, it was sure that the one on bottom was trying to devour the one on top. Anger filled the blob's body. It would not be denied its meal. Desire threatened to produce uncontrolled eyes and mouths across its glistening flesh, but it held them at bay and positioned itself over the two mortals as the one on top bucked and grunted, obviously trying to fight for its freedom like so many had done when it had devoured them.

But it was too late. For both of them. Shoggoth poured down on them, covering them like a sheet and tightened, crushing the pair of them together. They screamed, but it was muffled and only heard by the oozing creature.

"You will feed me instead," it told them inside itself as they screamed and bucked. It savored them. Let the hunger linger just a little, to make the meal last. The others had been just as delicious, but it had eaten them too fast. The man in black told it to appreciate its meals more. Now it would try to do that. The pair thrashed and bucked but it was no use. Shoggoth gurgled in pleasure.

Feeding on the mortals slowly, over the following day and night, had released their essences and minds gradually, a little more sharply. When morning came around, Shoggoth dragged the blanket from the bed onto the balcony and lay upon it while the sun shone down. It wanted the warmth of the sun on its flesh as it pondered new lessons. It learned the two mortals had not been feeding on each other, but "making love". With that knowledge came strange desires and new questions. Why was it so hungry, for instance? It had never questioned the need to feed before or why it was so intense. It pondered the dreams of one of the devoured lovers.

Shoggoth pictured making a home with the other person. Building it together. Making love. Making children. Similar notions had filled it before, from others, but these were stronger. They filled it with an odd sense of melancholy that confused it. This was like the first memories it got from Nahum and Maisy and Dar and their daughters. A fragment of a memory worked its way up, and it recalled the brief and overwhelming feelings as it had eaten Dar.

Guilt? Protectiveness? Sorrow?

Shoggoth had been barely more than an animal before eating Sheogorath. Now...now it was called demon. Abomination. Wrong. It knew, though, that it was something else. The man in black had said so. It wanted to ask the man what it really was now, but he wasn't around.

It reached out and looked down from the balcony, at the riverside. At the dock near the river. At the green skin of the orcs standing on the dock. Emerald and Grimluk. As Emerald kissed Grimluk's cheek, Shoggoth got another idea.

It would make the demon hunter tell it what it was. Grimluk would explain it. If anyone else could figure it out, it was the demon hunter. Grimluk would help Shoggoth. And when it was satisfied, then it would feast on the hunter and his friends. Or maybe it wouldn't. It didn't know.

Chapter 17

After his talk with Emerald, Grimluk spent the rest of the day taking care of small things as a form of relaxation and meditation. Mostly, he wanted to take the time to think about what needed to be done to stop the demon and Jakobs. So he started by focusing on repairing his coat, adding another small patch to fill his already sizable collection. The thick canvas was sturdy and had seen him through a decade of hunting. Bullet holes peppered it along with slashes both singular and grouped, from blades and claws. Sewing a small patch over a hole was easier than sewing his own flesh closed.

While he could take a bullet, or several when the need arose, it was never a pleasant experience. The coat simply let the bullet pass through it, but he had to pull the slug out and then patch himself up. Plus, the coat didn't bleed.

Much easier.

After that, he broke apart his revolver and set about cleaning it meticulously. After a quick soak in steaming water, he dug any buildup in the runes along the barrel out. A wire brush cleaned the barrel and cylinder chambers with brisk efficiency. While the metal dried, Grimluk set to oiling the holster. He treated the belt well, and in the years he'd had it, he'd never once suspected rot setting in. Under his coat, it remained protected from the elements and he kept the oil flowing to protect it from everything else.

As he worked the oil in, his throat rumbled as he pondered the situation. He needed to figure out the best way to protect anyone else from harm. He was still certain that ice magic and a demon trap were the best tools for the job. It was all he was certain of at the moment, but it was something. Though he did wonder at how he could employ them both. The demon would undoubtedly avoid the blanket after being burned like it had. A fact that also meant the trap wouldn't trap the demon.

He considered patrolling Cold River. He could leave traps and elder signs across the fort and search the whole of the town. Investigating a demon's activity was commonplace among hunters. This particular situation was more difficult only because of...well, everything, but especially the shapeshifting and body splitting. Grimluk could feel the paranoia gnawing at him and he hated it. Cults could spring up anywhere and even those failed to provoke this kind of response in him.

He still couldn't figure out exactly why it had chased him, either. True, the demonic visage that had pushed out of the pulsing, oozing flesh of the thing had appeared to be the demon from Arbor-town, but he had watched the beast crumble into a pile of bones, stinking of brimstone as its flesh burned away. He still had a piece of its horn to prove it.

Grimluk reassembled his gun, oiling it thoroughly, and prepared to go out into the town. He pulled fresh shells from his bag to refill the slots on his belt as he thought on his plan. Saloons and hotels would offer the most cover for the thing if it was pretending to be a person. He could check them first. He pulled out his chalk pen and checked it. With a fresh stick from his bag, there'd be enough he could leave marks to deter the demon. It might not help anything, but leaving traps and signs of protection could provide the edge he needed right now. Gear readied, he headed out only to be stopped by Manyara and Emerald in the courtyard.

"Where you off to?" Emerald asked.

"Had a mind to patrol the town, look for signs of the demon," he replied.

"Any way we can help?" came Manyara.

Grimluk considered this for a moment. "Not with that, but—" he took the blanket with the demon trap on it and handed it to them, "—study the demon trap and find paint or chalk and put it around this place as best you can. The sigils need to be exact. They can be difficult to memorize, but given the circumstances, it could mean the difference between safety and waking up…unpleasantly."

"What if you find it while you're out?" Emerald asked with a frown.

"Reckon you'll hear it. And I'm still better equipped to stand a chance than anyone else right now." He headed for the gate and pushed it open before pausing. "Emerald?"

"Yes?"

"Stay frosty," he said with a grin.

She looked like she would roll her eyes for a second before nodding in return.

His first destination was the old saloon where Roscoe and his friends had attacked him. He had no doubts about whether they were fakes or not. Two of them had dropped with the nerve pinch and Roscoe would not have bothered to gather support if he'd been the blob demon, or spout off about goblins and lessons. The thing could split itself into others, as he'd seen, but it had a simple focus and hadn't spoken much.

Still, a saloon had people and people were food and camouflage. At the least, Grimluk would find nothing and leave a trap.

The patrons of the little saloon mostly ignored him, though a few gave him scowls. He wasn't sure if the place even had a name. The sign outside simply said "Saloon". It was nothing more than a watering hole and a cheap one at that, though that didn't always mean the drink was of low quality.

The saloon was relatively sparse. It lacked any gaming areas and had only a few tables and chairs. Mostly, it was just the long bar running along one of the side walls with a dirty mirror behind it that was too dingy to be much use.

He approached the bartender, a human woman with thinning, greasy hair and a surprisingly friendly demeanor. The smile she wore faltered when he said he was a demon hunter, becoming strained as he asked his questions. Had she seen anything strange, any new people, heard of any disappearances? All she could properly say was that Roscoe, and Grimluk himself, had been the only new faces as of late and no, she hadn't heard or seen anything strange or about anyone disappearing. He thanked her for her time and, before moving on, he drew an Elder Sign above the batwing doors. It wasn't much but it would at least deter the damned thing if it came oozing this way.

He then found a small hotel at the other end of town, near a newer residential area and another road leading out of Cold River. The proprietor, a halfling with surprisingly pale skin, was less friendly than the bartender had been as he answered Grimluk's questions. The hotel, the Dozing Dragon, currently housed a few of the Conqueror's survivors. By all accounts they came and went at the usual hours travelers kept, heading to the Horned Court occasionally. Beyond that, he'd seen nothing remotely strange. Grimluk sighed and left half a bilt's worth of pennies for the effort. He left a demon trap on the roof of the hotel's porch before leaving.

The Horned Court was slightly more helpful, but only because more people there knew of what had happened. No one had heard of any disappearances or other strange things. Grimluk grew frustrated at a lack of signs, but it was hardly a surprise. This thing had begun eluding him almost immediately after appearing. He thanked them all and left, leaving Elder Signs around the door frame.

He stood in the street, looking around. The afternoon had gone gray and brought a chilly breeze with it. He sighed.

"Thing shows up and makes itself known as clear as day," he mumbled. "Now it's a gods-damned secret all unto itself."

He continued on down another street, occasionally asking shop owners what they'd seen or heard. When he could, he'd slip between buildings and put demon traps on the walls. Finally, he headed to the Rothwilde Hotel and inquired there.

Halfling and human bellhops in pressed blue uniforms and matching hats stood waiting to serve or else busying themselves elsewhere as he entered. Behind the desk was an elf with silver hair and eyes like polished jade who stood and nodded to Grimluk curtly as he approached.

"I am unsure if you're in the right place, sai, but all the same, how may I help you?" the elf asked.

Grimluk laid out his introductions and questions again, maybe a bit gruffer than he usually would have but he doubted the elf noticed. Rothwilde's appeared to be quite a fancy establishment. Much nicer than any place he'd ever stayed outside of his trip to New Gilead's capital. More often than not, he slept on the ground. He knew too well that it showed on him. If the establishment did not have any problem with orcs, it certainly had a problem with people covered in dust and dirt and with patches on their clothes.

The elf sighed and answered Grimluk's questions with strained politeness before asking him, with that same strained politeness, to kindly leave unless he could offer up payment for a room.

Idly, Grimluk pulled out a glut and twirled it along the knuckles of his hand. The elf's eyes widened slightly at the sight of the gold coin and actual politeness filled their face. Grimluk sighed through his nose and walked off, still guiding the coin over his fingers with long-practiced precision.

It was a trick Kort, one of his mentors, had taught the apprentices to build dexterity in their fingers. He could even do it with just about anything he could fit between his knuckles. Kort had even told them stories about a hunter he'd once known, a man named Roland or Walter, Grimluk couldn't quite remember, who could hypnotize people by moving a bullet along his knuckles.

Grimluk stood on the Rothwilde's porch and looked out at the town, twirling the coin and trying to decide on what to do next. Night would come in a couple of hours and the demon's oily flesh blended in with shadow too well for Grimluk's liking. Not that that was entirely worth caring about when it could also shapeshift, but no sense in giving it any help in killing. He put the coin away and wondered if it wouldn't be best to return to the fort and see how the ladies were faring with the task of painting traps.

Grimluk shrugged and headed down the street. "Fort it is," he muttered. As he neared the alchemist's pharmacy, he was surprised to see Emerald waiting near the path to the dock, waving at him from across the street. She had apparently changed back into her red and gold dress, which seemed a strange thing to wear for painting, but her clothing was her choice.

"Grimluk!" she called. Her voice sounded a little on the stuffy side.

He wondered if she might be catching a cold. After all the walking to and from Downingville and however long she'd spent painting outside today, he found the prospect probable. He'd worried about her health as they'd walked anyways, and if a cold was all she'd come away with, he was pleased for her resilience.

"Em, where's Manyara?" he called back.

"Oh, she's taking care of something. Come with me, won't you? I have something I'd really like to ask you."

"Sure," he replied. As he got closer, she turned and headed down the path to the dock. He followed her, watching as she seemed to glide down to the riverside. She stopped near the part of the railing they'd stood at earlier and waited for him, a placid look on her face.

"Everything all right?" Grimluk asked.

"It will be. Won't you come stand here with me?"

Grimluk looked her over, stepping slowly. Her voice really did sound stuffy. And just a little high. "Reckon this is a good spot for talkin'. Had a good talk this mornin', didn't we?"

"Very good, yes. I liked it. I want to talk more, please." She held out her hand. "Come."

"What did you want to ask me?"

She dropped her arm when he made no move to take her hand, but the placid look on her face never changed. She just turned away from him and picked up a brown robe from the ground. She slipped the garment over her head and let it fall. When she turned back around, Grimluk had his gun aimed at her head.

Except now it wasn't Emerald's face anymore. It was only the facsimile of a face, perfectly smooth and bulbous, without a nose. It glistened in the dim light of the overcast afternoon. Black, beady eyes met Grimluk's and then the small slit of a mouth moved and it spoke.

"What gave me away?" came the thing's warbling voice.

"I don't reckon you'd really take to it if I tried to explain." He pulled the hammer back. "Now, before this little shindig gets started, you tell me if Emerald's still alive or whether I gotta take this personal."

The face remained placid and unblinking. "I have not touched her."

Grimluk squeezed the trigger.

Gunfire roared out across the river in rapid succession. At such a close range, Grimluk's shooting was more than sure. It was inevitable. Bullets split the robe, opening up three holes. The placid face changed like a sudden storm, shrieking in pain and fury.

Grimluk's knife came out next, singing its blade song as it cut the air and bit into a robed limb. It sliced deep, making the beady eyes grow wide. The slit mouth widened along with the rest of the demon's head, expanding into a hood that lifted into the air, ready to come down on Grimluk.

He fired two more shots at where the face had been as he leapt back, loosing his last round into the demon's gut. The thing gurgled in pain but didn't move closer. Grimluk took the opportunity to reload, fingers moving nimbly and precisely. With one, fluid motion, he slammed the cylinder shut and raked the hammer back, ready for the oozing creature's counter attack.

It didn't come. Purple, oily flesh shrank back

into the robe and then the robe fell empty to the dock. Grimluk backed away from the dock as fast as he could, realizing the thing had slipped through the slits between the planks.

"I really do have something to ask you, Grimluk."

"If you're anything like any other demon, I reckon you're curious as to the flavor of my soul and if I'll scream as you devour it. Might be a little bitter for your liking."

"I do not know what a soul is, but if it can be eaten, I will eat yours with the rest of you. But not before you answer my question."

Grimluk held his weapons at the ready, gun out and searching, knife held with the blade pointing behind him, doing his best to keep notice of his surroundings. "Go on and ask then, demon."

A moment later, something slammed into his back and sent him rolling back toward the dock. He dug the knife into the dirt to slow his movement, thankful his instincts had taken over. Tendrils of oozing flesh had sprouted from under the dock as he neared. He rolled away and rose as quick as he could. The tendrils reformed into a rotund, glistening body as another walked over to join it.

"What am I?" the two bodies asked in one voice.

Grimluk's aim dipped for a moment. "What?"

"I told you. I really did want to ask you something. I want to know what I really am. I...don't think I'm supposed to be this. I was...was..." The faces seemed to be searching for something. "I was born in a rock that came from up there," it said, pointing to the sky. Neither body attempted to get closer to Grimluk.

"I remember it. I was small and hungry. Part of me was in water and someone breathed in the rest of me. I ate her from the inside out. And then I ate the animals that drank me. And then her family. And then I went looking for another meal and all I wanted was to eat. The red thing with the horns, the demon, helped me. And then it said it wanted to take me to find the one who killed its sibling."

"Me," Grimluk said.

"I didn't want to. I didn't care. I wanted to try new food. I learned things from the people I ate. I learned about venison. Have you ever had venison?"

Grimluk frowned. Deer was, in fact, one of his favorite meats. The thought of discussing the merits of venison with the abominable blob almost made him start laughing.

"Yes," he said simply, avoiding the laughter.

"I wanted that. But the—the demon, Sheogorath, it attacked me, tried to force me to do what it wanted. I ate it. It picked me up and tried to carry me and instead I ate it, and something happened."

Grimluk's brow furrowed. "You changed?"

"I don't remember much about it. People attacked me. I ate them. I learned your name and where you'd gone, and I knew I had to eat you. For vengeance. Wanted it more than…than venison!"

Grimluk stepped slowly to the side, moving closer to the path back to the street. "So you chased me and killed everyone who tried to fend you off."

"Killed? No, I ate them."

"Reckon no one put it in your head that eatin' requires killin'."

"I see," the voices echoed. "Then yes."

The two bodies didn't seem concerned with stopping Grimluk from moving around. He looked down the riverside, checking for signs of other people or any more of the demon thing's other selves. If there'd been any fishers still out, they'd fled at the gunfire. He was alone with the damned thing and that suited him just fine.

"Grimluk!" Emerald called from the street somewhere.

"Ah, shit," he said. His brain worked quickly at his approaching friends. Maybe he could keep the thing's attention. Maybe he could give Emerald enough time to try using her ice magic. Maybe.

"Hey, uh, shit, what the fuck do I even call you?"

"Shoggoth," it said in an even tone.

"You really keen on knowin' what you are?"

"I am. I must know. Tell me."

"You say you ate the sibling of the demon I killed. You're right, that don't necessarily make you a demon," he said, moving slowly back toward the river. "But it also don't necessarily make you somethin' else."

"I don't understand," Shoggoth said, a hint of frustration in its voices. "I don't understand!"

"Demons are tricky bastards," Grimluk continued, hearing his name called again. "Maybe eating a demon makes you a demon knight. Maybe you are somethin' else altogether. We could find out. I could take you somewhere and we could find out the answer."

Purple heads tilted in unison. "You would offer your help like this?"

"Despite how you know me, I do my best to help folks when I'm able. I would have to ask that you only eat animals along the way, though. Things that I caught for us." To his left, Emerald and Manyara appeared at the end of the path. He held up his hand to keep them back. "You can't eat people anymore. Not half a town's worth. Not even one. If you are something else, you can prove it. You can be different. You can be more than that thing inside you wants of you."

"Can I?" it asked slowly, the two heads tilting as they looked at him.

Grimluk hesitated for a moment before holstering his gun and dropping his knife into the loop on his coat. He didn't trust the thing, but maybe if he worked the situation right, he could get it to follow him, maybe even back to Hunter's Hollow where it could be dealt with more thoroughly. Whatever that actually meant.

"Life," he started, "is full of choices. It would seem you're learning that lesson now. The first time we met, you tried to run me down. The second time, you may well have killed me outright had the Preacher not stopped you. And since you put that robe on, you haven't been the one to attack. That was a choice."

"He told me to learn to hunt better. That fear made people taste better. That I was special." One of the bodies turned its head toward Emerald and Manyara.

"Maybe you are special. Truth be told, I've never come across anything that ate a demon before. That's special in itself. One thing that makes us mortals special is we can choose who we want to be. Sometimes those choices ain't so easy. Sometimes we can only make a choice that's less bad than another."

"What do I choose?" Shoggoth said quietly.

"You want to know what you are. I want to keep you from hurtin' anyone else. You could choose to take me up on that, choose peace. I chose a life of violence, but peace, when available, is usually the right choice."

"I do not understand," it said. "What does peace mean?"

"Like I said already, no more eating people. No more hurting anyone. You and I, we put our feelings aside. No more fighting. We show each other mutual respect and work together. And you would eventually need to make restitution for the people you've hurt."

"Restitution?" it echoed. "What does that mean?"

"It means you make things right. Accept the consequences of what you've done. Possibly punishment."

A burst of flame appeared behind Shoggoth. Marlowe Jakobs stepped out wearing a grin that looked like it would split his face in two. The man stepped between Shoggoth's bodies and leaned close to one of them, whispering. Grimluk's guts knotted up. He knew exactly what the Preacher was doing.

"No!" the twin bodies screamed. "No! No, I won't be punished! I won't!"

A growl rumbled in Grimluk's throat as the bodies collided and began thrashing, tendrils flying around wildly. Peace had been so close, but Jakobs had made good on his promise. Grimluk had failed.

Mouths gnashed across the massive, shining body, growling and spitting and bubbling like boiling tar. Each new mouth would pop out, screaming against punishment or about hunger or vengeance. Grimluk drew and fired from his hip, fanning the hammer, drawing more screams of pain. Shoggoth balled up and barreled down at Grimluk, sending him diving away, narrowly avoiding the lashing tendrils and the death they'd bring. He fired his remaining shots and set to reloading.

"Go warn the 'keepers!" he shouted at Emerald and Manyara. In truth, he was amazed they hadn't gotten over here yet. The peacekeepers should have descended on the riverside after hearing gunfire.

Before Emerald or Manyara could respond, the pair lurched forward with shocked cries, hitting the ground. Surprise ripped through Grimluk at the sight of Bringar standing over them. He turned to fire on the man on instinct, forgetting about Shoggoth for a moment. What felt like a brick slammed into his chest, knocking him away and sending him sliding across the grass. Grimluk didn't have the time to focus on helping Emerald and Manyara. The monstrous, many-mawed form of Shoggoth demanded the entirety of his focus.

Chapter 18

Demon traps were harder to get just right than Manyara expected. She and Emerald had readied the first pentacle on the fort gate and started with one of the easier looking symbols, taking their time to get the symbols right. Manyara did not want to be responsible for the demon getting to them. By the time they got to the last one, gunshots interrupted their progress, startling Manyara and causing her hand to jerk and ruin the effort.

It didn't matter, though. She knew immediately it was Grimluk's gun, and by the look on Emerald's face, her friend knew it, too. Manyara had heard at least a dozen different types of gunshots. Having heard Grimluk's gun in Downingville, there was little doubt. It was an unmistakable sound.

She dropped the paint bucket and brush and the pair hurried to find Manyara's gun belt. She insisted on giving Emerald a gun as well. Emerald was hesitant to take it. Manyara had offered, once, to teach Emerald to shoot, but her friend had simply insisted that if she couldn't charm or punch her way out of trouble then she wasn't going to live through it.

Mostly, it'd been a joke. There was no time for

jokes now. Emerald took the gun and clutched the demon trap blanket to her chest. The report of the demon hunter's gun had grown quiet by the time the two of them were running toward where they thought it'd come from.

The fort had an eerie silence to it as they left. Cold River was blanketed by that same silence. It made Manyara's guts tighten. When they saw the first person, standing perfectly still as a statue, she began to realize why things were so quiet. Bodies stood where they'd been as they went about their day. A group of peacekeepers down the street defied gravity, frozen in mid run.

Emerald called out Grimluk's name as they passed, her hat dangling by its cord from her neck. Manyara had left hers behind. Everything felt utterly surreal.

The sight of hunter and demon stole her breath. Emerald let out a sharp gasp. Bulbous, twin bodies stood in front of Grimluk, holding an echoing conversation with him while he moved away from them. A moment later, he held up his hand, signaling for them to stay where they were. After that, he holstered his gun.

"What on Arkod is he doing?" Emerald muttered.

Manyara listened. It sounded like Grimluk was trying to talk the monster out of fighting. It even seemed to be working until a pillar of flame erupted behind the slimy bodies. Manyara watched in quiet horror as the man in black casually approached the demon. When the demon began screaming, he turned to her and Emerald and gave an exaggerated wink.

She barely had time to react before something slammed into them from behind, sending the pair of them sprawling. Manyara rolled across the cold grass with a grunt as deafening gunfire filled the air again, followed by eldritch cries of pain.

The ranger shook off her fall and got to a crouch. A few feet away, Emerald was rolling over, gun and blanket lying in front of her. Bringar staggered toward her, a muffled scream trying to climb out of his throat. His face was a mask of pain as he dropped onto Emerald, pinning her to the ground hard enough to make her yelp.

Something snapped and crackled as Bringar's body split open like a massive maw, spraying blood and bits of flesh as it did. Something snapped in Manyara, too.

As a ranger, she'd assisted allies in fights many times, and been assisted as well. It was a soldier's duty. You saw your own in trouble and aided them as quickly and smartly as you could. Manyara saw Emerald struggling underneath what had once been Bringar and that instinct surged through her with the haste and power of lightning splitting a tree.

Bringar bent over Emerald, his chest cavity opening wide as a slimy tendril reached out, slowly forming into a misshapen hand.

Manyara drew her revolver with the speed and surety brought on by years of training and bolstered by her desire to save her friend. She fired once, knocking the slime-hand away. Emerald screamed and filled the air with a blast of ice that caught Bringar's ruined face.

Manyara dropped her gun after she fired and

clawed for the blanket. She remembered what Grimluk had said about putting the blanket on the fake Emerald and did the same, tackling her marshal with the trap side of the blanket.

For the briefest of moments, she was sure that at any moment, his ribs would bite into her. It felt like time had slowed to a crawl as she slammed through him, tumbling off Emerald. Manyara pressed the blanket down into Bringar as hard as she could, waiting for the mouth-body to kill her. He thrashed madly, cracking her elbow while she pinned him. Razors shot up her arm, bringing tears to her eyes, but she kept pushing with every ounce of grim determination in her body.

Behind her, thunder and screams rang out in equal measure. Under her, smoke and screams.

Bringar's thrashing weakened rapidly and then Manyara was holding a blanket against the unmoving corpse of her marshal. She stood, pulling the blanket with her. Charred chunks of slime filled the husk, while black lines rolled away from his eyes. She felt utterly sure the ruined sight of Bringar would never leave her but there was no time to focus on it. She hoisted Emerald up.

"Freeze the bastard, Em!"

Emerald took in a deep breath and let it out in a thick cloud of frost. They turned to see Grimluk dodging and rolling away from the massive, hideous thing swinging at him with mouths and tendrils. Manyara had no idea how much longer it would take before it caught him but it couldn't be much longer.

She took Emerald's hand and squeezed it. "Do it!"

Emerald let out a roar and thrust her hand toward the monstrosity, unleashing an icy gale that lashed out and struck oily flesh.

The demonic abomination tried to slam down onto his chest, but Grimluk rolled out of the way and spun to his feet. His gun shouted thunder as he backed away, keeping out of reach of snapping mouths and stringy, grasping fingers. With each avoided swipe, he fired a shot, taking off chunks from the screaming mouths or whipping tendrils.

Someone called out, but he didn't have time to see what was happening as Shoggoth hurled itself over his head, spreading out wide like a tarp ready to engulf him. Grimluk rolled his knife around and leapt, slashing along the dark, glistening body of his attacker just as gunfire caught his ears. Shoggoth let out a shriek, pulling apart where the knife bit it, pausing long enough for Grimluk to dodge out from underneath it, dragging the massive knife through the oozing thing's body as he did. Once in the open again, he fired three more shots and set about reloading, a task made more difficult now with his knife in hand. Precious seconds were devoured slipping the knife in and out of the loop on his coat while he emptied the chambers and slid fresh shells into place.

A line of worry traced the back of his mind,

that this creature would push him well beyond his abilities and finally end him. His training kept that thought at bay. He didn't have the luxury of fretting about death at the moment. There was only the battle.

The cylinder slammed closed, but before he could raise the barrel and fire, a wad of purple flesh flicked out and grabbed his wrist. With a flick of his knife, the flesh detached from its source but held on. Grimluk danced away and pressed the Elder Sign on his blade down into the flesh, searing it away. More mouths lashed out, sending him rolling away.

The murderous mound of ooze made to lunge at him again. Grimluk readied himself, preparing to fire just as a frigid, heavy blast of wind slammed into Shoggoth's side, accompanied by a scream. A wave of frost rolled off like a breaking wave and washed over Grimluk. He looked over to see Manyara and Emerald standing together as Shoggoth shrieked at the cold, Emerald's hand outstretched, a whirling aura of cold surrounding her.

Grimluk didn't wait for any more attacks. He rushed in, firing deliberately as he went, four peals of thunder sounding in between his footfalls. Another arctic burst of wind rolled over Shoggoth's body as Grimluk made it to the opposite side, dragging his knife along the length of the abominable body again as it shrieked from his bullets, the cold, and the steel.

Emerald roared again and when Grimluk came around the back of the boulder-sized creature, he could see she had both hands out now, sending sheets of rime and needles of ice out. Bones began to poke out from Shoggoth's body and Grimluk aimed and fired with the kind of precision elves told stories about, splintering the bone and any others in line beside it. He hurried to join Emerald and Manyara, reloading again as he did so.

"Blanket!" he called.

Manyara thrust it at him without looking away from what was happening. The icy wind began to falter. Grimluk looked at Emerald. She was panting, fighting to keep her eyes open, while two streams of blood trickled from her nostrils.

"It's too big," she gasped. "I can't...I can't do it..."

Grimluk looked at Manyara, her face a mask of fear and worry. She swallowed hard as she looked at Emerald. The ranger stepped behind her friend and wrapped her arms around the woman.

"Keep goin'," Manyara shouted. "We'll do it together. You lean on me, Em."

Grimluk watched as Emerald sucked in a shuddering breath and renewed her efforts, sending a new flurry of icicles and freezing winds toward the sluggish, moaning Shoggoth. Manyara's body was tensed as well. Gently, Grimluk pushed the women forward.

When Manyara's eyes snapped to his, he gave a quick nod. "Trust me."

She nodded back and slowly, one step at a time, the three of them marched toward the rapidly freezing form of Shoggoth. When they got within six feet, Grimluk rushed behind the thing again in time to see it trying to split itself once more. To escape.

Grimluk was ready, though, and held up the blanket. The sluggish second form jerked away, sending bits of ice tumbling to the ground. Grimluk held the blanket up as high as he could without blocking his vision and pressed forward, sending the form stumbling back, screeching and holding up seven arms to block itself.

"Keep on it, Emerald!" he shouted, hoping she could hear him. "Keep on it!"

He felt more bones pushing out from the lumbering bodies, trying to push him away, but he pushed back harder, grunting as the bones dug into the blanket and his body, grateful the thick blanket dulled their power. He just kept pushing back. They were so close.

Emerald and Manyara let out blood-curdling screams and Grimluk felt more waves of freezing air rolling around Shoggoth's body, biting into his skin now as well. Rime started to form on his hands. He ignored it, kept pushing, working every muscle in his body with every ounce of willpower he had. The bones started to give way, growing brittle and cracking. Grimluk let out a growl as he felt something soft against the blanket. He roared and willed his body on.

Shoggoth screamed as the blanket bit into it. Rancid meat sizzled and popped, filling the air with a stench worse than anything Grimluk could recall. It cried out as he pushed into it, a disgusting tendril making one final attempt at freedom slipping out and taking hold of his hand, biting into his flesh. The cracking of ice filled the air, rolling down from the top of Shoggoth's body, reaching out for more flesh. Grimluk's arms began to burn as he took a step back to stay clear of the ice. He kept the blanket up anyways, held whatever bits of the monstrosity that might be able to get free at bay as the mystical ice wrapped around the black, ruined flesh greedily.

A long, pitiful moan escaped from somewhere as the ice closed around the flesh and locked itself into a frozen fortress that gleamed in the light of the coming evening. Grimluk leaned forward, pressing the blanket into the ice one last time. Nothing moved. He let his arms drop and walked wearily around the frozen creature, wrapping himself in the blanket. The freezing wind died away.

"Did we get it?" Emerald asked, her voice hoarse and almost hard to hear.

"We got it," Grimluk replied, holding his hand against his coat.

"Fan-fucking-tastic," Emerald said as her eyes rolled back. She would've collapsed to the ground had Manyara not been behind her.

Grimluk helped them to the ground. Manyara was panting now as well, her eyes bloodshot and glassy. "You did good," Grimluk said, spreading the blanket over them.

Manyara opened her mouth like she wanted to speak but her eyes fluttered and she just nodded, shivering under the blanket. Shouts caught Grimluk's attention and he looked up to see a group of peacekeepers coming down toward them.

He nodded to them. "Evenin'."

"What...what in the good gods-damned is that?" one of them asked.

A sudden grin spread across Grimluk's face. "Ice scream," he said.

"What?" was all the reply he got.

He sighed. "You had to be there, I guess. It's a frozen demon."

"Y—you got it?" came one of the peacekeepers.

"Trapped it in the ice, at the least," Grimluk replied, trying to work warmth back into his hands, and wincing at his left hand. "And banged up like it wandered out of the Wastes to boot. What took you folks so long, anyhow?"

The foremost peacekeeper gave him a confused look. "We came runnin' just now, soon as we heard the gunshots. Expected to find a whole different sight."

Grimluk's throat rumbled. "I see. Well, only one thing left to do."

"What's that?" the peacekeeper asked.

"Need a hammer and a fine-point chisel so I can finish this job and make sure this thing doesn't hurt anyone else."

"Parker!" the peacekeeper called. "Go on and get what he asked for!"

"Sai!" came Parker, who took off from the back of the group.

"Anything we can do to help?"

Grimluk dropped to his butt next to Emerald and let out a long sigh. "Get some lanterns and bring me some food. Carvin' banishment circles on that much ice is gonna take some time and huntin' makes me mighty hungry."

"Right, yeah," she replied. "We'll be back shortly."

Grimluk touched the brim of his hat as they left and looked at the ice. "Reckon I could eat a whole damn cow right about now." He looked over his hand as he waited. It was an ugly sight, streaks of bloody, tender flesh down across his fingers. The only reason he could come up with that he even still had fingers was that the cold had slowed the thing down. When he'd found Denny, it had ripped the man's flesh off in about as much time as Shoggoth had his hand.

Small victories.

Once the peacekeepers returned with his tools and food, Grimluk set to work. After devouring some meat and biscuits with ravenous zealotry, he had lamps positioned to his sides so he could chisel with enough light to stay accurate. It took him almost two hours to do each side and then climb on top and make the mark there. Once the circles were finished, he put on a glove and held his hand against the ice, ready to speak the incantation to banish a trapped demon like he'd done so many times before when bullets hadn't been enough.

"We invoke the power and authority of mortal life," Grimluk began. "We invoke the strength of our will and the resolve of our spirits! We banish you, O Abyssal adversary! We banish your poisonous taint from this world henceforth. I cast thee from this realm, O fiend! BACK TO THE ABYSS WITH THEE!"

Flashes of light exploded inside the ice, making it all crackle and groan. As the light faded, cracks ripped across the ice's surface, sending crumbling chunks out in all directions before going silent.

With a sigh, Grimluk stepped away from the

block, happy to be done with the task. Manyara was awake by the time he'd finished but Emerald remained unconscious, breathing steadily. He helped the ranger up, steadying her when she wobbled. After that, he got one of the peacekeepers to help him carry Emerald back to the fort and into the infirmary.

As he gave Dr. Gamgee the details, Grimluk watched the doctor look Emerald over thoroughly, checking her pulse, her breathing. He went to check her eyes but as soon as he got her eyelid open, Emerald batted him away.

"In my professional opinion," the doctor began, "I'd say she'll survive. For now, she's just exhausted, but we'll keep watch. I would imagine there's a chance she'll be awake some time tomorrow morning, though it could be longer. I'm not terribly familiar with magical exhaustion."

"Take care of her, doc," Grimluk said. "She's a big damn hero."

Manyara just stood there, looking down at Emerald. "I'd like to stay here with her."

"You're welcome to, of course," Dr. Gamgee said with a nod.

"Reckon you oughta get some food, Manyara," Grimluk offered. "You can hardly stand guard or help if you're exhausted and hungry, too."

She nodded weakly. "Reckon you're right."

"Before you go, sai," the doctor said, looking at Grimluk, "I can see you favoring your hand there. I know you have your own methods but I would prefer to take care of it now, if I might."

Grimluk let out a sigh. "Yeah, might as well let you wrap it up.'

Dr. Gamgee nodded and set to work cleaning and dressing Grimluk's bloody hand. Once he finished, he turned Grimluk's hand over. "Make sure you keep watch of this joint here. It took a pretty heavy slice. Should heal up fine but if you don't watch it well, you might lose some use of your finger."

"Much appreciated, doc. Reckon if I can handle bullet holes, I can handle this. Now, Manyara, let's get some food. I'm still fuckin' starvin'."

Manyara once more led the way to the mess hall where the two of them ate in silence before finally parting. Grimluk wandered back to the room he'd been using and made no attempt to remove the demon trap on the floor. Once he'd disrobed, Grimluk climbed into bed and tumbled headlong into sleep.

CHAPTER 19

Blackness dissolved into light. Stone filled Shoggoth's vision as it looked around. Stone and the man in black. It let out a little moan, fighting back pain and a strange feeling of disconnectedness. It felt small now, no bigger than the man's fist. It couldn't remember how it'd gotten here or why. It remembered talking to Grimluk, thinking about agreeing to the orc's terms for help, and then the man in black had appeared.

"Punishment means death," he'd told it, setting a hand on the side of one of its bodies. "He means to destroy you."

Then anger had flooded Shoggoth's mind, almost like Sheogorath's lingering will had roared to the surface once again. Then gunshots and darkness. Now it was here, wherever here was, sitting in the man in black's hand.

"Dear Shoggoth," the man started, "I must admit to being tickled silly at your choice of name. Do you know why?"

"No," came its burbling voice, now small and weak. The man was walking somewhere down the stone path. Was this a cave? A tunnel? It didn't know.

"Eons ago, when this planet was considerably younger, there existed a race of beings who fancied themselves grand makers and tinkerers. Dared to view themselves in high esteem, defying the true gods of the cosmos. Fools, the lot of them. Their doom came in time, though, at the behest of one of their creations."

Noises came from farther down the tunnel. Strange voices and sounds. Shoggoth perked up, wondering if the man in black was taking it to feed. The weakness it felt made the hunger burn brightly, tearing through its diminutive insides with a fury that rivaled its once massive body. Despite sitting on the bare hand of the man in black, it could not feed on him. Or maybe it wasn't allowed to.

"This was once their grand city. A less than ideal area for you in the world above, what with the ice desert, but you'll be more than safe here. With your new family." The man let out an amused sound. "No, not family. Your subjects. Your vas-sals. Your beautiful citizens!"

The man stopped walking at the mouth of the tunnel and held Shoggoth out to see the sprawling ruins of the city. What Shoggoth assumed were buildings littered its view, shaped so differently from the structures it had come to know. There seemed to be a lack of corners among the still-standing structures. It didn't care about the view, though. It cared about the sounds from below. The strange voices echoing words it didn't know.

"Ah, here comes a citizen now!" the man in black said cheerily and stepped back.

An oily ball rose up, terribly vast in size, filling the mouth of the tunnel. Boiling across its black, luminously pulsing surface were eyes and mouths innumerable, forming and disappearing slowly. Tendrils reached out, grasping for the man in black but never quite reaching him. Shoggoth looked at the creature with curiosity. The sight of the swarming eyes and mouths echoed the feeling of them across its own body.

"Fffffffhtagn," came the creature's mouths. "Tekeli–li, tekeli–li."

"Your name, dearest Shoggoth, struck me so because of this. Because of the subjects of your new kingdom. This, my dearest, my smallest friend, in beautiful happenstance, is a shoggoth. The fatal creation of those, feh, elder things." The man in black set Shoggoth to the tunnel floor.

"Unlike you, these creatures are, to put it mildly, limited. They were created as servants, as living tools, merely to hear and obey their masters. A facet of their behavior that seems to remain true wherever you might wander. It seems to happen with remarkable regularity, you see."

Shoggoth looked up at the thing it shared a name with. It flattened slightly, seeming to peer at Shoggoth with a dozen eyes, reaching out to touch its small form.

"Unlike you, they are not truly capable of learning. Their shapes are versatile, but they cannot change as you change. Cannot mimic more than voices. They are, however, so much like you in other ways, as you can see. And, I dare say, their appetite rivals your own. Their intelligence allowed them victory over their wretched masters, though. So sure of their superiority, they were caught unaware when the shoggoths rose up and devoured them.

"Henceforth, Shoggoth, you shall be the Lord Shoggoth. You shall rule. You shall grow. You shall regain your strength and form, free from the interference of accursed demon hunters. I told Grimluk he would fail. I gave my word and here it is, my word: given and kept and cherished. The shoggoths, servants as they are, will be yours. And unlike their former masters, they shall know you as an equal. You may even take nourishment from them, if you so wish. Their regenerative abilities are as remarkable as your own. I dare say you could devour half of this creature right now and it would be whole again within a day."

Shoggoth, burning with hunger, tested this assertion, grabbing on to a probing tendril from the towering ball of flesh and devouring it. Within moments, the tendril stretched back out anew. Shoggoth took more from the shoggoth, relishing the taste, relishing the flood of strength that filled it.

"Eat. Grow strong. Learn to command your subjects. When the time comes, my lord, you shall be ready to make your return to the world above. You shall be ready to face Grimluk again, bringing glory to the Great Old Ones. Glory be, hallelujah."

"Fhhhhtagn," the shoggoth said.

"Fhtagn, indeed," the man in black said.

Then he was gone, disappearing into the shadows without word or warning, and Shoggoth was alone with the other shoggoth. It rolled around the massive form and down the wall. It wanted to explore. After all, this was its home now. It was the Lord Shoggoth.

The day after the battle was a mix of relief and the mundane tasks of a completed job for Grimluk. Given the situation, given the demon, he was happy he hadn't had to find a way to show the proof of the creature's death. The Cold River peacekeepers had seen him end the thing in the ice and Manyara and Emerald could vouch for what transpired given their help. The captain of the peacekeepers was relieved at the news but remained no more friendly than before. Once Grimluk had given his statement he went on to the mail building to retrieve his letter to his family and send word that his impromptu job had been completed.

He held the letter, staring at it as he walked. It would be wise to hold on to it. He wondered how long it would take before he might need it. He hoped not for a long time, but no one was guaranteed any life beyond the moment, especially when hunting demons.

Emerald was awake and talking with Manyara when he returned to the fort. Manyara was sitting in a chair next to Emerald's bed, holding the woman's hand in both of hers. Grimluk smiled as he approached.

"It's the hero of the day," Emerald half-croaked.

Grimluk shook his head. "You're the hero this

time, Em. Ain't no way I'd have finished the thing off without your help. Reckon I owe Manyara here as much thanks with her helpin' you finish the job."

The two women looked at each other and smiled. "We're a pair of aces," Manyara said.

"Ace of hearts?" Grimluk asked with a playful grin.

Emerald rolled her eyes at him, but a smile spread across her face all the same. She let out a long-suffering sigh that turned into a yawn. "Never doin' that again if I can help it, y'all."

"Gods willing, you shouldn't have to. I caught the thing before its other half could get far. You burned what was in Bringar." He paused, remembering Marlowe Jakobs. "Jakobs could have done something, but I reckon whatever his plans there, I won't know until he brings them to light. No sense in worrying about them just yet."

The three of them sighed. Grimluk's throat rumbled as he thought that over. He suspected the Preacher would focus only on him, but if he didn't – if he went after Emerald and Manyara after Grimluk left – he'd never know. He pushed that thought aside for the time being. The day was won. The people of Cold River and the survivors of Downingville were safe.

"It's safe to go back home now, right?" Emerald asked. "Is anyone even still there?"

"It's safe. Reckon folks will return shortly once word gets around. Downingville will need some fixin', though. Conqueror's seen better days."

Emerald frowned at that. "Suppose it has. At least the Guild will help cover the costs of fixing it.

The few buildings that need repairs are another story."

"I'll get my guild to help cover it. And I'll be happy to help with repairs. Least I can do to show my appreciation."

Emerald's face softened into a new smile. "Thank you."

Grimluk nodded. "What about you, Manyara?"

"Cap'n Van Cleef offered to promote me, have me take over for Bringar." She let out another sigh at that. "After all this, I don't know that I want to be a ranger anymore. Was thinkin' maybe...maybe I'll offer to take over as captain of the peacekeepers for Downingville."

"Reckon that's as good a job as any. Make good use of your experience. Should still get the occasional brawl, too. And—" he motioned to Emerald and winked at Manyara, "—you won't be alone."

"That was the idea," Manyara replied with a smile.

"It'll be nice to sleep in my own bed again," came Emerald. "I'm ready to get out of here."

"Tomorrow," Grimluk and Manyara said at the same time.

"We'll charter a coach. You're in no shape to make the walk right now," Manyara said. "Shit, I'm barely in shape to make it."

Emerald let out an overly dramatic sigh. "Fine. You hens."

"Get some rest," Grimluk replied. "I'll make arrangements."

With that, he touched the brim of his hat and

left the two alone. He could get the coach and send word to Hunter's Hollow about the money and let the other Companions know what had happened. The group was already a central part of the town to begin with, but now they might be its new core. Considering what he'd come to know about Emerald, and even the others, he felt like Downingville could only benefit from that.

Another thought rose as he walked. Marlowe Jakobs. Something else to message the Hollow about. He'd have to send several magi-tell messages to cover all the details. Might not be much but he was sure he could get Downingville some form of protection once he was gone.

It took almost a week to get things underway, but the Companions' eagerness to return their town to normal helped things go smoothly. Grimluk helped clean up the few bodies there were, digging graves for them. A piece of advice his cenka had once told him echoed through his head. You can't save everyone. He knew it, but it would never be easy to accept. In truth, he was okay with that fact. Suffering wasn't inherently noble, as a few philosophers had asserted through the years, but for a demon hunter, the pain of lost lives would keep them grounded. Keep them tethered to the world and not lost to the madness they fought.

Bonds were important. Bonds would keep your will strong in the worst of times. Grimluk was glad he had them, especially after everything that happened over the summer and recently.

Once the town had been cleaned of bodies and most of the debris, Grimluk and the Companions were able to retrieve the bar from its resting place in the office down the street with relatively few bruises. Once the Conqueror's repairs were under way, townsfolk started returning a family or two at a time. Manyara rode out looking for signs of camps and survivors. Many people had fled the night of the attack after realizing the peacekeepers had all been killed, and the ones who hadn't fled then – and hadn't been found by Shoggoth – fled when the rangers had shown up.

Grimluk stayed through the new year, joining Emerald and Manyara for the Day of Clarity. He had never been sure that the Day of Clarity, which capped off the end of the year, did much for him. The symbolic act of airing the good and bad of the previous year, making ready for a fresh one, was good for people in general. He suspected being a demon hunter just cut too deep. Most folks would talk about harvests or works of art they'd made, maybe a particularly wonderful meal. Or how they had cheated at cards or miscounted payment for something or hurt a loved one's feelings. Most folks were all too happy to forgive and forget the mundane negatives of their lives. Demons were anything but mundane, even for a hunter. Demons still got in you even after you killed them.

Regardless, Grimluk was glad to be with friends for the day and to share the good and bad. He hadn't been in any position to celebrate in years. After everything that had happened, he knew he could tell Manyara and Emerald about the events of the past year and they would understand. They'd fought beside him, been true heroes.

After a feast of a dinner, the three of them took to one of the larger rooms in the Coming Conqueror's hotel and the sitting parlor it contained.

"So," Emerald started, "who would like to go first?"

Grimluk thought about it. "I told you once the stories of my life weren't worth sharing, but I reckon after all of this, you've earned it."

"Oh!" Emerald said with a smile. "Okay, please!"

He drank a little of the holiday brandy and began his story, telling them about Greenreach Bluffs. About Gwen and her family. Told them how the little girl was every bit one of the good aspects of the last year, even if the reason she joined his family was bitter. Grimluk told them about the Hanging Judge, Parker Fenton, and his time in the jail. About Gwen's bravery. About fighting the demon out of his mind and ending Fenton's chances at amassing more power, and how close he came to ending the man and taking his first mortal life.

Once he'd finished recounting his tales, he took another sip of his brandy and looked from Emerald to Manyara. "Might not be my place or even my fault, but I want to apologize to the both of you for the nightmares you'll suffer. Most folks can put at least some of their dealings with demons behind them. Let the blasted devils go, but you... you will have to deal with what we deal with. It's trauma, pure and simple. But," he smiled, "you'll have each other.

"And I just want to let you both know, however short, however long, I'm glad to know you, glad to have fought beside you, glad deep in my heart to see you happy. It's most certainly a good thing to call you friend."

He held up his brandy to them in salute. "Here's to the both of you."

Emerald held her glass up in return, smiling and crying a little. Manyara did the same, a touch more stoic but still clearly moved.

Manyara went next, followed by Emerald. They each recounted their own highs and lows. Successful tracking of a gang of rustlers. Losing a drinking contest. Cooking an amazing meal. Emerald made special note of a year's worth of Roscoe trying to buy her services in the same manner as when Grimluk had met her. They both, of course, finished with the hurt of Shoggoth's attack and the joy of coming together.

"Guess we should thank you for encouragin' me to say somethin' to Manyara," Emerald said.

"Even if he hadn't, when I saw Bringar on you, it made it clear for me," Manyara added. "It made me realize then just how much I treasure you."

"So here's to you, Grimluk," Emerald finished, holding up her glass with Manyara.

A week later, as repairs to Downingville were in full swing, with carpenters bustling all around, Grimluk received a package and a letter from Hunter's Hollow. The letter, written by the guild's elven healer, Mint, and with instructions from his cenka, Bakhor, detailed the contents of his package. Along with another demon trap blanket and a dozen demon-killer knives, there were practice materials for apprentices learning to make the traps and other circles and signs. In his worries about protecting his friends after he'd moved on, he thought at the least he could arm the town a little bit.

"Hand out the knives to those you trust best," he told Manyara as he shared the package with her. "Peacekeepers, maybe the Companions, I'll leave it up to you. If Jakobs returns or sends a demon your way, you won't be caught unprepared."

"Reckon I can make a small task force for just such," she replied.

He helped her get the materials settled in the peacekeepers' building before slipping out and heading back to his room at the Conqueror. Man-yara was busy with repairs and finding new volunteers. He didn't want to take up any more of her time.

With his friends taken care of and the town mending, Grimluk readied himself to leave. Mint had sent some extra supplies for Grimluk as well, leaving only food to gather for his return to the road. Spring was rolling in full and bright, warming the air and stirring the land. Plants and animals would be plentiful as he traveled. He found Man-yara and Emerald in the Conqueror's saloon when he came down, wanting to see how things were going one last time.

"Leavin' already?" Emerald asked.

"Reckon it's time I get going," he said.

Manyara held her gloved hand out. He shook it while she gave him a simple nod and a smile. "Thank you."

He nodded back.

Emerald stepped forward and wrapped her arms around him, squeezing tight. "Stay safe out there, ya hear me? If you die, we'll beat yer ass. I don't care how big that gun is."

Grimluk smiled and gave her a proper squeeze back. "No promises on that front, but I'll do my damnedest." He pulled away and looked at her. "And I can promise that whatever kills me will wish I'd killed it."

He stepped out of the saloon, through the batwing doors and into the courtyard. "Take care of each other, you hear?"

"You bet your big green ass we will," Emerald said, wrapping an arm around Manyara on the porch.

He gave one last took to his new friends. They looked good together, Emerald in her red and gold and Manyara in her browns and greens, arms around each other.

The road beckoned him and Grimluk answered. He had food. He had bullets. He had money. He was prepared. It was his job to be prepared. He left Downingville behind, heading for Cold River once more and after that, deeper into Westlynth, into new places. There would be more people to help and more demons to kill. There always were. He would answer their calls and, hopefully, make the new year better than the last.

Grimluk was a demon hunter, and soon it would be time to hunt again.

THE DEMONS WITHIN

ASHE ARMSTRONG

RECOMMENDED AUTHORS

You've read my book now (and thank you for that!), and I'd imagine you'll be hungry for something new so here are a few recommendations for folks I know and enjoyed.

James Jakins, Author of *Jack Bloodfist: Fixer*.
Erica Lindquist, Author of the *Reforged Trilogy*,
Whisperworld, and the *Dead Beat*.
Luke Matthews, Author of *Construct*.
Rachel Sharp, Author of *The Big Book of Post–Collapse Fun*.
Edward M. Erdelac, Author of the *Merkabah Rider* series
and *Andersonville*.
Krista D. Ball, Author of the *Tales of Tranquility*, *The Dark Abyss of Our Sins*, and *Spirit Caller* series.
Christopher Ruz, Author of *Century of Sand* and *Rust*.
K.S. Villoso, Author of *The Wolf of Oren-yaro*.
Tim Marquitz, Author of the *Demon Squad* series.
S.M. Reine, Author of The Descentverse books and stories.

Happy reading, everyone!

THIS BOOK WAS MADE POSSIBLE BY...

Eric DiCarlo
Steven Latour
Andrew Paterson
James Jakins
Thomas Moore
Bryan Young
Rachel Sharp
William Stafford
Shayna Wark
Steven Pope
Garrett Schmigle
Melissa Schumake
Samantha Tohtz
Dee
Alyssa Riggs
Cliff Tohtz
Benet Reynolds
Asher Stephenson
Jacob Townsend
Kibret Gordon
Nick
Matthew Mueller
Alex Haigh
Lisa Richardson
Rebecca Roth

Anonymous
Christopher Hayes-Kossmann
Leigh Peterson
Krista Ball
Rachel N.
Jonathan Dean
Satya
Robert Woods Tienken
Prodigal
Mega Ninja Publishing
Justin
Michael Adam Childers
Jeff Lewis
Asher Stephenson
Nick Kilburg
CaffeinatedZombie
Kerri Regan
Margaret Beldyk
Ryan H
Amalia Dillin
Andrew Barton
Benjamin Savell
Wes Hillman

THANK YOU ALL!

ABOUT THE AUTHOR

Ashe grew up watching and reading about adventures and having horrible nightmares. He spent most of his young life wanting to know more about what scared him but also doing so from between fingers and from under the covers. Eventually, the realm of nightmares became home. Heroes and villains and the struggle of Good against Evil, combined with Horror, helped mold him into the weirdo lover–of–the–strange that he is. Ashe lives in Tulsa, OK with his partner.

Where you can find Ashe on the web

ashearmstrong.com
patreon.com/ashearmstrong
ashearmstrong.tumblr.com
twitter.com/ashearmstrong
facebook.com/ashearmstrong
goodreads.com/ashearmstrong